COAT OF ARMS

Rupert Sylvester was a happy social success, the man to admire in the village of Alderbury. Of course no one knew that he was linked with a sinister political plot and a series of murders disguised as suicide. A man was pushed from the top of a tower block, another man was killed with a shotgun in a remote Welsh cottage, another drowned in a bath in a Park Lane hotel. But when death reaches out for Sylvester it is Jack Quinn, individualist, who picks up the trail. Obstinate, pig-headed, with his own brand of honour, Quinn's quest eventually leads him to recognise his own mortality in the eyes of a professional killer . . .

COAT OF ARMS

George Sims

JAN 1 5 1991

ATLANTIC LARGE PRINT
Chivers Press, Bath, England.
Curley Publishing, Inc.,
South Yarmouth, Mass., USA.

Library of Congress Cataloging-in-Publication Data

Sims, George, 1923–
   Coat of arms / George Sims.
      p. cm.—(Atlantic large print)
   ISBN 0–7927–0413–4 (softcover)
   1. Large type books. I. Title.
[PR6037.I715C6 1991]
823′.914—dc20

90–42462
CIP

British Library Cataloguing in Publication Data

Sims, George *1923–*
   Coat of arms.
   I. Title
   823.914 [F]

   ISBN 0–7451–9951–8
   ISBN 0–7451–9963–1 pbk

This Large Print edition is published by Chivers Press, England, and Curley Publishing, Inc, U.S.A. 1991

Published by arrangement with the author

U.K. Hardback ISBN 0 7451 9951 8
U.K. Softback ISBN 0 7451 9963 1
U.S.A. Softback ISBN 0 7927 0413 4

COAT OF ARMS

The Duke of Wellington always maintained that when the man-in-the-street started to question the political and religious assumptions of European society the world would go through a 'very bad half hour indeed'.

'One can face any danger fearlessly, even court it recklessly, so long as it is far enough off.'
The Duke of Wellington

CHAPTER ONE

The darkly handsome, restlessly energetic Rupert Sylvester was a very popular man in the Surrey village of Alderbury; most of the villagers considered him to be a wholly admirable character; only a handful felt that perhaps he was just too good to be true. But for Judy Browning, Captain Sylvester, as he liked to be known locally, clinging to an Army rank he had held briefly in the mid-1970s, epitomised everything she disliked or hated. For Sylvester was a self-proclaimed right-wing member of the Conservative Party, an arch-conservative who resisted all changes in Alderbury including the building of council houses, and a disciplinarian always ranting on about the sloppiness of young people; even worse from Judy's point of view, Sylvester was a militarist who believed in keeping a nuclear force. Judy's own fiery radical views matched her unruly red hair. She was on her own in actively disliking Sylvester, but she was used to being out of step with the people who lived around her: an outspoken atheist and republican, the only active CND supporter in the neighbourhood and the only person who always refused to buy a poppy for Remembrance Day, she tended to be ignored

1

or shunned by the villagers generally.

Rupert Sylvester, on the other hand, was usually in the limelight where village affairs were concerned: aged thirty-eight, he was chairman of the Parish Council, captain of the cricket club and a star performer on the Vicarage's lawn tennis court, as well as being a regular churchgoer and contributor to charities and the proprietor of a handsome, double-fronted antiques shop which was scrupulously maintained.

Sylvester's energy was legendary—every moment of a long day was filled with work or exercise. He maintained a very large garden with a little help from his wife Polly and also looked after his beautiful black mare called Night which was kept in an adjoining paddock. He did all the buying for his antiques shop and if the cleaning woman failed to turn up he was not above washing the shop windows or even a stint of floor polishing. For such manual tasks he wore dark-blue jeans and freshly laundered, tropical khaki shirts from which it appeared medal ribbons had been removed. Rupert Sylvester and all his possessions, from his black mare to his old, racing-green Bentley, were always immaculate. If one of the ladies of the village, collecting for some charity, called late in the evening when it might be expected that the man of the house would be lounging with his shoes off, she could not fail to be impressed by Sylvester's prompt appearance at the front door looking as if he had just been scrubbed and polished himself.

Court Antiques, the shop with the glistening bow windows, so admired by the inhabitants of Alderbury and any motorists who stopped on their way to Guildford or the south coast, was not equally admired by dealers who occasionally looked in to see what Sylvester had been buying. Members of the trade tended to write off his stock generally as 'expensive tat' or 'nice-looking rubbish'. Sylvester had not served any kind of apprenticeship to the business by working for another dealer or even by being a collector; he had sprung into the field unarmed by knowledge, relying on his energy, good looks and confident manner, buying things purely on their surface appeal. Charlie Saunders, an expert Cockney dealer, rudely said of Sylvester 'he knows fuck-all' but continued to call in at the shop from time to time because, as he remarked, 'Where there's total ignorance you can sometimes make yourself a pound.'

The attractive black and white shop was divided into two parts with antiques on one side and old books on the other. Sylvester knew very little about the insides of books and largely bought what book-dealers call 'furniture', volumes prized solely for their bindings. Such a mixed shop could easily

3

have fallen between two stools and become a jumble, but in Court Antiques the proprietor's energy and the diligence of his two assistants, Miss Rogers and Mrs Stratton-Smith, prevented that from happening. One of them was always at work in a back room, polishing either bindings, furniture or brass objects. Brass and copper items were a speciality and they glittered so much that they brightened the premises even on the gloomiest November day.

It was said in the village that 'poor Miss Rogers thinks the sun shines out of the Captain's eyes'. A faded blonde, probably fifty years old rather than the 'forty plus' she acknowledged, Adele Rogers was indeed a willing slave to Sylvester and would become quietly hostile if ever a word was said against him. She always arrived a quarter of an hour before the shop was due to open at 9 a.m. and she left unwillingly when Sylvester finally decided to call it a day, which might be at 7 or 8 p.m., two or three hours after the shop was closed. They worked on, sustained only by a dry biscuit and a glass of very dry sherry.

Pamela Stratton-Smith was nearly as diligent, but not at all 'silly about the Captain'; an attractive brunette, the widow of a British Airways pilot, she worked only part-time at Court Antiques. Her knowledge of what she sold was as sketchy as that of the proprietor of the shop but she was a good saleswoman and managed to convey the impression that if you did not buy the over-priced objects on offer it would be due to your own stupidity or lack of taste. Sylvester too, unlike many dealers, was very good at selling and unhesitatingly pushed items which he had been told authoritatively were 'wrong'. But his pleasant appearance and charm were such that customers served by him usually emerged from the premises lovingly clutching their purchase and buoyed up by the vague feeling that somehow or other they had done rather well with the dashing Captain Sylvester.

Rex Bealby, a taciturn, lame widower, who lived the life of a semi-recluse at Alderbury Hall, never set foot in Court Antiques. He had a very poor opinion of the highly polished stock displayed in the shop windows and reserved his judgement about Sylvester. And Rupert, usually so sociable, was inclined to avoid Rex Bealby. For Brigadier Bealby DSO MC, late of The Rifle Brigade, who had been on the sharp end of the Second World War in Italy, France and Belgium before being badly wounded in Holland, never made personal remarks and rarely asked questions; but when he did so they were very much to the point. Rupert had even been known to make a sudden dash across the ever busy A281, on which Court Antiques was situated, in order to avoid an encounter with the Brigadier, who had cold blue eyes, a discerning glance and a knack for putting his finger on anything suspicious.

The attractive antiques shop, two old pubs, the White Rose and the Green Man, a tiny cottage where Judy Browning lived and a small baker's shop were the only buildings on the A281 since the village of Alderbury had, as it were, its back to the main road. Motorists on their way to or from the south coast who stopped at one of the pubs might pause to look into the windows of Court Antiques, might even succumb to buying a brilliantly polished copper bed-warmer or some horse-brasses, but they were usually unaware that a picture-postcard village lay just at the back of the tiny High Street. They did not see how delightfully the River Alder meandered round the village on its way to join the larger River Wey at Godalming. They did not admire the spick-and-span, white, wooden bridge across the river, nor the clear water of Alder Pool where white ducks lived with mallard, moorhens and a family of swans, nor Sylvester's most prized possession, his Elizabethan Vine Cottage; nor glimpse Alderbury Hall, a rather dark, old house tucked away at the end of a faintly gloomy lane. But they often carried away with them one memento of Alderbury, a postcard showing Court Antiques centrally positioned in the High Street, with sunshine gleaming on the windows and a darkly handsome, faintly military-looking man in hunting jacket, cord breeches and boots opening the glistening black door.

A village ceremony which Sylvester did not attend was the Remembrance Sunday service at the church which dated back to Norman times. It was the only Sunday on which Brigadier Bealby could be relied on to put in an appearance, slowly limping round the Alder Pool, soberly dressed in a bowler hat and dark suit but eschewing the opportunity to display his many medals. It seemed that there was always some distant auction sale which it was imperative for 'the Captain' to attend on the November weekend when the Remembrance service was held. It was the only thing that Sylvester had in common with Judy Browning, not attending the most popular church service of the year. But it was dimly felt that Sylvester must have his reasons, possibly unhappy memories connected with the Army, though it was apparent that his memories could not be of the war-time epoch which the Brigadier remembered.

Sylvester was vague about his service career and his reasons for resigning his commission. He tended to imply that he had not seen eye to eye with the War Office, or 'the War House' as he called it, over some matter; he mentioned 'idle fellows', 'bloody slackness',

7

'part of the general malaise that infects this country', and maintained, 'It is a bloody disgrace that the Army has to fight with one hand tied behind its back in Northern Ireland.' But any conversation with Rupert Sylvester touching on his former vocation would turn sooner or later to his hero, the first Duke of Wellington. One came away from talking to him with the impression that if Captain Sylvester could only have served under the Iron Duke all would have been well.

CHAPTER TWO

On a particularly fine day in early June, when the sky was cloudless and a brilliant blue, Judy Browning went for a walk round Alderbury. Her closest friend, Sarah Levey, was staying with her at Street Cottage for the weekend and they got up early on the Saturday morning as Judy had something more than just a stroll in mind. Judy and Sarah agreed on all political matters and believed that Britain would not be a happy or successful country until it had taken a sharp turn to the left, imposed a truly socialist economy, withdrawn from NATO and the Common Market, disarmed unilaterally and welcomed more coloured immigrants—all the things, in fact, which Rupert Sylvester bitterly opposed. Judy knew that Sylvester, like many Tories, was a man of fixed habits, and that he unfailingly rode his mare early on a Saturday morning before putting in a long day at his shop. Judy had talked about Sylvester with Sarah and she wanted her best friend to see her implacable political enemy.

Alderbury and the surrounding countryside looked at its best that morning. Even Sarah, who loved living in London and rarely left Hampstead when she was not working, had enjoyed waking up in Street Cottage to the sound of birds and thought the blossom on the trees and the lush hedges were beautiful. Larks sang high above them and zephyr-like breezes wafted faint delicious scents as they strolled by the river.

The two girls passed a neat lime hedge and then a glistening, white, picket fence.

'Talk about obsessive neatness,' Judy said. 'I'd like to hear a psychologist on the subject of Master Sylvester and his compulsive behaviour. You see he keeps his grass clipped as brutally short as his fingernails.'

Judy realised that the walk had been well timed as she heard Sylvester's unusually deep voice, though he was hidden behind a stretch of box-hedge shaped by topiary to resemble a row of birds. Then the girls looked up the wide gravel path to Vine Cottage and saw him, dressed in a black roll-neck pullover,

9

white breeches and glossy black boots, astride his black mare, calling out something incomprehensible in a sharp tone. They also spied Sylvester's pretty blonde wife, who was a few years younger than her husband. She was holding up a newspaper so that Sylvester could have a closer look at it. Momentarily he appeared disconcerted by what he read for he tugged suddenly on the reins and the big mare reared up.

'Too much to hope for that he'll fall off,' Judy whispered to Sarah. 'It's a remarkably mild-mannered horse for such a tough guy. What an idiot! And would you believe a horse-blanket with an embroidered coat of arms? *And* a signet ring with a coat of arms?'

Judy Browning was unable to say any more on a favourite subject as Sylvester trotted his horse down the gravel path towards them, his handsome face set in a smile. He waved his crop and called out in the deep voice which many of the ladies of Alderbury considered rather sexy, 'Morning, Miss Browning. What a day, eh?'

'Yes. Very nice,' Judy said, tugging at Sarah's arm and walking off briskly so that there was no chance of further conversation or an introduction.

Sarah said, 'So that's the famous Captain. But only a glimpse.'

'Yes, sorry about that, but I just can't stand him. What a show-off! And the biggest joke is that he's not even a good rider. Last autumn I was out with a group protesting about the local hunt and you should have seen the cautious way he took his fences.'

'The blonde woman—is she his wife? She looks quite nice.'

'She is, but of course he treats her like a doormat. Your authentic chauvinist pig. Polly hardly ever seems to say a word and never in his lordship's presence.'

'You didn't mention that he's rather dishy.'

'Oh, for God's sake!'

'I didn't mean . . . I just happen to like that very coarse black hair and coal-black eyebrows.'

'Sarah! You are abso-bloody-lutely hopeless!'

CHAPTER THREE

Rupert Sylvester jogged his mare only a short distance along a grass bank before allowing her to settle down to the ambling pace she preferred. He was frightened! He could admit it frankly to himself even if to no one else. He was very scared indeed and it was a time when he needed all his wits about him. What he didn't need was a fall from a horse or any other stupid accident which might crock him. He was in a veritable trap! It was like being

11

on a road which at first appeared wide and open, but kept on narrowing all the time and inexorably leading on to palpable danger. All his thoughts were of the threateningly oppressive situation, but no matter how long or hard he puzzled he could not hit on a possible way out. He exclaimed aloud: 'God! What a fool I am! What a bloody idiot!'

Hearing his angry voice, the mare moved her head slightly as if she would like to look back at him with her big mild eyes. I need someone to confide in, Sylvester thought, with the bitter knowledge that there was no one he could turn to in such trouble. For years he had longed for a truly sympathetic and unshockable confidant; just one person with whom he need not keep up any pretences, but could bare his soul and admit his inadequacies and failings, the greatest of which he considered was cowardice. But such a person would now be more than a longed-for luxury—such a friend might even be able to help him to escape.

Night suddenly whinnied and began to trot quite briskly along the wide grass verge that lay outside the rotting chestnut palings marking the boundary of Brigadier Bealby's copse. Then, perversely, the mare came to a halt just at the end of the shady lane leading down to the Hall and Sylvester spied Rex Bealby standing in the lane, dressed in a white shirt and old-fashioned grey trousers, scything down the tall couch grass.

Sylvester acknowledged Bealby's presence with a vague wave of his crop. Surprisingly, the Brigadier greeted him with a faint smile and said, 'Good morning.' For a moment it looked as if he might be going to put down his scythe and walk up the lane.

'Come on girl!' Just using his crop to flick the horse on her great behind was enough to startle her into a canter and in a few moments Sylvester was safely away from the perceptive, thoughtful Brigadier. One thing I don't need at the moment, Sylvester thought, is a heart to heart chat with old Bealby. Another is a broken leg.

He tugged on the reins and the mare showed by a tetchy movement of her large head that she did not like first being flicked and then tugged. She came to a halt again on a particularly lush bank and began to munch the grass, which was mixed with loosestrife growing over from a ditch that ran into the river. Sylvester looked down into the ditch and, instead of seeing teasles, comfrey and ragwort, his eyes were offended by unsightly rubbish. It was plain that some townee lout had made a special trip to dump a load of miscellaneous junk, together with the contents of a stinking dustbin. Sylvester was so furious that momentarily his haunting fears were forgotten. He dismounted and looped the reins round a branch of a wild plum tree.

There was a foul-smelling, rotting mattress, a large doll lacking its head, a rusting pram, a transistor set that appeared to have been smashed in a tantrum, empty tins and beer bottles and a wide scattering of greasy packets and smeared papers that had once enclosed 'convenience' meals. The fish-finger offerings of the so-called 'working' classes, Sylvester thought, the too-lazy-to-even-cook-a-meal class! The typically foul leavings of louts who continually lounge in front of their beloved 'tellies' watching their heroes, the ghastly beer-bloated darts' champions and primping soccer players. This is the one thing they can produce—stinking trash!

Sylvester bent down and used his crop gingerly to turn over the slimy wrappings and tins and a filthy vest, in the hope of finding an envelope or anything addressed to the former owner of the nauseating rubbish. With that evidence in hand, what pleasure he would have in loading all the muck into his horse-box and returning it. But the only papers to be found were those in which fish and chips had been wrapped, junk mail and football pool forms.

Staring down at the mess, Sylvester fitfully clenched his fists, fuming with impotent rage. When would the politicians face the facts? That so many of their 'workers' were in fact useless loafers! With a set, stony expression

14

that would have surprised the customers of Court Antiques, Sylvester remounted his horse and urged her to trot again. The mare reacted to all the hurry-up-and-slow-down treatment she had received by breaking into an uninhibited canter. He found the rapid movement through the fresh morning air exhilarating and concentrated on trying to control the powerful beast who could do them both damage.

When the mare swerved into a field known as Ten Acre he allowed her the rare opportunity of a gallop, managing to slow down and turn just in time to avoid a rough patch at the far end by a hawthorn hedge. As he did so an unexpected image slid into his mind, a mental snapshot of Rex Bealby's face: the long, aquiline nose, the thin, brown cheeks, and eyes the colour of diluted blue ink, but with a less guarded expression than usual. Yes, there was no doubt that the old man had been on the point of leaving his scything and actually saying something more than good morning. It was puzzling, even faintly disturbing, that the enigmatic Brigadier should have some reason for dropping his habitual reserve.

Another irritating memory of the Brigadier intervened in Sylvester's mind and he spoke out loud again. This time he imitated Bealby's lighter timbre and throw-away delivery. He said, 'A place called Arnhem.' A

15

place called Arnhem indeed, he thought. The publican at the White Rose had asked the Brigadier where he had been so badly wounded that his Army career had ended. Bealby had diffidently replied, 'A place called Arnhem.' Talk about backing into the limelight! Typical inverse boasting by that old snob. 'My God! What a country!' he exclaimed to his horse and a hawthorn hedge. 'Bloody well riddled with snivelling won't-workers and ghastly old snobs!'

CHAPTER FOUR

After Rupert had trotted his horse down the drive, Polly Sylvester decided that she would scrutinise the front page of the *Daily Telegraph* in the hope of discovering which item had caught his eye and apparently startled him. She thought it was typical of Rupert that he had recovered in mid-air, so to speak, and ridden off to chat up two girls even though he knew that one of them disliked him. Any girl was a challenge to his ability to charm and Rupert was always *acting*: that was the key to him though it had taken her years to discover it. But once that was understood a lot of other things made sense. In any given situation Rupert would simply be acting the part, whether of lover, soldier, sportsman, husband or business-man—only on rare occasions would he be faced by circumstances where acting was no good, like the time when they had seen a child drowning in the sea, and then he stood exposed as being merely an actor.

The headlines of the newspaper were concerned with Israel and an air raid on Lebanon which might lead to wider trouble with the movement of the US Sixth Fleet, but Rupert was usually indifferent to such international affairs although he had widely proclaimed his loathing of the Soviet Union. Polly carefully read each item on the front page: the Queen had paid a visit to a children's hospital; a gang had used a stolen Rolls Royce to carry out a daring jewellery raid in Bond Street; a militant miners' leader had committed suicide in a remote Welsh cottage; a young tennis champion had behaved badly at London Airport. The smallest paragraph concerned a rare silver spoon sold for thousands of pounds at auction.

Polly took the newspaper through the cottage into her bright, spotlessly clean kitchen to make herself a cup of instant coffee. It was typical of Rupert that he had erased all signs of his meagre breakfast before attending to his mare. One of her closest friends had shaken her head knowingly when commenting on Rupert's 'compulsive tidiness', but it was only recently that a number of such memories had come together in her mind as his behaviour became noticeably more odd and she had begun to judge him. The phone calls which obviously worried him, the time when he had replaced the receiver halfway through a sentence as she descended the stairs into the hall, his increasing abstraction, the faces he made when he thought she wasn't looking, the letter he had blankly denied having received.

Sighing deeply, Polly took the newspaper and her cup of coffee out to the paved patio at the back of the cottage. Seated on a gleaming white wooden bench, she read the smallest paragraph again. A rare Edward IV spoon, made about 1465, had been sold for a record price at Sotheby's; but it was a foreign dealer who had bought the spoon and his name was not one she had heard of. Anyway that kind of thing was out of Rupert's field. The expert Cockney dealer, Charlie Saunders, a bald man with nice eyes, had once said to her in the shop while looking round approvingly at the gleaming stock, 'Your husband certainly knows his customers.' And it was true that Rupert had a definite flair for knowing exactly what he could sell. Rare old spoons which commanded thousands of pounds at auction were not his cup of tea.

Polly put down the paper still feeling very puzzled; she knew that in his present anxious

18

mood it would be quite hopeless to ask Rupert what item in the paper had surprised him. He would lie, or 'fudge it' as he said—his ability to 'fudge it' had been only gradually revealed over the years. It seemed he took a perverse pleasure in misleading people and he would quite often lie when there was no need for it. Confronted by any difficult situation he would always lie his way out of it—he could look anyone in the eye and smile while doing so. Only recently had that knack deserted him a little, particularly over the letter that he declared had never existed.

A movement in the strawberry bed caught Polly's eye and she put the cup down with another sigh. The prolific strawberry plants were guarded by nearly invisible green netting and a family of young thrushes had been taking turns to become trapped in the close mesh. One had been so badly entangled that she had had to cut it free and then she had been uncertain as to whether it would survive the ordeal.

As she stepped over to the spot where she had seen the luxuriant plants stir, a cock blackbird hopped out of the net and on to the grass path, regarding her calmly and showing no anxiety to fly away. She saw a fragment of ripe strawberry disappear into its yellow bill and then the bird slowly hopped away, more like a pet than a wild thing. Polly stood still, sensually enjoying the heat of the sun, listening to the mellow fluting from another unseen blackbird and watching half a dozen butterflies ministering to a buddleia bush. The prospect of sky and trees beyond the hawthorn hedge was quite glorious. The only sign of human habitation was the eccentrically tall chimney-stack of the Hall, partially screened by great oak trees. I must always remember that I owe all this to Rupert, she thought; to his initiative and hard work. Rupert had taken the gamble of buying Vine Cottage and it was he who had decided to make an old English garden with rare types of apple such as Ribston Pippin, Michaelmas Red and Rosemary Russet, he who had planted the great beds of lavender, moss roses, stocks and forget-me-nots; even the herb garden had been his idea.

The sound of a horse whinnying and a female voice, disturbed Polly's pleasant reverie in the sun. She walked slowly round the side of the cottage, not too worried if she missed her caller for she thought she recognised the 'frightfully horsy' voice of Louise Simpson. It really was a great irritation to have a husband who acted the rôle of a ladies' man and attracted women round him like butterflies to a buddleia bush. If only they knew the truth, that Rupert had never been very enthusiastic about the physical side of their relationship and seemed to be growing ever less keen. Thinking hard, she could not be sure when they had last come together for sex; it might have been as long ago as the Hunt Ball and that had probably only happened because they had both been stimulated by excitement, champagne and the attention of other people.

'Coo-eee—it's only me!' Polly turned the corner of the cottage and saw Louise Simpson looking very slim and attractive, standing on the gravel path and holding her dappled grey gelding, Lucky. She was wearing a gentian blue silk blouse, dove-grey breeches and black boots that were as highly polished as Rupert's. The blouse was modestly buttoned but well tucked down into the breeches so that it clung to her small, high breasts.

Polly grimaced, felt in her jeans' pocket for the carrot she had forgotten to give Night and called out, 'Sorry,' fudging it for once like her husband, 'you've just missed him. He went off a little earlier this morning.'

Louise Simpson had an unusually pale face that went well with her long, dark brown hair. She never seemed to catch the sun or show emotion, but her brown eyes were suddenly smudged with disappointment. She said, 'Oh, I'm definitely brand X this morning,' then realised she was making her feelings plain and added, 'Not to worry though. I wanted to see both of you.'

Liar, Polly thought, saying, 'That's good. Do you have time for coffee?' She walked up

21

to the handsome grey horse and gave it the carrot.

'Alas, no. I'm afraid I'm doing the rounds, begging again—for the church fête this time. Do you think you could possibly manage the white elephant stall? And it would be wonderful if Rupert would be our auctioneer again. He was such a success last year.'

Amazing, Polly thought, the woman's amazing. Can't she hear the difference in her tone when she talks about me and then about the wonderful Rupert? She said, 'You can sign me up right now, I've nothing at all on that Saturday. I'm not so sure about Rupert—it's a particularly busy day for him...'

'Well, I shall pester him anyway. I thought of popping into the shop this afternoon. I was tempted by an oak settle I saw there on Thursday. I also wanted to do some checking...' She left the sentence unfinished and hanging between them, with a slightly mysterious expression that irritated Polly who asked, 'You mean on something else in the shop?'

'No, I was having an argument with Patience about Rupert's height. I said six foot. She said slightly less.'

'Five foot nine actually,' Polly said promptly.

'Really?'

'Absolutely. Of course, he does look taller,

because he's slim.' And, she thought, because he wears slightly built-up heels.

'I'm amazed. So I lose my bet?'

'Definitely. Sorry. But, you see, Rupert thinks tall.'

Louise did not dignify this somewhat tart remark with a reply, but looked about her saying, 'Oh, I do envy you this place.'

Polly had to smother a desire to shake her head disbelievingly. The Simpson family owned a great brewery concern; they also owned the largest estate in the Alderbury neighbourhood. Louise lived on it in an elegant, small Queen Anne house every bit as attractive as Vine Cottage, but with the bonuses of a tennis court and a swimming pool. Why should she possibly envy Polly for having the cottage, apart from the fact that Rupert also lived there? I wonder what fantasies about him take place behind that calm, pale brow? she thought.

'That tree, for instance,' Louise said, pointing to a great mulberry tree with huge, heart-shaped leaves. Some of its gnarled old branches had touched the ground and re-rooted, so that it looked like a group of trees. 'Did Rupert plant that?'

Polly thought, How she loves to bring his name into the conversation, but she said, 'No. Some old chap in the village said it had been there for as long as he could remember. And they don't fruit for about ten years after they are planted. But you can still get them from a few nurseries. You have to ask for *morus nigra*, the black mulberry. The white kind is only good for silk worms.'

'Ah, I see. I must remember that. Oh well . . .'

Louise looked vaguely round again, obviously having run out of things to say to Polly, but loath to depart while Rupert might return at any moment.

Polly smiled and said, 'Oh well.'

'Yes, I'll be off. Don't mention that auctioneering chore. I'll tackle the Master myself this afternoon.'

'Okay. But you can pencil me in anyway.'

'Good. I'll do that.' Louise smiled and walked off, leading her well-trained gelding. She waved her left hand, then turned as if struck by some afterthought, but said nothing, giving Polly a rather serious, judging look.

Polly was not allowed to brood on the significance of the look because a Post Office van pulled up outside the picket fence and the youngest postman in the area got out. He was a ginger-haired, cheerful youth who was another member of the Rupert Sylvester fan club because of Rupert's ability as a batsman and as captain of the cricket team.

The postman sidestepped the large grey horse, grinned at Louise and walked up the path waving several letters. 'I spotted the

24

Captain,' he called out, 'but he raced off into that Ten Acre field.'

Hearing this tip as to Rupert's whereabouts, Louise promptly mounted her horse and jogged down the path.

Polly grinned back at the youth, who said, 'These should keep you busy.' She thanked him and glanced through the letters quickly before going back to the cottage. One was from her mother and there was a card from her sister in Yorkshire who thought of staying in London while Wimbledon was on. All the others were addressed to Rupert and some looked like bills. But would one of the ordinary, white, typed envelopes disappear, like the letter over which they had had the argument?

Polly walked into the cool hall of the cottage, which had a floor of highly polished red bricks and looked even nicer than usual with so many flowers in bowls and vases. There was a handsome walnut grandfather clock in the corner, but the area was dominated by a brilliantly coloured reproduction of the coat of arms of the first Duke of Wellington, embroidered on Irish linen for Rupert by another of his tribe of adoring females, the shy and undemanding Adele Rogers. Polly gazed at the colourful design, in which two large gold-chained lions were shown on either side of the royal insignia, standing on a scroll which bore the

25

Iron Duke's motto: *Virtutis Fortuna Comes*. It seemed that only she knew Rupert's secret—that he admired the Duke of Wellington, not because he resembled him in any way, but because he was so unlike him.

Turning to place Rupert's letters on a small table, Polly encountered her reflection in the old mirror. The dark glass reflected a distorted image but the eyes were plainly scornful. She knew that she was bad at hiding her feelings; it irritated her that she always flushed when complimented. When she had noticed her husband's sudden fearful look over something in the *Daily Telegraph* had her eyes shown suspicion and a hint of scorn? He knew that she knew he was a coward. Would he now feel that he could not possibly tell her if something really serious was troubling him?

CHAPTER FIVE

A verdict on Frank Shields often expressed by his former neighbours and other people who had known him when he lived in Heygate Street was, 'Young Frank—he lives for his pleasures.' It was said in the flat, faintly joyless voice of those brought up in the Elephant and Castle area, but sometimes was tinged with envy or admiration. Even in his early thirties Frank was referred to as 'young' because people wanted to show a familiarity with the former boxing champion and because the Elephant was where Frank Shields spent the first twenty years of his life.

Most of the people who were at school with Frank had not made much of a success of their lives and they were intrigued as to how he had done so well with a similarly inadequate education and not much help, as far as they could judge, from anyone. If he had climbed out of the South London district by a series of well-paid boxing bouts, they could have understood and approved. It was true that he had once been poised on the verge of turning pro, on the advice of the well-known boxing promoter, Sammy Coyne; but Doreen, whom Frank had married at the age of twenty, had been against it, and eventually Frank had said no. So what puzzled his old friends when Frank returned south of the river and stood rounds of drinks in the Walworth Road pubs, was how he had managed the move to a terraced house in Chelsea and various other trappings of success such as foreign holidays, Doreen's smart clothes, a Volvo station-wagon, and sending his son Gary to a private school, and all from a 'potty little business' dealing in old stamps.

Even his mother-in-law, Marge, who thought that she understood Frank and certainly liked him, was puzzled by that, but then her stereotyped verdict on the kind of people who collected tiny pieces of coloured paper and stuck them in albums was, 'They wants their heads examined.' Her opinion of Frank was much more generous; for one thing, she thought that he looked a lot like a film star she had admired years before, but being a wise woman of mature years she kept some of her thoughts about Frank to herself, particularly when she got into bed and viewed the enormous behind and gross neck of her husband, Joe. She never bothered to disguise the fact that Frank was her favourite son-in-law. 'Always so cheerful,' she said fondly. 'Always'—and then that characteristic South London pause—'content. He never complains. Like Sunny Jim he is.' And Frank knew just how to cuddle a mother-in-law with a hint of sexual interest.

Marge also said that Frank was very generous. Certainly he was open-handed in pubs and often took flowers or chocolates to his mother, Eileen, who continued to live in Heygate Street and to Marge who lived round the corner in Wansey Street, near the Town Hall. Oddly enough, Frank's wife Doreen, who received her fair share of gifts, did not have such a high opinion of him, but she kept it strictly to herself. For Doreen had come to realise that Frank had a very cold heart indeed, though it was well disguised by his surface charm, and that he was intensely selfish. She had other dim suspicions about him as well, but you would have had to know Frank as well as she did and be much more articulate in order to put them into words.

It did appear that Frank lived for his pleasures and devoted little of his time to making a living. If someone offered him a chance to go shooting, for which he had a definite talent, he was off at once. He was also available for a number of other sporting activities and some of Doreen's girlfriends found that he had the time to call on them. For these and other reasons Frank found it essential to keep one hundred per cent fit and he took some form of exercise every day.

Frank did not welcome questions about how it came about that he had so much leisure and tended to head them off one way or another. 'Leave it out, girl,' he once said to Doreen. It was said in a light, flat tone, for he sometimes relapsed into his old manner of speaking; and it was only a mild rebuke, but then he hardly ever needed to rebuke anyone. The four words were enough for Doreen to 'button up'.

When Frank was fifteen and leaving school, all the jobs open to him appeared equally unattractive. In the next ten years he had a dozen occupations and never took one of them seriously or devoted a fraction of his energy to carrying them out. But after his twenty-fifth birthday his Uncle Fred, who single-handedly ran the Old Kent Road

Stamp Company from a poky little shop, offered him a position. Fred Haswell had been suffering from rheumatoid arthritis for years and was becoming crippled by it. He badly needed someone to act as his legs in attending stamp auctions and calling on other dealers, as well as tackling humdrum tasks like keeping the shop tidy and making the tea. The job appealed to Frank as the duties were light and he could have time off whenever he wanted for training or boxing contests.

The Old Kent Road Stamp Company had always been something of a joke in the Shields family circle and they were amazed when Frank stuck to it after chucking up a dozen better jobs. But he had changed things around to suit himself after a few weeks in the little shop. Fred Haswell had to keep on doing the tidying and making the tea as his nephew spent nearly all his time out, at auctions or meeting other dealers and stamp-collectors and finding out what made them tick, or seeing what was going on in London generally. Frank quartered the metropolis on foot and came to know it as well as a taxi-driver. He accumulated a mass of other knowledge which was to prove useful to him later on.

For Frank Shields was an unusual young man, not at all like his lazy, bullying father or his petty-minded mother. He had a keen eye and brain, as well as fast fists and he took a long cool look at everything going on about him. He believed profoundly that the world did not make sense from a human point of view—for one thing he could see that there was no sensible system of reward and punishment. Good people often died agonising deaths while some villains passed away peacefully in their sleep. Many men spent tedious lives working for a pittance, while others were handed a fortune just for being born in the right bed. Frank came to an important decision: that there was no way to make sense of the world in general, but sense could be imposed on a very small portion of it. He decided that he would live exactly as he chose, taking every pleasure he could find, but that he would be willing to pay any price that might eventually be asked of him. Doreen was right, as wives usually are about their husbands—Frank Shields, as well as being an intensely private person, was a very cold character indeed beneath that surface charm.

When Fred Haswell died Frank inherited the stamp business and for a while he kept it going much as before. But it was widely known that he was 'looking round for something a bit tasty' and such an opportunity was given to him through the generosity of two men. The first was Sammy Coyne, the boxing promoter, who had

31

prospered mightily since the time when he had suggested that Frank should turn pro. Sammy Coyne had become an entrepreneur, with various interests apart from boxing, he had also acquired a large flat in Hay Hill and an estate near Snape in Suffolk with good rough shooting. Occasionally Frank was invited to the Suffolk manor house for a shooting weekend, as he never wasted a shot and obviously enjoyed joining in the slaughter of pheasants, partridges, hares, rabbits and anything else foolish enough to be moving about in the fields.

One misty autumn morning, in the middle of a field of barley stubble with only a few dead pheasants as witnesses, Sammy Coyne suggested to Frank that it might be worth his while having a few words with Ben Sutro: 'So listen to him, maestro. You could be well pleased.'

Ben Sutro was a very big wheel in the wonderful Soho entertainment world, with numerous interests. In fact, no one, apart from Ben, knew quite how widely his interests were spread. He was mean when it came to words, rarely giving anyone more than a dozen and those were chosen with care. He spread himself a little with Frank and even addressed him as 'My son', but only after having looked him over carefully with old, bloodshot eyes that were surprisingly keen. Ben Sutro regarded people silently and they tended to become uneasy in the long silent moments as he pushed aside their pretences and isolated their weaknesses, while revealing nothing of himself. But Frank did not become a jot uneasy; he had an inner self-confidence that could only have been shaken with thumbscrews. Putting a plump hand the colour of a good cigar on Frank's shoulder, Ben confided that it might be worth his while having a few words with a man called Denis.

A week after returning from the Suffolk manor house Frank exchanged a few ambiguous sentences with Denis in a dingy room over a pornographic cinema in Dean Street. Then a similarly spare conversation took place between Frank and an unusually large man called Phil in a tiny office that was to let in Goslett Yard, during which a new and lucrative vocation for Frank was outlined. Frank took another week to think it over and then accepted in his give-nothing-away voice, so that it was hard to tell that he was indeed 'well pleased'.

The proposition put to Frank was extremely simple, like many good money-making schemes: he was to do some odd jobs for which he would always be paid cash in advance. It was suggested that it would be wise for Frank to keep the Old Kent Road Stamp Company afloat, as it provided him with a visible source of income

33

and an excellent means of 'laundering' quantities of ten pound notes. It seemed to Frank that behind Phil and Denis there lurked the shadowy presence of Ben Sutro, a veritable prince of London's night-life. And he had the vague impression that behind Ben there were other shadowy, powerful men who saw to it that their names never got into the newspapers. But these were only Frank's thoughts. What had been put to him quite forcefully was that Phil was to be Frank's only contact and even telephone calls with Phil were to be kept to a minimum and very little said. Equally plain was the knowledge that if anything ever went wrong with a job for which he had already been paid in advance, then Frank would be on his own and no one would know him. All this suited Frank very well: he was the quintessential loner, he hated working with other people and he was always prepared to pay for any mistakes he made.

After agreeing to Phil's proposal, Frank disposed of the lease of the shop in the Old Kent Road; but he was not disregarding Phil's good advice. He explained that he simply wanted to move his stamp business from a depressed part of Newington to the more prosperous venue of the City. He took new premises there, just one room at the back of a tea-jobber's office in Silver Street, off London Wall. The tea-jobber was a boxing

34

enthusiast and a one-time fan of Frank's and trusted him enough to let him have a key to the premises to use out of normal business hours. Frank had a special lock fixed to his own door. In this small room he installed a telephone, a chair, a desk, a typewriter, a steel filing-cabinet, a waste-paper basket and a superior type of safe which was highly recommended by experts. It amused Frank to keep a few conspicuous signs of his stamp-dealing activities in evidence, including a battered, well-thumbed group of Stanley Gibbons stamp catalogues, a framed set of Queen Elizabeth II Coronation issues and a magnifying glass.

Subsequent to moving to the City premises, the stamp business became even more of a puzzle to Doreen. On one occasion she raised the matter hesitantly with her mother. 'Mum, I know you think I'm silly to worry about Frank and his business. But he takes so much time off—you know—for his hobbies. And he's never at that office—you try ringing him there—you never get a reply...'

Marge did not interrupt her daughter, though she listened with barely concealed impatience. A strange but delightful thought had flitted in and out of her mind when Doreen mentioned phoning Frank at his City office: she imagined doing just that one day, and going up West to meet him, having shed a few pounds. But she quickly censored further erotic fantasies about Frank's strong hands and his slim hips and waited till her daughter's diffident sentences fizzled out. Then she gestured at Doreen's handsomely furnished drawing-room and the quiet Chelsea street outside the window, saying, 'Honestly Reen, I can't understand you. Reely girl! How you can ever complain about a man like Frank! Just 'cause he never worries you with his business problems. A man like that—'course he's too proud to bother a woman with his ups and downs, he just gets on with them hisself. Look round you girl—tell me one thing you lack! Didn't you say lunchtime, when you mentioned wanting a Mini to take Gary to school, Frank said "Right, go down Piccadilly, doll, choose yourself a colour." Does that sound as if business can be bad? Honestly, you girls today . . .'

Frank's accountant, Julius Myers, another boxing devotee, had his own suspicions about the stamp business. In a way the accounts appeared to make sense, but Myers had not been examining profit and loss accounts for thirty years for nothing. 'It stinks' is what he succinctly said to himself on occasions while looking at the Old Kent Road Stamp Company's ledgers which were written out in Frank's neat but rather childish hand. Myers permitted himself the odd ambiguous smile, but never when he was with Frank. Myers was very shrewd and Frank admired him, even liked him—as well as he liked anyone. Myers gave him excellent advice, including the tip that he should not put down too large a deposit on the house in Chelsea: 'Be like everyone else. Have a big mortgage. Wince a bit.'

The Old Kent Road Stamp Company operated in a decidedly eccentric fashion from its more prosperous City address. Hardly any transactions were done by post and callers were never allowed into Frank's private office. He simply bought a few rare stamps from a handful of dealers whose winning little ways he knew well. He was sure that, by paying them cash 'to simplify the book-keeping', the said sums of cash would promptly disappear and never be mentioned to the tax gatherers. Such deals were quite often a matter of 'giving gold for gold', as dealers described transactions where there is no profit margin, but that did not worry Frank who did not want to spend his time looking around for bargains. He also bought a few stamps by cheque and every month took his more valuable rarities to well-known London dealers who paid for them by cheque. These cheques were entered into a ledger in Frank's careful hand, duly audited by Julius Myers. They then formed a visible, taxable income.

CHAPTER SIX

Frank Shields' step as he walked up King Edward Street towards his obscure City office was definitely bouncy. For one thing it was a perfect June morning without a cloud in the sky and the weather had an effect on several of his pastimes. Secondly, he was feeling particularly fit, absolutely on top of his form. And it was going to be one of his rare working days, which had come to give him more of a charge than anything else he experienced, even a session with Doreen's best friend, Betty, who was 'a right little raver'. It also happened to be a Saturday, but he never complained about having to work at weekends or in the evening. For, as he had patiently explained to Doreen more than once, if you had a one-man business then you just had to do the work when it was there to be done.

At breakfast Frank had smiled inwardly, as he did most of his smiling, when Doreen asked him about his plans for the day. Frank had taken up sea-fishing as well as shooting and had acquired a rowing boat which he kept moored on a creek in the strange, desolate area of marshland on the Thames estuary stretching out beyond Gravesend. And he had become as much of an expert on the Halstow Marshes and the St Mary's Marshes as anyone who lived in the villages of Cooling and High Halstow. But he never boasted about that, for boasting was not his style. Doreen had said that as it was such a nice day she wondered if Frank might be going sea-fishing and would he take Gary along as a special treat. He grinned to himself and explained that he must work and had no idea how long this particular deal would take.

Frank's mother-in-law, Marge, once confided to her closest friend Elsie that she enjoyed seeing Frank walk down a street 'looking just as if he owned it'. Frank dressed quietly in dark suits and eschewed flamboyance, but there was just a hint of a swagger in his walk. He always looked what he was in essence, an athlete in tip-top condition. He was five foot ten, but much taller men often stepped out of his path. Marge had seen him deal with a veritable giant of a man, a bullying Swedish sailor who was making a nuisance of himself in one of her favourite Newington pubs. Frank had quietly warned the sailor once—he never warned anyone twice—and then got him in a corner and cut him up till he needed a dozen stitches. 'The speed of it, Else. Fair took your breath away,' Marge said.

It was 9.40 a.m. when Frank cut through Little Britain on his way to Silver Street, but there was no one about to admire the way he walked because that part of the City was always deserted at weekends. He enjoyed being on his own and hearing his steps ring out in the empty, echoing streets. He was dressed in a lightweight, brown suit and a cream, cotton shirt, with a brown, knitted, silk tie. He carried an empty, brown, hide briefcase. The pleasing sensation of solitariness continued as he opened the front door to the tea-jobber's office and picked out the meagre amount of mail addressed to himself from the pile that awaited the tea-jobber's attention on Monday.

There was only an electricity bill, two stamp catalogues and one letter addressed in a shaky hand which had been forwarded from the Old Kent Road shop. Frank unlocked his own door, locked it again and sat down behind his imposingly large desk. He threw the stamp catalogues unopened into the waste-paper basket and left the electricity bill on the blotter while he studied his single letter. It was from one of his Uncle Fred's old customers who, at the age of eighty, had lost interest in hoarding tiny pieces of gummed paper and wanted to sell his collection. Painstakingly typing with two fingers, Frank replied that it would be best to put the lot into auction; he then shredded the old man's letter into the basket.

With his stamp business concluded for the day, Frank opened a secret drawer in his desk that was extremely difficult to find and virtually impossible to open unless you knew the trick. The contents of the drawer would have surprised any of his acquaintances in the philately business: there were three automatic pistols, a steel flick knife, a clean yellow duster, rubber gloves, two pairs of sunglasses and a pair of heavy horn-rimmed spectacles with plain glass lenses since Frank had 20-20 vision. Only one of the automatics, the very efficient American PPK/S, had been used to kill anybody because the other two guns, a .357 Snub Magnum and a 8mm Nambu, were facsimile models, though they looked just as deadly as the PPK/S.

Frank thoughtfully weighed the Snub Magnum facsimile model in his hand for a moment before wrapping it in the clean yellow duster and placing it in the briefcase along with the pair of rubber gloves. He slipped a pair of sunglasses with amber lenses in to his pocket. After locking the secret drawer Frank looked around his room and then left it with a jaunty step.

When setting out to do an odd job for 'the corporation', as he mentally referred to the shadowy group which he could visualise lined up behind Phil and Denis, Frank always felt that he was living at about ten times the rate of anyone he saw in the street. During the next few hours he was going to walk a tightrope and his own life might well be in the balance.

Walking towards Wood Street, Frank appeared to be strolling haphazardly, smiling to himself and swinging his briefcase. In fact he had a telephone-box in Gresham Street in mind, but there was no rush, so his step was leisurely and he enjoyed the sunshine. When he entered the phone-box it was 10.25 and he passed the next five minutes idly thumbing through a directory. No one in his right mind was going to ask Frank Shields to vacate a phone-box.

At precisely 10.30 Frank dialled the number of a phone-box off Frith Street. Phil was there to answer it, in his breathy Cockney voice, at the first ring and the two men began a conversation which would have sounded decidedly dull to anyone who happened to overhear it on a crossed line.

Frank: 'Has that item arrived then?'

Phil: 'It has, but it's not an export item.'

Frank: 'So it's a home, do-it-yourself job then? Right?'

Phil: 'Definitely.'

Frank: 'Fine. I like it.'

Phil: 'But there's nothing to be done till after lunch so I'll see you, say, half two? Corner of Park Lane and South Street? Right?'

Frank: 'Half two it is.'

At 10.35 Frank stood in Gresham Street, looking up at the church and enjoying the warmth of the sun. He had approximately four hours to spend before his important appointment in Park Lane, but that was no problem. If Frank had not known what to do with spare time he would not have devised his life with the purpose of having a lot of it. Within two minutes he had decided to walk across the heart of London in a westerly direction, buy some cheese rolls in a Health Food Shop in Baker Street and enjoy a couple of hours of leisurely rowing on the lake in Regent's Park.

CHAPTER SEVEN

'Julia.' It seemed to Rex Bealby just as if his dead wife's name had been said somewhere in his head, very quietly but in a tone of intense longing. Expressed thus the name was like an abracadabra, a code-word that set free all sorts of pent-up feelings including both hope and despair. Julia, I long to be with you, he thought; life is an empty thing without you. Bealby found the idea of suicide alien, even repugnant, but he had to acknowledge the persistence of a death-wish in himself. The previous evening he had sat out in a deck-chair watching the wonderful changing colours of the sky as the sun set. There had been a moment when part of the sky was deep purple and another part a pale duck-egg green, while the area near to the sun had an orange glow and was fire-bright. Just before the sun vanished from sight the sky was extremely beautiful and the peace of that vision quite overwhelming. He had experienced a profound desire to step into the sky and leave the world. He wanted above everything else to find Julia again—that was his hope. But despair followed hard on the heels of hope, for he could not believe in the promise of immortality held out by the Christian religion.

Bealby put down his scythe and stood with his hands on his hips, resting his aching back. Although Julia had been dead for over five years, he would still sometimes wake up in the bed they had shared for so long and put out his hand to touch her or murmur her name before the horrid realisation sank in that she had gone away forever. Then memories of her cruelly painful death from cancer would come into his mind and leave him disturbed and angry. She was often in his mind, though usually with happier memories. So he was sometimes lost in a day-dream and hardly aware of what was going on about him. He knew that he had an increasingly remote, abstracted air and that some people must think he was on the verge of losing his wits. Two weeks ago he had been introduced to a young Coldstream Guards officer at his club.

44

The fool who had made the introduction had babbled on about him being 'a hero of Arnhem' and he had glimpsed a fleeting expression of incredulity on the young man's face. He had imagined the Coldstreamer's mental comment: What, this puny old buffer?

Looking at the banks of the lawn which he had largely cleared of couch grass, cow parsley and the ubiquitous ground elder, Bealby was thinking how impossible it was to tell the young of all the changes that come with time, transforming vigorous lithe bodies into feeble old ones and stealing away ambition, love and hope. And so it should be, he thought; quite soon enough when the next generation have to make these sad discoveries for themselves. But it was certainly a bad sign that he should have appeared an impostor in the Coldstreamer's eyes because he was usually at his best in London. In the familiar City streets or in his office in Old Jewry, dealing with his family's shipping business, he could often manage to put thoughts of Julia out of mind and be reasonably competent at the work which he still enjoyed to some extent. But it was not possible to escape the many ghosts of Julia haunting the old house and garden she had loved so much.

Picking up his scythe again, Bealby glanced at some tall nettles he had spared from habit. Julia had always asked him to leave a clump or two because they attracted butterflies. He had no taste for poetry himself, but he could remember a few lines about nettles written by a soldier poet of the First World War which Julia often quoted. He summoned up all he could remember of the poem and said it aloud:

This corner of the farmyard I like most:
As well as any bloom upon a flower
I like the dust on nettles, never lost
Except to prove the sweetness of a
    shower.

As he spoke the words Bealby could hear his wife saying them and his eyes became misty. Let the tears come, he thought. In public he always preserved a poker face when her name was mentioned and strove to reply without a sign of emotion, but alone he did not have to keep up any pretence. If one could not shed a few tears over the loss of a lover and friend who had shared all his good years, then emotion must truly be dead. Despite the pain of memories he did not want that. Tears ran down his face silently for a few moments and ended in a sob. He sniffed and wiped his face with his handkerchief, then looked at his watch. Eleven o'clock and he had been hard at it for over two hours. It was time for a break. When Julia was still alive this was about the time he would hear her call 'Darling' and she would come out with a jug of fresh lemonade for them to drink while sitting in deckchairs near her favourite hedge, the wild one composed largely of hawthorn but interspersed with wild rose and ivy.

Limping back through the garden, Bealby was aware of how much his knee had been aching in recent months, but he was more concerned about his ludicrously thin arms, revealed by short-sleeved shirts. Normally he was most aware of how painfully thin he was when sitting in the bath and it was plain that he lacked flesh to cushion his spine. Gradually, in his seventies, he was being transformed into another persona, that of a pathetically thin and feeble old man. 'Without the strength of a louse,' he said aloud, quoting a favourite First World War saying of his father's. If one ate very little, then such a course of events was probably inevitable, but he just could not enjoy his solitary meals. He had never been a gourmet, but even the ordinary savour of food had vanished with Julia's death. Mrs. Gideon, who came to the house every weekday and prepared his dinner, was a good cook, but often he found no enjoyment in what she had left for him.

Bealby could not be bothered to find the rarely used lemon-squeezer in order to make lemonade for himself, just as he could never take the trouble to make himself a proper meal at the weekend and always settled for cheese and biscuits, or soup and toast. He poured himself a glass of water, realising that he had overdone the scything and made himself weary. It was when he was very tired that he was most plagued by thoughts of Julia's death. When she was a young woman there had been a kind of macabre dress-rehearsal for her last illness; she had a hysterectomy because a large fibroid had grown in her womb. 'As big as a grapefruit,' the surgeon had remarked cheerfully. Then in her sixty-third year a carcinoma had been diagnosed, but the opinion of three surgeons had been that it was inoperable. The first illness had brought them even closer than many couples, he suspected, because it had meant that Julia could not have children. The second, so painfully cruel . . .

The melancholy reverie was interrupted by the sound of the telephone and Bealby decided to take it in the hall where he could sit down, as he thought it would be his sister calling with a long narrative of family news. But instead of his sister's voice, which was rather like his own, it was the lilting, slightly honeyed tone of Barbara Owen, the Vicar's wife, whom he liked though he found her husband pompous and long-winded.

'Rex, it's Babs. Are you in the middle of your elevenses, dear? It's the church fête again. We wondered if you might possibly spare something for the auction.'

48

'Of course, Babs. I'll look something out today. Any suggestions?'

'Anything, as long as you are quite sure you don't want it. Hold on—Arthur's saying something . . . Rex, Arthur says you are *not* to be as generous as you were last year. You remember, you gave us the lovely Japanese painted screen and the Kyoto bowl. Arthur says they were both snapped up by dealer friends of Captain Ty Wester. We're very grateful indeed for anything, but we don't want to deprive you of your treasures and then have dealers benefit most. Arthur says—'

'My dear girl, do tell Arthur it is not possible to have an auction and then prevent dealers buying items—if they wish. And you can't possibly have reserve prices at a charity sale . . . Don't worry, Babs, I shan't bankrupt myself and this old house is too full of things that are never looked at. Besides I like to support the church . . .' He was going to say, 'because Julia liked to', but suppressed it, and said, 'Even though I'm usually a defaulter on church parades.'

Barbara Owen giggled and passed on the last phrase to her husband. 'Arthur says there has to be some dispensation for someone as generous as you are to the church.'

'Very good. Then I'll make a search this afternoon. You know there are rooms here with things I never look at from one year to

49

the next. But I promise not to donate another Kyoto bowl.'

'Fine. No hurry, old boy. That very nice girl, Louise Simpson, will be calling on you one day about the auction. Don't tell her I phoned, but Arthur thought the request should come from us first.'

'Yes, understood. I shall try to be discreet.'

'As ever, Rex. Now do remember that we are still waiting for you to propose yourself for dinner here.'

'I know, my dear, and so I shall, very soon. Goodbye, Babs.'

'Goodbye, Rex.'

Bealby limped back into the kitchen thinking that his wretched knee was becoming unusually painful and wondering whether he should take some aspirin. When he read of the IRA criminals 'knee-capping' their victims he knew just how much pain was involved in that simple phrase and how the pain would inevitably go on for years. On principle he was against too much drugging and decided against the aspirin as he had taken some the previous day.

Picking up *The Times*, Bealby thought that he would take a break from gardening and have a session of reading and perhaps snoozing in a deckchair, near to Julia's favourite hedge where shade was provided by the ancient apple trees. Walking to the front door, he reflected on how easy it was for him

50

to appear generous regarding the church fête auction. There had been many travellers and collectors in the Bealby family over the years and most of their possessions were still in the old house named Alderbury Hall that had been built to the directions of a Joshua Bealby, a merchant of London and Guildford, in 1750. Rex Bealby was not a connoisseur nor a collector and thought that material possessions were relatively unimportant as long as one had somewhere comfortable to live. But the fact was that he owned enough things to stock two or three antiques shops and they would be valuable items, not like the flashy stuff Sylvester had on show at Court Antiques.

On his way to the favourite spot by the straggly hawthorn hedge, Bealby gave Rupert Sylvester some thought. He had nothing against the chap, indeed he admired his energy, his self-confidence and his determination to get on in the world, just as he admired the delightful appearance and charming personality of Polly. The breach between himself and the young Sylvesters was a silly, awkward business, but it was entirely of Rupert's making. Bealby knew just how it had come about and thought the reason quite absurd, but now that he felt he should approach Rupert he was not sure how to do it.

Placing his deckchair by an ancient

Bramley apple tree with boughs supported by crutches made out of other boughs, Bealby looked round appreciatively, thinking how lovely the hawthorn was in June. His gardener's eye noted that the ivy was getting too much of a grip on the hedge and would have to be cut back, but that could wait. What was the point of having a pleasant garden if one could never sit down and enjoy it?

As Rex Bealby dropped his newspaper and lay back in the deckchair, the pain from his knee that had been shattered on the bridge at Arnhem became less severe. Smelling the faint but sweet scents of flowers, listening to a blackbird singing in an ash tree, he gave his mind to the absurd and annoying business regarding Rupert Sylvester. When he was first introduced to the young couple he had been glad that they were going to be his nearest neighbours. The wife, Polly, was pretty and had a delightful, very feminine manner. Rupert had appeared likeable too; he seemed to be genuinely interested in the history of the Hall and had seized on the fact that the Bealby family could be traced back to Norman ancestors, which accounted for the simple coat of arms cut in the stone lintel over the front door of the Hall. Indeed, he had once made a copy of the shield with its crossed swords and the legend *La Garde Noir*, saying that he would do some research on the de Bealbie coat of arms. Bealby's relationship with the young and attractive pair seemed at that time to be set on a pleasant course.

Then there was the ludicrous occasion when both he and Sylvester had turned up at the church fête wearing Old Etonian ties. The scene in the refreshment tent that afternoon had indeed been a comedy of errors. Jokingly he said to Rupert, 'Will you sock me a strawberry mess?' using the Etonian slang for 'Will you treat me to an ice-cream sundae?' but was met by a blank stare. Then he asked Sylvester if the tuck-shop in his time was still called Jack's, named after Jack O'Connor, the cricket professional who had run it. Another perplexed, embarrassed look from Rupert. Finally, and still quite innocently, he asked whether Sylvester had been at the school under the Claude Elliott or the Robert Birley regime. When there was still a blank response the penny finally dropped and he realised that Sylvester had not in fact been to Eton. He had accordingly made some other footling remark and moved away to get a drink. But Sylvester must have been seriously embarrassed by the questions and possibly thought that Bealby had deliberately set out to expose him.

Bealby shook his head vehemently as if once more to disclaim any such notion. Nothing could have been of less interest to him than exposing Rupert Sylvester as someone who wore a tie to which he was not entitled. In Bealby's mind such a pretence was a silly piece of snobbery not worth thinking about, let alone brooding on, but Sylvester must have done so and had studiously avoided contact with him from that day.

'My God!' Bealby exclaimed aloud. 'What kind of chap does he think I am?' He knew that since the war there had not been the slightest trace of snobbery in his own attitude to people; the war had made him a real democrat as well as revising many of his other opinions. Ever since that fateful day in October, 1944, when he was serving with the airborne division and was informed that the drop at Arnhem was to take place over two days and he had known in his bones that 'Operation Market Garden' was going to be a planned blunder and monumental cock-up, he had been able to see clearly what was important in life and what was trivial. Love, courage, friendship and loyalty were important in his eyes; many other things were quite unimportant. Personally he did not give a damn if someone wanted to pretend that he had been to Eton, but he did mind that this silly act on Sylvester's part meant he never saw the young couple. And now that he felt he should warn Rupert about the dangerous man, Roscoe Starr, he was placed in a dilemma. If they had been on normal friendly terms he could have done it quite easily. But when he had moved towards Sylvester that morning in the lane, the young chap had looked quite startled and raced off on his mare.

Bealby muttered, 'Damn it!' opened his eyes and glared about the garden, feeling irritable and unsettled. Then the sights and sounds of a perfect summer morning soothed him again. He watched a bumble bee passing from bell to bell on a foxglove and how the bee's weight made the flower dip down. He glimpsed a jay and was taken by its delightful colouring. He gazed at the wild rose bush in bloom and mused on what a beautiful world it was and how particularly lovely was his own little corner. Then he lay back in his deckchair once more, feeling soothed by Nature's balm. As he closed his eyes to sleep he thought that he heard Julia calling 'Darling!'

CHAPTER EIGHT

'No, nothing's wrong, Mother.' Polly Sylvester spoke sharply and then was annoyed with herself for sounding irritable. Her mother was extremely perceptive about people and her perceptiveness seemed to work just as well when she was on the end of a telephone line two hundred miles away in Yorkshire.

'And Rupert's fit and thriving as usual?' her mother asked astutely. It was a trick question in that she would divine a good deal from the very tone of Polly's response.

Polly decided to fake liveliness by giving a mass of information that her mother did not want and could not possibly query. 'Blinding with science' was how Rupert described this technique. 'He's immensely busy just now. He bought a large cache of crested china. He says it's the kind of thing that was popular in the 1930s and sold very cheaply then at seaside resorts. Every piece bears the town crest of places like Scarborough and Margate. Anyway, he hit on this large collection, all in absolutely mint condition. Adele Rogers put a lot of them in the window and they've been selling like hot cakes to motorists passing through . . .'

Her mother appeared nonplussed by this loquacious reply. 'How clever of him,' she said, 'he does seem to be doing well. Do give him our love. So, darling, you'll let me know your plans for the first two weeks in July as soon as you can?'

'Of course, Mummy. Love to Daddy.'

'Goodbye, darling.'

Polly put the phone down knowing that her mother would be replacing her receiver with a puzzled expression on her face. It was the

56

first time that Polly had not responded eagerly by saying yes to a suggestion that her parents should come to stay at Vine Cottage. Normally she looked forward to their annual summer stay at Alderbury, to long talks with her mother and to taking both her parents off in her Mini to visit Rye and Tunbridge Wells. But this year she felt she just could not face having them in the house while Rupert was subject to such strange moods. At times he seemed full of pointless excitement, as if all keyed up for something to happen, while at other times he was on edge and very depressed. Her father would be particularly baffled by Rupert's odd behaviour as he was such a cheerful, positive man himself, always on the same optimistic level. She knew that her parents had been rather wary of Rupert from the first. To a bluff Yorkshire farmer like her father Rupert must have seemed a very unusual, rather exotic young man. His extreme good looks for one thing—she could vividly remember her mother's immediate reaction. Going into the kitchen, she had said how much Rupert resembled Tyrone Power, a film star of the 1940s and added that he was 'nearly too good-looking'. Her father made no comment, but Polly had sensed considerable reserve in his silence. At that time Rupert looked particularly dashing and handsome in his army uniform. In her parents' reaction, in those early days, what had seemed to loom large was the fact that both of Rupert's parents were dead and he appeared to have no living relatives. She could imagine her father saying, 'Very odd that, Mary. Quite pe-culiar in fact.' Polly suddenly remembered Edith Evans as Lady Bracknell in *The Importance of Being Ernest* declaiming in a stagey voice, 'To lose one parent, Mr. Worthing, may be regarded as a misfortune; to lose both looks like carelessness ...', and made herself smile even though she felt edgy and down.

Polly went back to the kitchen sink where she had been washing the first lettuce of the season picked from her garden. She contemplated it, thinking about supper and how to tempt Rupert into eating. He had always been fastidious, only picking at small helpings, but recently he seemed to have completely lost his appetite. She decided on a salad made of all the tiny vegetables she could find and then perhaps a pie made of the first gooseberries which were not properly ripe yet but would taste all right with some brown sugar. And a bottle of hock ... Her mind wandered away from planning a meal as recent images of Rupert appeared in her mind as if on a television screen. A strange, flustered smile; his worried expression as he answered the phone with a voice choked by nerves; his usually bright eyes blurred by fatigue; a strange look of naked fear once when the telephone rang just as they were going to bed.

Leaving the lettuce in a colander Polly moved aimlessly about, doing some pointless tidying, unable to settle down to her usual routine. She was brooding on how much she now believed of Rupert's stories about his life before they had met. His account of his childhood in India must be true—he told too many convincing stories of life in Lahore as a schoolboy and family holiday trips to Simla and Dehra Dun. He also conjured up vivid descriptions of misty mornings in the Kashmir mountains and had such a large repertoire of tales about the decaying estate of an Indian prince who had been a friend of his parents that she felt as if she knew the charming, weak but amiable prince who had been obsessed with keeping the princely trappings of his life after the cash that paid for them had gone. But it was decidedly odd that, if both Rupert's parents were dead, he should not have any of their possessions. And now she knew that he had lied to her about his reasons for resigning his Army commission—there was no doubt that he had been in trouble in Ireland, but had 'fudged' what the trouble was...

The telephone rang again but this time she walked slowly towards it as Rupert did. When she answered the call she heard the pipping noise signifying that it came from a public box and momentarily she experienced a feeling of nervousness at the thought of being suddenly enlightened as to the cause of her husband's strange moods. There was another delay as a coin was inserted and then a masculine voice asked if she would kindly inform 'the Captain' that Bill Edwards would definitely be fit for the cricket match on Sunday afternoon. Her first 'Yes' was so faint that she had to repeat it. Once the phone had been replaced she made up her mind to do something she had never even contemplated before: to look through things in Rupert's study to see if she could discover any clues as to what was worrying him. She felt certain it was nothing to do with his business which had been particularly successful in recent months. Nor did she suspect that he was involved with another woman. Women flirted with Rupert but he always shied away, as he had done from Louise Simpson and her friend Patience Chalmers.

To spy on another person was alien to Polly's nature and she flushed and felt guilty as she walked through the hall, deliberately avoiding looking at herself in the mirror there. She ran up the stairs and walked quickly into the scrupulously neat room that had been set out as an act of homage to the first Duke of Wellington. One wall was fitted with white bookshelves and these housed a comprehensive collection of books and pamphlets about the Iron Duke. The other walls were hung with prints, paintings, photographs and framed autograph letters illustrating the life and times of the Duke: a copy of the James Thorburn painting of the family man with his grandchildren, a copy of the handsome Sir Thomas Lawrence portrait, an original watercolour of Apsley House, a large photograph of the gravestone of the Duke's horse, Copenhagen, an architect's plan of the Duke's country house at Stratfield Saye.

On Rupert's walnut desk a bronze bust of Wellington regarded with a straight stare anyone who entered the room, looking as if he was just about to ask one of his typically forthright questions. Polly imagined him saying to her, 'And just why are you prying among your husband's things?'

She sat down nervously at the desk, the surface of which was bare apart from the bust and a green morocco-edged blotter. She opened the central drawer carefully so as not to disturb anything inside. The contents were very orderly as if thought had been given to the arrangement, completely unlike the jumble of her own desk where she could never find anything. On a piece of card Rupert had written out in his careful, large hand two lines of poetry with the author's name:

They have given us into the hands of
　the new unhappy lords.

Lords without anger and honour, who
dare not carry their swords.

G. K. Chesterton

A large piece of paper was covered with
drawings in Indian ink—designs for coats of
arms. One of these bore the inscription *La
Garde Noire* as over the front door of
Alderbury Hall; another was inscribed *Ardua
Molimur* and beneath it Rupert had written,
'*Ardua molimur; sed nulla nisi ardua virtis*—We
attempt the difficult; for there is no virtue in
what is easy.'

Polly shook her head. A detective might
make some sense out of such things, Sherlock
Holmes would immediately deduce from
them what was disturbing Rupert, but she
had no talent in that line. There was no point
in further ferreting and if she was not careful
she might disturb something and Rupert
would be bound to notice. She must either
ask him outright or wait and hope that the
trouble would go away.

Polly glanced at her watch as she left
Rupert's study. It was half past one but she
did not feel inclined to bother about making
herself lunch. She decided to change into a
dress, pick the gooseberries for the pie and
then sit out in the glorious sunshine. The
weather forecaster had said that high pressure
ensured that the good weather would last for

a few days, but she had no faith in such predictions. Tomorrow strong winds from the west could easily bring back the rain which they had endured for weeks.

In the kitchen Polly jotted down a note to remind herself to put a bottle of hock in the fridge at teatime and picked up a dish for the gooseberries. She looked in the mirror on the wall over the sink. The nervous flush had departed but her eyes had a worried expression. What had changed in her face since she was in her twenties? The change had been a subtle one, imperceptibly taking place over the years she had been married. Her complexion was still good and her skin free of lines, but she no longer had an open expression; she looked disillusioned, as an older woman might who had become used to a succession of disappointments.

Going out into the lovely garden revived her spirits as little else could have done. It was impossible to feel depressed when the sun was shining from a completely cloudless sky and the birds were singing like a celestial chorus in the row of trees which marked one boundary of their garden. She thought she would change into a bikini later on and sunbathe while she had the chance. The dark earth looked in a very good state and if they now had a period of hot sunshine they should have a truly massive crop of strawberries and raspberries.

Polly walked down the grass path between two vegetable plots, turning over in her mind the problem of how to put her parents off visiting Vine Cottage in July without upsetting or mystifying them. Rupert was obsessed with his work and he loathed taking holidays, particularly since that weekend at Budleigh Salterton when he had panicked as the child drowned, so the excuse of their being away then would be suspect. Should she simply put her mother's request to Rupert and leave the matter to him? Undoubtedly he would not want them to come and would be able to 'fudge' a good reason.

Pausing to sniff a lavender bush, Polly urged herself to put that particular problem and everything else to do with Rupert out of her mind for the afternoon—turning these matters over and over did no good and was only making her feel bitter about the man she had once loved passionately.

The neat row of gooseberry bushes looked in splendid fettle. Rupert was obsessive about weeds and could never rest until each bed had been inspected for the odd shoot of ground elder. She began to pick the small berries but had only a dozen or so in the dish when she heard some kind of commotion just over the hawthorn hedge. It sounded like someone falling and calling out something incomprehensible at the same time and it startled her. She put down the dish and ran to the hedge. She had to get down on her knees to peer through a gap. Brigadier Bealby was lying prone on the ground and looking round warily, his startled cornflower blue eyes appeared very wide and large. For a ghastly moment she thought he might have had a stroke or heart attack, but he smiled on glimpsing her and said, 'Oh, Polly, it's you. Sorry, my dear. I—I feel such an idiot. Fell and twisted my ankle, and it's the good leg, you see. Feel quite helpless, damn it.'

'I'm coming through.' The gap was small and Polly pushed at the springy hawthorn branches knowing it would be a struggle as the spikes would catch on her dress. Nettles in the hedge stung her hands and arms and halfway through she was momentarily caught so that she had to twist round, hearing her dress rip. Eventually she scrambled through on her bottom, having to lean over backwards like a limbo dancer. 'Not exactly a modest entry, I'm afraid,' she said.

'My dear, your dress!' Bealby said. 'I'm sorry.'

'Oh, bother the dress. It's an old one anyway.'

Polly knelt by the Brigadier, putting her hand on his shoulder and feeling surprised at how thin and shaky he was. 'If I help push and pull do you think you could get up? Or what should I do?'

65

'Oh, I could manage with your help, my dear. Sorry, indeed I'm sorry about this. Lord, I am an old crock!'

Polly put one arm round Bealby's shoulder and pulled him with her other arm. She was strong herself and was amazed at how frail and relatively weak he seemed to be. Knowing his reputation as a soldier who had won two medals for bravery, she had always presumed that he was strong although he had a slight figure.

'That tumble knocked the breath out of me,' Bealby explained. 'I got up on that stool to tackle the damned ivy. What a fool!'

When Bealby was on his feet again, Polly asked, 'What do you think? Shall you be able to walk with me helping? Or should I send for the doctor?'

Bealby laughed and Polly was surprised again at how agreeable she found his laugh. He had very white teeth and his blue eyes looked unusually bright against his brown cheeks. She thought he was attractive even if he was older than her father.

'Send for the doctor?' Bealby repeated in an amused voice. 'By God, I might die right here if we waited for that man Benson to turn up. I can see you've never bothered with him yourself. Very wise, that! I wish I had no experience of Freddie Benson. No, my dear, I shall be able to hobble over to the house with your assistance. And a little rest with my leg

66

up should soon cure a sprain.'

'Good,' said Polly. 'Then that's what we'll do. And when we get there I'm going to make you some coffee or tea. Or what about something to eat?' She looked round into his eyes. 'Have you had any lunch today?'

Bealby laughed again. 'These direct questions. No, my dear, I didn't bother with anything today. Seemed too much of a fag.'

'Nor did I, so we'll have something together.'

'That would be nice. I hate to bother you further, but that would indeed be very nice.'

They began to walk across the lawn at the slow rate dictated by the Brigadier, who was obviously in some pain as he winced a little. But his mind did not seem to be on his sprained ankle because he said, 'An omelette. Now that would be a treat. Julia—my wife—we often had an omelette for luncheon on a day like this. Or would that be too much trouble?'

'Omelettes just happen to be a speciality of mine.'

'What a treat!' Bealby exclaimed. He smiled again and then gave the matter some thought. 'First time you will have had a meal at the Hall. So I must open a bottle to celebrate. Well, how nice, but then they say that clouds have silver linings sometimes!'

CHAPTER NINE

'Now are you sure you'll be all right? You can manage that parcel?' Rupert Sylvester asked the unnecessary questions unctuously, thinking, Stupid old cow. His face felt quite stiff with a false expression of interest. The large North Country-woman veered in the general direction of the open front door of Court Antiques, but she had already approached the door and turned back twice. She moved in a stately fashion; she was as tall as himself and a good deal bulkier—it was rather like getting an ocean liner out of dock—but he was going to persist in dancing attendance on her until she was gone.

'Yes, I shall be quite all right. My Daimler's just there.' She indicated the large car parked outside the shop with pride, then stared hard at him as if trying to get his measure. Fat chance, he thought. He smiled back, feeling that the smile was glued to his mouth, amused at her for trying to size him up when so many had failed to do so. No one had ever suspected that there was Indian blood in his veins and that back in Simla he had an Anglo-Indian mother with whom he had not been in contact since he was nineteen.

'I just love that little table,' she said,

hesitating again and pointing to the George II mahogany tripod with a circular top on a birdcage support.

For a moment Sylvester had the impulse to say cheekily, 'Yes, but there we're talking about real money.' Instead the instincts of the market-place triumphed, and he said, 'I can see you've a dealer's eye for quality. Circa 1750. Particularly fine carving at the knees—those acanthus leaves . . .' He stopped the sales spiel when he saw he was leaving her behind. He wanted to be rid of her. She had managed in a short time to let drop, first to Adele Rogers and then to himself, that she was the Lady Mayoress of some town in Lancashire and her high and mighty airs were beginning to get him down. Now that she had made two purchases she must go. He exulted in thinking that the neat parcel contained fire-bellows which he had 'aged' himself and that the Lady Mayoress had paid twenty-five pounds for a china model of the Blackpool Tower for which he had paid less than a pound. Lovely, he thought. Be sure to call again when you can spend more cash and less time.

'Such an interesting shop,' the woman said. 'I must tell all my friends. A veritable Aladdin's cave.' She had the habit of closing her eyes while talking as if to display the tremors in the closed lids. Her light blue eye-shadow was a mistake; it had caked on

69

her dry, ageing skin and made her look older rather than more attractive.

Sylvester made an effort to pull himself together. Worried and frightened as he was, with the prospect of danger or a prison sentence looming before him, he was showing his nervous state by behaving badly to everyone and possibly damaging the business that he had worked so hard to build. For Christ's sake! he admonished himself mentally, have a little guts for once and try to behave more normally. Earlier that morning he had spoken irritably to Adele, of whom he was quite fond in a funny sort of way and nearly reduced her to tears. What was that saying about a coward facing a hundred deaths while a brave man met only one? He put his slim, brown hand on the woman's fat arm. 'Now, do let me take that parcel, at least while you get in the car. We don't want any minor tragedies.' He laughed inwardly as he said it, knowing that he would be getting two more fire-bellows the following week from a man in Firle who made them exclusively for the trade and that he had six more Blackpool Towers, all in equally mint condition.

'Well, yes, perhaps. Thank you.' She fluttered her watery grey eyes and tremulous lids in a faintly flirtatious manner. Sylvester held her arm as they walked out of the shop as if she too were a precious china model and waited patiently while she searched in her jumbo-sized handbag for her key to open the handsome lime-green car.

'The back seat, perhaps?' he suggested tentatively as if it were a matter of great importance. 'Then I could wrap that rug round the parcel to keep it quite safe.'

'How very thoughtful of you,' the woman said. 'I'm so glad that I decided to pull up here for a snack. It's all been most enjoyable and I *shall* tell my friends. So you can expect a veritable invasion from North Lancs. Well, goodbye.'

'No, *au revoir*.'

'Yes, *au revoir*.'

Sylvester continued to smile falsely as the Daimler was driven away and then tried to relax by taking in deep breaths of fresh air, wanting to still his mind which threatened to boil over again with unsettling thoughts and frightening possibilities. It occurred to him that it would be rather nice to pop into the White Rose and have a large gin. Never before had he had such a thought during the day. He glanced at his watch to see that it was ten minutes to two. He had gone without lunch, as he normally did when at the shop; fasting during the day usually suited him, but today he had to acknowledge feeling empty and low. Yes, low-spirited was the best phrase to describe his present state. But that would be normal for any coward faced with danger.

71

Turning to go back into the shop, Sylvester saw the Trotskyist, Judy Browning, poised on the doorstep of Street Cottage and gave her a wave. 'Still perfect—the weather I mean,' he said, smiling broadly. She frowned as if she did not understand, shrugged and stepped into her cottage.

The display of crested china which Adele had set out in the main window of Court Antiques did indeed look very attractive. In a month they had sold over three hundred of the pieces at prices ranging from ten to thirty pounds and he had paid just one thousand pounds for twelve hundred of them. And to think that cheeky know-all, Charlie Saunders, had dismissed them as 'fairground stuff'. Buying that collection had been a stroke of genuine serendipity: calling in to see a grandfather clock at a terraced house in Reigate, he had been very disappointed at its lamentable state, but then the owner had told him confidentially that her husband 'had travelled in China before the war'. He had climbed up into an untidy attic and found a dozen dusty cartons of the stuff, with all the pieces still wrapped individually in brown tissue paper. The old woman had been delighted to receive a cheque for a thousand pounds and he had probably turned over five or six times that amount already.

Adele Rogers tapped on the shop window. She was standing with the handsome curly-haired youth who had driven up in a brand-new Morgan and looked capable of spending a few pounds.

'Captain Sylvester,' Adele said as he walked through the front door, 'Mr Hughes here is very interested in the console table...'

'I can see you've an eye for quality, Mr Hughes,' Sylvester said briskly, staring hard at the table. 'Genoese, probably late eighteenth century.' The table was one of the most expensive items in the shop: giltwood with a white marble top supported by three cherubs, one of whom clasped a cornucopia spilling flowers and fruit, and standing on a rockwork base. The Cockney dealer, Charlie Saunders, had got quite excited on first seeing it, but after a close inspection had declared that it was a good deal restored.

'I wondered ...' the young man said hesitantly, 'if it was all original...'

'Oh yes, indeed,' Sylvester replied hastily. 'We had an expert opinion on it. A leading West-End dealer no less. That table is the chef's special here—if I might put it like that. I mean if I were going to buy just one item from the stock on display then that table would be it.'

'I'll take it,' the young man said. 'I want it for my mother—her birthday.'

'How nice—such a lovely thing,' Sylvester said in a tone that implied admiration mixed with longing and regret that it was to pass

73

from his sight forever.

'Will a cheque be all right?' Hughes asked, producing a Coutts cheque-book.

Sylvester smiled reassuringly. 'A cheque on Coutts Bank is an excellent reference in itself, I always say. Rather like having what I consider to be the ultimate in credit cards—an MCC membership card.'

'Aha!' The young man grinned and fished in the inside pocket of his expensive-looking suede jacket. 'There!' He produced the membership card which had eluded Rupert Sylvester for ten years though he had made two attempts to be elected.

The shadow of a rueful look passed over Sylvester's face, but he threw both arms out in an expansive gesture. 'What more can I say!' he exclaimed.

Adele Rogers' face was wreathed in smiles. Sylvester knew that it was not just the sale of an expensive item; she was happy that Sylvester appeared to be in a better mood again after he had snapped at her over that trifling matter.

'Now as to packing . . .' he said.

'I kept that stout carton aside—the one you brought it in,' Adele volunteered. 'With some corrugated card and plenty of shredded paper . . .'

'Fine, fine,' Sylvester said. He knew that Adele liked to fuss over an important purchase, lavishing loving attention on it, over-doing the packing as she tended to over-do everything. 'I'm glad, Mr Hughes, that such a choice piece has found a good home. And I'm sure your mother will be pleased.'

'Yes, thanks,' said Hughes, squatting down again to study the giltwood cherub holding the cornucopia which Charlie Saunders had said was suspect.

Sylvester strolled round the shop which even to his critical eye appeared to gleam with polish and care. He walked up to Pamela Stratton-Smith who was keeping a close eye on an elderly clergyman known to be liable to drop things.

'Pam, I've got to work on some catalogues and my calendar. You and Adele can hold the fort for half an hour? Unless anyone particularly asks for me.'

Pamela nodded. She had a more happy-go-lucky attitude towards the shop than Adele, but compensated for that by being a first-rate saleswoman.

'Of course. Would you like me to make some tea? There's a new packet of Earl Grey.'

'Not at the moment, thanks.'

Sylvester went to the back of the shop, turning to survey it a trifle wistfully as though for the last time. Soon, he thought, there might be a last time. If the shop were to close, Pamela would shrug it off and find a similar part-time job, but poor old Adele would be

75

lost. Adele did get on his nerves a bit even when he felt quite normal, what with her anxiety always to please, her over-sensitivity and her dentures that occasionally clicked, but he felt sorry for her nonetheless.

At the back of Court Antiques there were three rooms and a W.C. One room contained a sink and a gas-stove where they made tea and coffee and where Adele occasionally prepared a meagre lunch for herself. A larger room was used for minor repairs to broken items and for polishing and packing; it contained a large bench, a roll of corrugated card, piles of boxes and miscellaneous packing material—it was the one place where Sylvester did not continually strive for tidiness.

Sylvester opened the third door, that of his small office, with an unusual feeling of relief, glad for once to escape from the shop. His office was marked Private in large letters and no one was ever allowed to enter, even though members of the antiques trade occasionally tried, mistakenly believing that he must have some treasures hidden away there; he remembered Charlie Saunders trying to wheedle his way in and how he had been fended off by Adele. In fact the room contained only a desk, a chair, a waste-paper basket and some shelves of reference books such as Macquoid's *Dictionary of Furniture* that Sylvester found invaluable and to which

76

he would sometimes refer halfway through a conversation.

Closing the door, Sylvester sat down at the desk on which there lay an unopened copy of *The Times* and an auction catalogue. The catalogue was not elaborately produced and had few illustrations, but he knew the contents of the sale listed in it were quite exceptional. It was the sort of compilation over which he would normally have pored for hours, fascinated by the technical descriptions and having to search in the dictionary for some of the recondite words. As it was he had barely glanced at a few pages. The cover simply stated: 'Broomhill Park, Bucks. Sale of the contents by order of the executors of Lord Mallalieu.' The auction was being conducted by a small firm, Duckworth & Son, of Stony Stratford. A newcomer to the business would probably think that such an event, which had not been advertised, might not attract much attention, but Sylvester had enough experience to know better. First rumours and then hard information about the property of this famous old Catholic family would spread like wildfire through the trade and on the day of the view dealers from all over the country would turn up, together with the big boys from London who would inevitably take most of the treasures.

Oh, to hell with it, Sylvester thought, I

have more pressing matters to deal with. He put the catalogue out of sight in a drawer of the desk and then sat for a few moments in a most unusual posture for him, holding his head in his hands, in a mood of unrelieved gloom. To himself he said quietly, 'Idiot, idiot, idiot.'

Then, sitting with his chin supported by clenched fists, Rupert Sylvester reviewed his life. He was thirty-eight years old and it divided neatly into two halves. The first nineteen years he had spent in India being brought up by his doting mother. His English father, a Major then serving with the Indian army, had been killed in Burma while Sylvester was still in the cradle. When he was a boy his mother had always praised everything British, as if anxious to forget that she was Anglo-Indian herself, and she had made a fetish of anything to do with what she called 'Home' and 'the old country'. Sylvester had been nourished on stories of the British army with photographs of his father in uniform or playing polo and cricket. His mother had urged him to make a break with India one day, taking advantage of his British passport, not realising that when he did so the break would be final.

Nineteen years before his present dilemma Sylvester had landed at Heathrow with a bank credit of eight hundred pounds, but no introductions as his father had no living relatives. Since that day he had not been in contact with anyone in India and had managed to elude the enquiries that had been made about him there. His whole life from the bleak November afternoon when he had booked into a cheap hotel in Paddington had been a tissue of lies. Someone had said, 'All that I am, I taught myself.' It had struck a chord with Sylvester, who felt that he would have changed it slightly to, 'All that I am, I invented.' First he had constructed a largely fictitious background for himself and then a veritable pyramid of other fictions. No, he thought, not a pyramid, which was broadly based, but a crazy, ramshackle building, liable to totter a bit at times because it had no foundations. He could visualise the shaky tower-like erection, a rabbit warren of a place like some Indian houses he remembered, with steps that went first up and then down and passages leading nowhere. Fortunately he had an excellent memory, essential to anyone who lied consistently.

Sylvester said to himself, in a Peter Sellers-type Indian voice, 'Very truly sir, a complete lack of foundations, sir. And that is the trouble, sir,' making himself smile despite his despairing mood.

After an accident, he thought, one always saw how easily it could have been avoided if only certain steps had been taken or if some chance event had not occurred. The same was true of his present, dangerous plight. If he had told the truth about the circumstances in which he left the Army, which was because he had been in a visible panic at the idea of being posted to Crossmaglen and his colonel had offered him the chance to resign rather than be cashiered; or if he had ever admitted to having been terrified while on patrol in West Belfast, then Terence Boyle would have had nothing to do with him. Without being friendly with Boyle he would never have been introduced to Roscoe Starr, and so on. His involvement with Boyle, Starr, Moilliet, Pearson and other people he did not even know, in a secret, extreme right-wing organisation, had been accomplished in gradual stages, without him ever thinking hard about what it really meant. One of Wellington's sayings came back to him as being remarkably appropriate: 'One can face any danger fearlessly, even court it recklessly, so long as it is far enough off.'

Getting up from his desk, Sylvester began to pace the small room restlessly like a caged tiger. He could see that he had acted in the same manner as some foolish youth in the Middle Ages, who joined the Crusades in an impulsively romantic mood, carried away by the idea of the thing without ever visualising the bloody hand-to-hand fighting that would eventually be his fate. While he had been engrossed in the ridiculous trivia of designing a coat of arms for the group, Roscoe Starr had been planning a series of political murders. And what he had taken to be merely wild talk by Starr was in fact a blueprint for a campaign of assassinations that were to be disguised as suicides.

Sylvester stopped pacing up and down and ran his hands nervously through his thick hair. Then he picked up *The Times*; it had the fascination for him of something forbidden, because although he wanted to read the news item which he had spotted on the front page of the *Daily Telegraph* at the same time he dreaded doing so. He found that even the sober pages of *The Times* were full of violence. He glanced at stories of a riot in Brussels, a bomb going off in Rome, a hijack attempt at Orly Airport. Then he came on a paragraph on page four which told of the discovery of the corpse of Dai Llewelyn-Rees, the Communist miners' leader. Llewelyn-Rees's body had been found by a shepherd who had called at the miners' leader's remote country cottage in the Black Mountains. A shotgun had been found beside the body which the police said must have lain undisturbed for a week.

Throwing the newspaper into the waste-paper basket, Sylvester sat down at his desk again and took a large sheet of paper from the drawer. The paper was covered with doodles and drawings of coats of arms and armorial shields. The image of a mailed fist was incorporated in several of the sketches. He gave the drawings a baleful look and then shredded the sheet of paper into tiny pieces and put them in the basket too.

Sylvester's mind raced about pointlessly as it always did when nervous tension amounting to panic overwhelmed him. He was a conspirator in a murder—no, at least two murders because of the press story of the Militant Tendency man whose body had been found at the bottom of a Shoreditch tower block. The police would no doubt regard him as being an accessory to the killings although he had played no part in arranging them. And no matter how cleverly the murders were disguised as suicides the police would soon put two and two together. He had asked Roscoe Starr to come to see him but he had no idea what to say to Starr if he did turn up. He could put an ultimatum to the group that unless the murders stopped immediately he would go to the police. But Starr was a dangerous, reckless man who had proved that he was willing to risk his own life on several occasions. And Starr had said something about 'having protection in high places'. Did that mean that members of the police belonged to the group? And even saying that he now wanted to leave the group posed a threat to them which they could not ignore.

Tension had so boiled up in Sylvester that

he could not bear to be confined; the small, neat room made him think of a prison cell. But once outside it he hovered at the back of the shop because a coach from Birmingham had disgorged a crowd of talkative, middle-aged women who thronged the orderly premises.

Sylvester stood still, thinking of how he longed to share his impossible burden with Polly but knowing that it would be a mistake to do so. It would be like putting too much weight on a slender branch. Married people often made mistakes like that, revealing something damaging on an impulse and then regretting it. He felt too that he would get no help from Polly, only recriminations.

Moving slowly through the crowd of women, Sylvester spotted a tall man just outside the shop window. For a moment he did not recognise the averted face, taking in only the dark blue blazer, crisp white shirt and striped tie. Then he saw it was Colonel Moilliet looking, as he always did, poised on the edge of irritability. So Roscoe Starr had not taken Sylvester's threat seriously enough even to discuss it himself! And Roscoe had not sent Terence Boyle—but thought that the irascible, foppish Moilliet could deal with the problem. Pushing past three women who blocked an aisle, Sylvester made an unintentional noise that sounded like a groan.

CHAPTER TEN

It was a golden June afternoon and the start of a heatwave, or so the newspapers said, with a high pressure area seemingly anchored between the Azores and south west England. In London the unusual heat was making people lethargic and somnolent after their midday meal. At the heart of the metropolis crowds of sunbathers were exposing their pale arms, legs and backs in Hyde Park, as Frank Shields walked briskly into the park by Speaker's Corner. Frank had enjoyed a two-hour session of rowing on the lake in Regent's Park, followed by some wholemeal cheese sandwiches and a carton of fresh orange juice. After that he had been to Selfridges for a wash and brush-up.

Frank looked very chipper and swung his briefcase with what seemed an excess of energy to other Londoners who sank back languorously into deckchairs or stretched out sleepily on the grass. He felt on top of the world, like an athlete who has reached absolutely peak condition just before a contest. For a few minutes he stayed in the park, killing time, because he always wanted to be on the dot when meeting Phil. He stood looking round at the pale, unhealthy bodies knowing that he was superior to the great mass of people who thronged the London streets.

At 2.25 Frank strolled through the subway leading to Park Lane. There were three husky-looking West Indian youths hanging about in the middle of the tunnel. Frank took off his amber-tinted glasses to give them a hard look because this would be an inconvenient time to fight off a mugging, but one youth produced a guitar and another held out a greasy cap. Frank threw a 10p piece into the cap and emerged from the tunnel whistling. Apart from feeling in peak condition physically, he was also particularly alert and seeing things very clearly, nearly as if in slow motion and enjoying each passing minute. Anticipated pleasures, in his experience, rarely came up to expectations, but in his odd jobs for the corporation Frank never knew what to expect because any vague plans he might have had were subject to hasty and often drastic revision. Each, job was quite different, too, and full of interest, oddity and danger. For sheer excitement there was nothing comparable in his experience.

With his sunglasses on again, Frank walked along Park Lane in a detached mood that was just right for what he had to do. He felt quite remote from the workaday crowd around him; he watched a group of giggling girls going in the Piccadilly direction, an old couple staring over at the shady trees in the park, a copper who appeared to be hot and bothered in his uniform. Everyone else was doing ordinary things, but Frank Shields was preparing to go up on the high wire where a single slip could be very dangerous indeed.

Once he had crossed Upper Grosvenor Street Frank spotted Phil walking up Park Lane close to the South Street corner. Phil stood out in the crowd, being built like a brick wall, though his bulk was a little disguised by a carefully constructed three-piece suit. Phil was also as solid as a wall when it came to loyalty to Ben Sutro and whoever else it was he worked for, a real boss's man without a thought of his own in his rather small head. Frank regarded the heavy figure in a light grey suit with an alert, malicious expression which he had changed to the facsimile of a smile by the time they met on the corner at precisely 2.30, as agreed.

Phil smiled back, saying, 'Hi, champ.'

Frank said, 'Lovely day.'

'Glad you like it. Too hot for me.' Phil did indeed have a moustache of sweat on his florid face, but Frank knew that it was not just caused by the heat. Phil was always sweating at their meetings. Partly it was due to the large sum of cash that was about to change hands and partly the prospect of the job itself for which Phil plainly did not have the bottle.

Frank shrugged. 'So our friend's here, then?'

Phil nodded, breathing a little harder. Frank saw that Phil's nose looked as if it had been varnished red and was liberally sprinkled with open pores.

'He's in there.' Phil squinted in the bright sunlight as he stared up at the Aldford-Plaza Hotel which towered over Park Lane. It was a featureless block of white concrete, a newish American-style place of the kind which Frank had figured as a tourist trap, providing luxury of a kind for couples on dirty weekends, businessmen on liberal expense accounts, rock stars and other people too rich or careless to check their bills.

Frank grinned, saying in his flattest voice, 'I've a good head for heights.'

'I know, but our friend got hisself booked into a nice room on floor two. You could fall out that window and just sprain an ankle.'

'Diabolical.'

'So?' Phil's low brow furrowed; for a moment he looked a bit dolly dimple, like a punchy boxer who could not figure out what had happened in the last round.

'So, no problem. I'll improvise.'

Phil shook his greasy-looking head. More sweat was oozing out of his lank hair, giving him lamb-chop sideburns of moisture. He said quietly, 'Good for you, maestro.'

'And our friend's name? That's an

important little detail.'

'It's Big Billy MacShane. Room 205.'

All sorts of wry thoughts, quips and jokes began to surface in Frank's brain. Previously he had done odd jobs which he could understand were for the good of the corporation: removing a greedy gang-leader, a maniac, a talkative pimp, a book-keeper who had done a little ballet with the books. But this sudden flurry of communists and far left union bosses puzzled him. Big Billy MacShane was a notorious trouble-maker, a dockers' union man reputed to have been responsible for the closing of several docks. What could the corporation possibly have against him? Frank suppressed these thoughts and concentrated on the business in hand; he wasn't being paid to make jokes. He said in a dead voice, 'So he's up there now, in Room 205?'

Phil nodded. 'Billy had a very early lunch, likes to get his trotters under the trough smartish, does our Billy. He had an awful lot of meddy too.' With a brief gesture of his right hand Phil indicated that it was the kind of medicine taken in a glass.

'Be handy.'

'Thought you'd be pleased. He's due out again about half four—some meeting. He's probably having a quick kip now.'

'By himself?'

'As far as we know.' With an enigmatic
88

smile Phil implied that he wasn't in the business of giving guarantees.

'If it was easy they'd all be at it. And?'

'And it's here.' Sweat ran freely down Phil's heavy, lugubrious face as he handed over a crisp copy of *The Standard* folded in half. 'Five grand. They're well pleased.'

'See you then.'

'Be lucky, champ.'

Frank grinned, saying, 'Dull it isn't.' He turned on his heel and walked off briskly, using his left hand to transfer a thick white envelope from inside the newspaper to a capacious inner pocket. He hummed a tune that years before had been a favourite of his Grandma's after she had consumed a few bottles of stout. It had a simple, repetitive lyric: 'Today I feel so happy, so happy...'

It was a busy afternoon at the Aldford-Plaza Hotel, with guests continually arriving and departing in a queue of taxis at the Aldford Street entrance. The porters were all occupied and the head doorman, dressed in a grey frock coat and topper, was having a confidential word with a cabby. Frank took a small, red suitcase from a glamorous blonde and walked with her into the foyer, putting down the case as her bald-headed escort bustled in with a porter and two more cases.

Frank nodded at the blonde and took a seat on an iron-grey couch, standing his briefcase on the floor between his legs. He held *The*

Standard open as if he were reading it, but his eyes flickered round the foyer to see what the drill was regarding security. At the same time he was recalling old television images of Big Billy MacShane. Billy had been out of the public eye for some time, but there had been a period when he had been hamming it up on TV news programmes or seen briefly emerging from a meeting and pausing to say 'No comment' or 'More cash on the table, that's what I want' to the waiting reporters. Frank remembered Billy as a shambling, top-heavy character with a head of curly hair like a gippo's and a truculent manner. Forget your worries, Billy, he thought, Frank's here to solve them for you—at a stroke.

There was a bustling, excited atmosphere in the hotel foyer as men booked rooms with women who were not their wives, or paid grossly inflated bills: a rich compost of money, lust and nervous tension in the scented air.

Frank was alive to the tension and knew that it was bound to be helpful to him. With so much going on there would be little attention directed towards him. Sitting on the couch, he realised that *if you didn't care* you could get away with nearly anything. But there was one person to watch out for, a manikin employed as a page, with the body of a ten-year-old boy, a face like a withered apple and cynical, observant eyes.

As soon as the page had gone up in the lift, Frank walked across the foyer to the stairs. He felt particularly remote and detached as he did so, like an Angel of Death who had been sent to seek out a victim. He knew that life was only a paltry thing: faces of dead men—one with dry, parted lips and a rigid smile—another with a blue, waxen pallor as if frosted over—danced before his eyes.

Once on the thickly carpeted stairs he was alert for any sounds. On a landing between the first and second floors he put on rubber gloves which were colourless and barely noticeable. He looked round before knocking on the door of Room 205, but he knew he had to take some risks. As he waited by the door he was prepared for anything, even for the job to go badly wrong. There was silence on the other side of the door and Frank rapped again, harder. Then there was the sound of a lavatory being flushed, so he knocked a third time.

A blurred voice called out, 'Yes? What?'

Frank said, 'A message.'

'Message? What kind of message?'

'A message,' said Frank enigmatically. He had a lot of experience and knew that while people were often suspicious they were usually curious too.

The door to Room 205 opened a little and Frank saw green, bloodshot eyes and a liverish face.

'A message from Frank. It's private.' It amused Frank to say this, and most men knew a Frank.

'You better come in then.'

'Billy MacShane was dressed in a mussed white shirt and dark grey trousers with the top part of the zip undone. He had a lot of carefully tended curly, ginger hair; his chest had largely slipped down into his stomach.

Frank stepped through the doorway holding the open briefcase in his left hand. He closed the door with his right elbow.

Billy looked a little cagey at being disturbed by a stranger, but not unduly worried. He was the kind of man who expected telephone calls and messages while staying at a London hotel. He was breathing heavily but that was because he was badly out of condition, most of his recent work having been done with a knife and fork. There was a half-smothered belch and Frank smelt a mixture of beer, garlic and red wine.

While saying nothing Frank's eyes wandered all over the room and he noticed that the bathroom was open and empty. An Alka-Seltzer tablet was fizzing away in a tumbler on a bedside table, next to a well-filled wallet.

Frank took the facsimile Snub Magnum out of the briefcase with his right hand and let the case fall to the floor.

MacShane exclaimed, 'Oh Jesus! No!' His

92

large tongue forked out to lick his dry lips. Something glittered on his chin. He was a strong man and did not lack courage, but he had enough experience of tough guys to recognise someone who would go all the way, even to firing a gun in a busy hotel.

'Now listen a minute. Listen!' Frank's voice was quiet and persuasive, not threatening. MacShane's brain was dimmed by alcohol so that he could not think clearly, but the tone of voice gave him some hope of buying his way out of this trouble.

MacShane asked, 'Cash? You want my wallet?'

'Yes, John, and I'll take the watch.' Frank pointed to MacShane's gold Rolex watch on a heavy, gold-mesh bracelet.

MacShane licked his dry lips repeatedly while he fumbled with the bracelet. In his anxiety he couldn't get it off and moved his brows as if trying to refocus his tired eyes.

Frank caught him with a left upper-cut to the point of the chin, a favourite punch that had twenty years of experience and all his weight behind it. MacShane's face lost its shape and he crumbled at the knees, falling over as if in slow motion without making much noise. Frank went to the bedroom door and put a 'Do Not Disturb' notice on the handle outside before locking it.

The body was dragged into the bathroom in a matter of seconds. MacShane showed no sign of coming round but Frank lifted his head and cracked it down on the tiled floor. Then he removed the gold watch and undressed the inert body. It was an unpleasant chore but Frank set that off against the staggering amount of pay he was earning per minute. He turned on both taps in the bath while keeping an eye on the unconscious man's face which was flushed and blotched with drink; he saw to his surprise that there was a small, bruised swelling on MacShane's forehead on the left side, which puzzled him.

Getting Billy into the bath was not an easy task and the heavily built man was beginning to stir. As soon as he was in the water Frank banged his head against the end of the bath. Once more Frank had a ringside seat to watch Death at work; he knew from experience that it would probably be a casual affair, rather like watching a spider disappear down a plughole.

When the bath water was six inches deep Frank turned off the taps, then got hold of MacShane's feet and lifted them up by the horny heels so that the big man's head sank down below the surface of the water. As Billy began to drown in a flurry of bubbles he stirred again, but not violently; just a series of slight shudders that ran through his thick legs to Frank's taut arms. MacShane's mop of curly hair waved about in the water like

94

seaweed and he opened his eyes in an expression of mild surprise; his mouth was open too as if he wanted to say something, but he could only expel a string of bubbles that became smaller and smaller.

When the bubbles had stopped Frank hooked Billy's ankles on the edge of the bath and surveyed his victim. MacShane's flaccid white body and gross stomach showed how long it had been since he had done any manual labour in the docks. He seemed to be grinning even though his face was three inches below the surface of the bath water, as if he had had the last laugh, or knew something that Frank didn't.

But it was not Billy's strange smile that stayed in Frank's mind as he got on with the rest of the job, it was the unaccountable bruise and bump on MacShane's forehead. He unhooked MacShane's ankles from the rim of the bath and let him slip down into a natural position, then he put the dead man's underclothes neatly on the stool in the bathroom. He took the gold watch, trousers and shoes into the bedroom, placing the watch conspicuously next to the wallet on the bedside table. He hung the trousers over a chair and left the shoes beside them.

Putting the Snub Magnum away in his briefcase Frank walked back into the bathroom, unwrapped a new bar of soap and slipped it into the bath, leaving the wrapping screwed up on the floor. Since being moved the dead man's expression had changed slightly, but there still seemed to be the faint curl of a sneering smile on his thin lips.

Frank looked round the bedroom carefully, making sure that he had not left anything and kneeling for a moment on the carpet where MacShane had fallen. Everything looked all right, so it would appear that Billy had simply slipped on the soap in a half drunken state and struck his head against the bath.

Satisfied that he had made no mistakes, Frank carefully opened the door of Room 205 and stepped out into the corridor. He left the 'Do Not Disturb' sign on the door handle and walked briskly away, glancing at his watch. The job had taken about fifteen minutes. He removed his rubber gloves on a landing between the second and first floors.

The foyer was even busier than when he had entered the hotel. Apart from a steady press of people at the reception desk, a lot of attention was focused on some freakish young chap with a girlish face, probably a rock star, who had arrived with a large entourage including a middle-aged man sweating like Phil. The cynically observant manikin page was not to be seen.

Frank left the Aldford-Plaza Hotel in a good mood. He had put the perplexing bruise out of his mind, reckoning there were bound to be a few little mysteries when you had an unusual occupation. He smiled to himself in the bright sunshine that greeted him in Park Lane. He was mentally working out the rate of pay for the job. Say twenty minutes for five grand—£250 per minute—even that ace union negotiator, Big Billy MacShane, would have had to agree that it was generous.

CHAPTER ELEVEN

It was becoming stiflingly hot in the greenhouse and the smell of the geraniums was oppressive. Rupert Sylvester's forehead was greasy with sweat. The June heatwave had lasted for ten days and an ever increasing amount of space in the newspapers was devoted to stories of workers refusing to stay in over-heated factories, soaring temperatures and fires in heathland areas. In Sylvester's mind the period of unusual heat had somehow become linked with his period of growing tension over the ultimatum he had put to Roscoe Starr. For no good reason he thought they might end together, that a sudden thunderstorm would clear the air and he would hear that Starr had called off the campaign of political assassinations. In the meantime his feeling of nervous tension was becoming ever greater and more difficult to hide.

Sylvester used a dead geranium stalk to jab at some powdery putty and traced the outline of a shield on a dusty windowpane, then erased it with an irritable movement. Suddenly exasperated, he exclaimed, 'Why, may I ask, are we all standing round here like spare pricks?'

There were five antiquarian book-dealers with Sylvester, standing in the greenhouse at the end of a rose-arbour behind the west wing of the elegant, stone house called Broomhill Park. Eric Willert, Dr Arbeit, Mickey Harland, Peter Rawlins and Sidney Stretham, all of them considered small fry who had been frozen out of the auction sale by the big boys on the understanding that they would get a cash payment from the settlement that was to take place after the public auction.

'Because, ole man ...' Eric Willert always spoke slowly and stared hard at the person he addressed as if he were afraid they would miss his point. He had a bloated face with heavy shadows under his eyes. He was rumoured to have a flighty young wife who led him a dance. 'Because we are waiting to be informed about our humble payments of cash. The divi, ole man ...' There was a fleeting glimpse of Willert's bad teeth. 'To be handed down to us by our betters. But you don't have to wait, you know—if you have something better to do.'

Sylvester's expectations about the auction

sale at Broomhill Park had descended in stages. He had welcomed the sale as a good excuse to get away from his shop for two or three days, but on the previous day, during the view, he realised he would have no hope of buying any of the items he had marked in the catalogue, since every major antiques firm was to be represented there. So he had transferred his hopes from the superb collection of furniture and porcelain to the library of books, only to learn that 'the ring' would be operating there and he would have no chance of buying the books at prices that would allow a profit.

'Yes, I do realise that, Eric,' Sylvester said. 'But why do we have to stand here, cooped up like this?'

'It's not much fun, in such heat,' Dr Arbeit, a sardonic, sad little Jew, admitted. 'But be patient, my dear, it should not be long now.'

Sidney Stretham said quickly, 'Got to be some place, don't we? I mean somewhere out of sight. Tucked away like. Private. So the punters don't catch on.' Stretham had worried grey eyes and a swollen-veined forehead. He tended to gobble like a turkey when he became excited. 'It's just till Victor puts us in the picture,' Dr Arbeit added in a placatory tone.

'But will it be worth waiting for?' Sylvester queried. A comparative newcomer to the world of auctions and country sales, he had no first-hand experience of 'rings' which he knew operated only on rare occasions.

'Ah, that's the gamble,' Willert said with a shrugging movement.

'Everything's a gamble,' said Dr Arbeit with unusual firmness.

'But I still don't get the hiding away bit,' Sylvester said. 'It's not as if we were doing anything illegal.'

'Illegal.' Mickey Harland repeated the word in an amused voice. 'Of course it's illegal. Why do you think we've all got this furtive look? Eric, be a pal, give us a child's guide to the law as relating to the ring.'

Willert grinned widely for once, displaying a mixed bag of bad teeth, a gold filling and one tooth that was too white to be true. He said, 'An act ... to render illegal certain agreements ... affecting bidding at auctions ... 1927. Para one, sub para one—if any dealer agrees to give, or gives, or offers any gift or consideration to any other person as an inducement or reward for abstaining...'

Peter Rawlins, who looked as hot as Sylvester felt, said, 'Oh, speed it up a bit, for fuck's sake.'

Willert looked sulky but continued, 'A fine not exceeding one hundred pounds, a term of imprisonment for a period not exceeding six months...'

Mickey Harland interrupted him. 'But let's

look on the bright side. Jack Quinn's in there, bidding away against the ring I'll be bound. By the time he's finished there may not be any profit left for anyone. No profit, no divi, no fine or term of imprisonment...'

Sylvester said in an irritable tone, 'Oh, Quinn, that Irish hobbledehoy...'

'Rupert, why you persist in this silly fiction about Jack being Irish is beyond me,' Mickey Harland said. 'Jack's father ran a second-hand shop in the Hammersmith Broadway for thirty years and his grandfather was a London copper. Now, how far back do you have to go?'

Sylvester sniffed. 'The last story I heard about Jack Quinn was that he had pushed two policemen through a plate glass window.'

'That's not how Jack tells it,' Dr Arbeit said.

Peter Rawlins fanned himself energetically with both hands, saying, 'It's too hot to argue.'

The conversation was diverted by an outbreak of the harsh coughing that was Dr Arbeit's trademark. When he had finished he said in a thick voice, 'Sorry, I'm sorry, my dears. I must get some fresh air.'

Rawlins lifted a finger to catch attention. 'Hold on a sec. I think a message cometh from our masters. If it isn't Jacob Marley, the ghost of Christmas past.'

Looking along the rose-arbour, Sylvester

saw Victor Sorensen in a funereal suit stopping to pick a small white rose.

'Beg a little, steal a little,' Mickey Harland said in an amused voice. 'But Scrooge's conscience looks well pleased. Maybe there will be something for us after all.'

Victor Sorensen acknowledged the presence of the small group standing in the greenhouse with a discreet wave, then entered in his usual guilty fashion and casting uneasy glances with his eyes rolling. His black suit and unusually pale face did make him appear rather ghost-like.

'Well, what news, Victor?' Peter Rawlins asked. 'We're all feeling somewhat over-cooked in this little oven you kindly selected for us.'

'Not long now, boys,' Sorensen said.

'Oh, terrific!'

'No, I mean, well, less than half an hour.' Sorensen's large brown eyes were continually moving: he had an envious expression, as though he knew something more interesting was happening elsewhere. 'Say twenty minutes to the last lot of books. Then I'll nip back here and give you the gen about where to meet later on. It looks good, well, not at all bad.'

Stretham gobbled in his excited way, 'Quinn, Jack Quinn, now, is he giving you much trouble?'

'No, not much, nothing we can't handle.

He's been raising his hand quite a lot but I don't think he's bought a single book. Anyway, I must get back. See you soon with all the gen ...' Sorensen retreated to the door, moving sideways like a crab, with a guilty look.

'So now there's no need for you to hang on here, Rupert, if you don't want to,' Mickey Harland said. 'I'll stay till Victor comes back. I'm told there's an interesting little chapel you could look at and a lake somewhere. Then we can meet later by that pub down the road, the Crossed Keys.'

'Are you sure?' Sylvester had noticed that Willert gave off a faintly stale smell as if he did not change his underwear often enough. He could hear the distant, enticing sound of church bells. The suggestion of a walk round Broomhill Park was attractive.

'Yes, off you go.' Mickey Harland's tone was authoritative but world-weary, as if he thought nothing really mattered one way or the other.

'Well, are you going to stay or what?' Rawlins asked petulantly. 'There's only a limited amount of oxygen in here, you know.'

'Okay, okay. Thanks, Mickey, see you at that pub.'

As Sylvester stepped out of the greenhouse he thought he heard some sly, *sotto voce* comment by Rawlins. He did not glance back. Antiquarian book-dealers formed a tightly knit community, living in each other's pockets: 'taking in each other's laundry' would have been his mother's way of describing their incestuous behaviour. No doubt Rawlins and the others objected to his being among them; they did not regard him as being a book-dealer even though half his shop was stocked with fine bindings. It was just jealousy really, because he was successful whereas some of them were struggling to make a living. But he was used to jealousy and to envious looks and he didn't give a damn whether they objected. To leave would mean giving in to them—he would wait and salvage something from the fiasco.

Sylvester paused at the end of the arbour, smelling the roses and listening to the church bells. It was a Stedman ring on the front five bells, with the largest, called the tenor, covering:

12345
21345
23145
23415
23451

He had made it his business to learn something about bell-ringing, as he had mastered other subjects in his determination to be more English than the English. But he genuinely liked to listen to the bells and to see them, surprisingly vast and ancient, often engraved with the names of princes and saints as well as with rhymes and prayers. How unfair it was that he, who appreciated such things and so valued English traditions, should have a mixed background which he had to conceal unendingly whereas most English people took their heritage for granted and thought nothing of it.

As Sylvester slowly made his way round the stone terrace overlooking a vista of lawns sloping down to a shimmering lake, he was brooding on all the difficulties that had been put in his path and how he had overcome them. In his early days in England there were certain words that were liable to pop up in his conversation, words that were second nature to him such as 'shroff', 'peg', 'dibs', and 'Simpkin'—the Hindustani corruption of 'champagne', and threaten to trip him up, as did certain gestures and mannerisms. But he had mastered all that and now his vocabulary and mannerisms were impeccable. For a moment he was agitated by the fact that, nevertheless, his second application to join the MCC had been turned down; but that was in turn forgotten as his mind was suddenly flooded by a much more serious matter.

It was deeply ironic that it had been his ability to lie and deceive which had enabled him to achieve several ambitions but which now threatened him with a truly perilous situation. He was in no doubt at all about the danger. Colonel Moilliet was an irascible fop, Terence Boyle a mindless thug, but Roscoe Starr was a very different kind of man—one of that rare breed who are completely indifferent to danger and therefore willing to take any risk. Roscoe Starr had inaugurated a daring series of political assassinations and undoubtedly he would also be willing to kill anyone who threatened his plans.

For a moment Sylvester had to stand still. His chest was moving up and down agitatedly, and his hands were wet with sweat as they had often been in that short but terrifying period when he had been on patrol in Belfast. Danger was all about him, vague yet palpable. Yes, those veiled threats of Moilliet's could lead to his actual extinction, as a bullet might have done in the Falls Road area.

Very slowly Sylvester moved forward again, gradually bringing himself under control by keeping his mind blank. An old woman was making even slower progress towards the stone wall at the edge of the terrace, walking with two sticks and grimacing with pain. He forced himself to smile at her and gestured at the broad sweep of parkland. 'Quite breath-taking, isn't it?' The old woman nodded and smiled sweetly, and for a moment Sylvester was ashamed that his behaviour was always false and that he never had a genuinely sympathetic feeling for anyone else. 'Have you had enough of the sale?' he said. The woman shook her head. 'Oh no, there are some marvellous things coming up this afternoon. I just felt like a breath of fresh air before lunch. You can get sandwiches and coffee here you know, in the tent.'

'Yes, thanks, I know,' Sylvester said. 'And the coffee smelt very good. Perhaps I'll see you there later.' He walked off feeling a little puzzled that saying what he did not mean had become such a habit with him: it was as if he was now a prisoner of years of systematic lying and incapable of ever being honest.

It was a windless afternoon—one tiny cloud had appeared in the west but it stayed in the same position. Broomhill Park looked splendid in the bright sunlight with just a few towering trees to break up the vista of rolling grassland. Swallows were flying to and fro overhead and dipping down to the mirror-like surface of the lake. Sylvester thought that in such an idyllic spot he should be able to feel at peace for a while, but then his mind reverted to Colonel Moilliet's story of the powerful ramifications behind the extremist right-wing movement: the General whom Moilliet had mentioned and the powerful supporters in high places. Was it really possible that such a desperate conspiracy could have some backing in the army, the police and even among members of the Government, as Moilliet had said?

Turning round to look back at the large stone house, he saw with a start that instead of the old woman on the terrace there was now a male figure, dressed in a dark blue blazer like the one Moilliet had worn. But as he concentrated his gaze the man disappeared. Sylvester again found himself unable to breathe properly. Could it possibly have been Moilliet, and if so, why should he be there? He felt profoundly weary and as if he lacked the energy to walk any further. He sat down and took off his jacket; his pure linen suit had been made by an uncle who lived in Simla and was of unusually fine quality—even the old-fashioned bone buttons were good to look at. This suit was the only relic of the clothes he had brought from India and it was ideal for such a hot day; wearing it proved that he had not added half an inch to his waistline in nineteen years, something he was sure that big oaf, Quinn, could not say. He folded the jacket with great care before laying it down with the sale catalogue.

The grass had recently been cut in unusually wide swathes and gave off a fresh, sweet odour. Stretched out full length with his head pillowed on his arms, listening to the song of the larks high above, Moilliet, Boyle, Roscoe Starr and the shadowy General all came to appear like the grotesque characters of a bad dream. A small aircraft was droning away in the distance and its faint steady noise had a hypnotising effect, so that it was difficult for him to think straight. Heat and sunlight were also conspiring to make him want to sleep. More than anything else in the world, Sylvester longed to feel free of fear. How wonderful, he thought, just to nod off and then awake to find his frightening dilemma had vanished like a nightmare. He tried to follow a swallow's erratic pattern of flight but his eyelids had become so heavy that he knew he must close them for a moment or two.

CHAPTER TWELVE

'Six hundred and fifty. Six hundred and fifty pounds then.' The auctioneer repeated the sum in a satisfied tone. He knew his business back to front and realised that he was unlikely to get a more generous bid. He smiled amiably at Jack Quinn, who held a big, scarred hand up in the air a good deal higher than anyone else who had been bidding that day. Quinn looked more like a heavy-weight boxer than a book-dealer and his far from handsome face had not been improved by an encounter with a plate glass window: the pattern of scars on his face made it appear as if he had stuck his head through a barbed wire fence. The auctioneer paused significantly and then drew out what he expected to be the final bid: 'So . . . six . . . hundred . . . and . . . fifty . . . pounds.' The fact that Timothy Duckworth, the auctioneer, repeated the figure yet again underlined for Jack Quinn the undeniable fact that he had made a mistake: he had been goaded into taking the bait and had finally succumbed, paying a hundred pounds more than the coded buying figure he had noted in his catalogue.

Duckworth absently murmured, 'Six hundred and fifty' under his breath, as he looked round his silent, captive audience with practised skill. An easy-going, plump man in his late forties, Duckworth had been conducting house sales for twenty years and knew exactly what had been going on during the dispersal of the Broomhill Park library. Jack Quinn had been the main opposition to Trevor Wynant who was buying for 'the ring', but Quinn had only been successful on the present lot by paying too much. Duckworth's gaze paused for just a moment on two black-suited Catholic priests who had previously made a few bids, but they were whispering together with their heads down. Then he stared hard at the burly figure of Trevor Wynant who had so far dominated the book sale. Wynant prolonged the by-play in pretending to check on something in the catalogue before looking up with a broad smile and shaking his head vigorously from side to side, implying that anyone who would pay six hundred and fifty pounds for that particular book must be mad.

Duckworth nodded at Quinn, saying, 'Then that's yours, sir.'

Quinn, encumbered with a tweed sports coat that was too thick for such a warm day, half rose in his seat. 'Books International, sir.'

'Yes, I know, Mr Quinn. Books International, six hundred and fifty pounds.' The auctioneer banged his gavel sharply on the top of the high rostrum which he always brought to house sales, making him look like a preacher in a pulpit.

Quinn said, 'Well, that's it,' his annoyance obvious. He got up clumsily. He was over six feet in height and the small chairs had been arranged in neat rows for people with shorter legs. He walked along the row, banging into the backs of a few chairs. There was a murmur of irritation at this disturbance before the sale was ended and Quinn was aware of this, but he had been impulsively propelled out of his seat by his annoyance at having made a beginner's mistake and at the sound of Trevor Wynant chortling away to a crony.

Quinn pointed at the small calf-bound

volume with a scarred forefinger. 'I'll take my little bargain now if I may.'

The young porter working beside the auctioneer was an indolent youth with ginger hair, as Quinn's had once been before fading to its present sandy shade. The boy regarded him with an impudent grin. To remove lots during the sale was against the rules, as was plainly stated in the catalogue. He made no move to touch the book. Quinn paused in scribbling out a cheque to give him an unfriendly look and say, 'What about a bag, sonny?'

The youth's expression became plainly rebellious and he glanced up at the auctioneer for guidance. Duckworth appeared to be absorbed in his ledger but he nodded hastily. The boy frowned and fumbled among the clutter under a long table, triumphantly producing a messy jiffy-bag that looked as if it had made a dozen journeys through the post. He smirked and dropped the little book into the bag. Irritation was a catching infection and Quinn decided to stop spreading it about. He nodded his thanks, acknowledging defeat, as he handed over the cheque and a fifty pence piece.

Quinn was nearly at the back of the large room before Duckworth cleared his throat loudly and recommenced the sale by saying, 'Now, lot 205—the Douai Bible. Now, this is the first Catholic translation, 1609, and a fine copy. So can I say five hundred pounds to start it?' Someone plucked at Quinn's shirtsleeve and he looked down to see his friend, Charlie Saunders, whom he had known since he was a schoolboy, when Saunders used to call in at his father's second-hand shop. Saunders was a leading London antique dealer and a veteran of countless auction sales, with a hundred tales of battles won and lost at the fall of the hammer. He scrutinised the pink scars on Quinn's face but did not comment on them. In a stage whisper loud enough for Wynant to hear he said, 'Well, my son, they certainly tucked you up there, bang to rights. I could see it coming a mile off . . .'

'Yes, well, thanks a lot, Charlie.' Quinn shrugged. 'Sometimes you lose you know. But I certainly dug myself a nice big hole to fall into. Are you staying on here to the bitter end?' It was a pointless question, since Quinn knew it was Saunders' invariable rule to sit stolidly through every lot in a house sale no matter how little interest they had for him, methodically taking down the prices so that his catalogue provided a complete record.

'Yes, Jacko, and then I've got to have a word with Tim. Why?'

'I'm just off to the local. Thought you might join me in a swift pint?'

Saunders shook his head slowly while keeping an eye on the bidding for the Douai

113

Bible, which was developing into a battle between one of the black-suited priests and Trevor Wynant. The priest appeared much more determined than on previous lots, while Wynant called out his bids in a loud, contemptuous voice as though to show there was not a chance of his being unsuccessful in the end. Saunders lowered his voice to a genuine whisper as he said, 'Thanks, but no thanks. You see, after I see Tim, certain boys here have to meet up and come to certain decisions about this afternoon. *Compreney?*'

'Of course, Charlie. Well, I'm off to down a pint. So, see you.'

'Right, Jacko. Why don't you come round one evening and have some supper? I heard Madeleine and your girls had gone off to America. That right?'

'That's right,' Quinn said, automatically grimacing though he did not intend to. He waved farewell to Saunders and walked out of the beautifully proportioned room which had been the Mallalieu library for hundreds of years before it had become the venue for the auction.

When Quinn walked through the hall his heavy footsteps echoed on bare wooden boards. Broomhill Park was in a state of sad disarray, with some of the carpets rolled up, discoloured patches on the walls where paintings had been removed and the furniture pushed round to odd positions to catch the eye of prospective buyers.

At the open front door Quinn turned round to have a last look at what had been the stately home of the Mallalieu family for several centuries. Their long tenure had reached a high point in the Victorian and Edwardian epochs, when royalty had often been entertained, but had come to an end when the last Lord Mallalieu had died an aged bachelor during the previous winter. Now, over a three-day sale, all the family portraits including one by Holbein, all the other valuable paintings and porcelain, some twenty clocks, many unique Catholic relics, all the furniture, even potted palms, odd pots and other dust gatherers would come under Timothy Duckworth's hammer. The final day included a rounding-up of minor items descending from garden statuary and servants' furniture to antique prams and lawn-mowers, with an unusual postscript in the form of two ancient Daimler limousines, the larger of which had not been driven in forty years.

Quinn walked out of the door and down the steps plunged in thought, immersed in the atmosphere and history of the fine old house, thinking of all the dramatic scenes that had been played out within its stone walls, the births and deaths and the savage raid by Cromwell's soldiers. He imagined it as a Catholic stronghold in the sixteenth century, when Edmund Campion was said to have found a temporary refuge there only a year or so before his public execution at Tyburn in 1581.

But as Quinn strode quickly along the gravel drive leading down to the main road through an avenue of horse-chestnut trees, his irritation over the book sale surfaced again. He had foolishly banked on buying most of the early books and particularly the Edmund Campion items which included the rare pamphlet, *Rationes Decem*, said to have been surreptitiously printed behind a chimney piece in another Catholic mansion. In fact Quinn had taken the purchase for granted and planned his own specialised catalogue with informative notes about each book listed. These hopes had been buoyed up over a period, since he had been given an early tip-off about the sale by a girl who worked in the Duckworth office, and he knew that the old-fashioned firm never advertised their sales adequately.

Quinn tapped his forehead, indicating that he had a screw loose, and laughed at himself. There was no one in sight on the long drive so he felt free to say and do what he liked. 'What a nerk! What a maroon!' he called out. His plans for the catalogue were so advanced that he had even designed the cover.

'What a supreme twit!' After all that ludicrously optimistic planning, in the event he had bought a single volume and paid too much for it. With a groan Quinn acknowledged that his behaviour over the previous twelve months had been downright stupid on several occasions. To be outwitted at bidding by a veteran dealer like Wynant was not all that bad, but then to make his annoyance plain and leave in a huff like a silly girl! He should have played it cool, as Mickey Harland would have done, and smiled back at Wynant as though he was delighted with his solitary purchase.

'Oh, sod it!' he said. His temper was getting out of control—he had behaved like a madman over that trouble with the police. He knew exactly what was at the bottom of such incidents—his marriage was on the rocks and he could not see any chance of it getting better. He and Madeleine kept up the pretence of a marriage, but they only did so for the benefit of their daughters. They led separate lives, slept apart, and when they were on their own moved about their house like strangers, putting on an act when Dolly and Liz came in. Their occasional cool kisses were only for the benefit of their little girls. He pondered on what his daughters must think; it was impossible to know how much they were taken in by the charade, and equally impossible to ask them. So his frustrations, including those of a sexual kind, boiled up inside him and found an outlet in sudden bursts of temper, not with Madeleine but with strangers. He knew there had been occasions just after she had made a withering remark, when anyone calling at the house at that moment might have been punched on the nose. It was madness!

At the end of the gravel drive, just before a dilapidated lodge gate-house, an area of grass had been roped off to serve as a car park for people attending the sale. Among the cars he noticed the vintage racing-green Bentley belonging to Rupert Sylvester, gleaming in a shaft of sunlight through the chestnut trees. He walked up to it and spent a few minutes admiring the way in which it had been restored and lovingly polished. He had to give Sylvester full marks for energy and willingness to work, even if some had to be taken off for quirkish behaviour. Quinn's Mercedes was an excellent car which had clocked up a huge trouble-free mileage but it looked in sore need of a wash; he unlocked the car door, threw his tweed coat and catalogue on the back seat, placed the scruffy jiffy-bag next to them, and took out a large envelope which he had received in the post that morning.

The massive gates of Broomhill Park were supported by great stone piers surmounted by griffons. There was some indecipherable lettering on the piers, and he decided to re-read the introductory notes in the catalogue to see if anything had been said about the gates. He had become fascinated by the ancient Catholic mansion and wondered about its fate—who would want a house with twenty-five bedrooms but only three bathrooms, an antiquated heating system and a vast subterranean kitchen that looked more like a dungeon and torture chamber?

Quinn waved to a silver dealer, who apparently had given up hope of the sale and was driving away, and turned left out of the gateway. He kept in close to the grass bank on his left and walked on it when possible as the road leading to Stony Stratford was reasonably busy. He felt distinctly hungry—he had not bothered with breakfast, he rarely did when Madeleine and his daughters were away. Now hunger was adding savour to the prospect of a snack lunch at the Crossed Keys—he visualised a plate of bread and cheese and pickles, with a tankard of bitter.

In places the bank was relatively low and easy to walk on. As he made his way to the pub he opened the large yellow envelope he had taken from the Mercedes. The envelope had a stiff cardboard back and was adorned with a 'fragile' label though the contents were not worth five pence to anyone apart from himself and possibly his daughters. To Quinn the four flimsy enclosures were invaluable; they were photographs of his mother, father and grandfather, sent to him with a brief note from an old friend of his mother's. Quinn's mother had died when he was two and he had only the haziest memories of her. The photographs included two of his mother which he had not seen before and one of them was identified on the back as being of 'Stella in Holland Park. June 1944'. He stared at the print, trying to imagine the time in the park with his mother as she was two months before his birth.

The sound of a car braking behind him brought Quinn out of his day-dream about Holland Park at the time of the 'doodle-bug' raids, one of which had killed his grandfather. On hearing jeering voices and laughter, he turned round. The car was a luxurious new BMW, metallic blue in colour. It was being driven by his friend, Charlie Saunders, but there were four other occupants, all top antique dealers whom Quinn either vaguely knew or recognised. Saunders had his window down and his bald head half out, calling, 'Go on, go on, get a move on!'

Quinn said, 'I thought you said you couldn't spare the time for a drink.'

'No more we can't, my son. Fancy us catching you up. What's the matter with you?'

'So you're not having a drink?'

'No.' For a moment Saunders did not

expand his reply, but maintained an air of mystery while keeping the powerful car at a crawling pace.

'All right, why not?'

'Because, Jacko old lad, we are all bound for exotic Stony Stratford, playground of leafy Bucks. Now get a move on! What you got those long legs for then? Mooning about like a great dozy girl.'

As his passengers laughed and made derisive gestures Saunders drove past Quinn in an eccentric fashion, weaving about as though the BMW were out of control. Then he put his foot hard down and accelerated away with a great turn of speed.

Quinn shook his fist at the speeding car, calling out, 'Bloody show-off!' He put the photographs back in the envelope, realising that it wasn't a good idea to walk in a day-dream along a road where there was no pavement and cars did tend to speed. Having lunch by himself there would be plenty of time to study the ghostly, sepia-tinted prints.

The Crossed Keys was an attractive black and white building with a garden at the front and on one side, where there were several benches and tables. They were all empty and it looked as if he was going to be one of the first lunchtime customers, which pleased him as he hated waiting in a smoky atmosphere.

The pub was equally attractive inside, with only a handful of locals standing under the old black beams. He asked for a pint of best bitter and a ploughman's lunch and in a few minutes emerged into the sunlight carrying a tray on which was balanced a brimming glass, a large plate of French bread, butter and cheese and a small one with lettuce, tiny radishes and spring onions. He took a seat under a cherry tree, put down his tray and enjoyed a drink of beer. He looked round appreciatively. The sale had been a write-off which he could chalk down to experience. But the day was by no means a waste of time. He had learnt a lesson or two, enjoyed seeing Broomhill Park and lunch in such surroundings was a definite bonus.

After he had eaten most of the bread and cheese, Quinn pushed the plate away and opened the yellow envelope. The two photographs of his mother and the one of his father were rather poor snapshots that looked as if they might fade away completely in time. The large photograph of his grandfather was quite different, a portrait taken at the Addison Studios in West Kensington, on a gilt cardmount and covered by a flap of fancy paper.

Jack Quinn knew that he had inherited his height, large frame and plain face from his paternal grandfather, Daniel, though he had never seen him. He had been told by his father that they were as alike as twins. Studying the portrait, he had to concede the similarity: the blunt face of an Irish navvy, square chin and sharp pugnacious nose. His grandfather had been a police constable patrolling a beat in Hammersmith, twice promoted to sergeant and twice reduced to the ranks. He had been killed by a 'doodle-bug' in September 1944, but his reputation lived on after that: the notorious 'Danny Q' who had ruled the roost in seedy streets where there were more pubs than shops and who was best remembered for his talent for laying out unruly customers with his tightly rolled oilskin cape. 'Danny Q' was said to have controlled 'his' streets like the policeman played by Charlie Chaplin in the last reel of *Easy Street*.

The portrait showed Daniel Quinn in plain clothes, a dark suit that was tight across his big chest, looking at the camera with an unhappy expression; ill-at-ease and anxious to be elsewhere. Quinn sighed. It was from this ugly mug that he had inherited his liking for alcohol and his quick temper, the two things that had caused most of the trouble in his life and had no doubt contributed to his frozen marriage.

After a long look at the photograph, which was rather like staring into a mirror, Quinn put it back in the envelope. There was no point in blaming his faults on someone else. Finishing the pint of beer, he stretched out his long legs and slumped down on the rustic bench to relax before driving back to London; but once relaxed, the tedious calculations about his marriage began again. He visualised leaving the house in Barton Street, which had been bought with his father-in-law's money and had never seemed like his own home. He imagined renting a tiny flat and trying to change an unhappy marriage into a reasonably friendly relationship, with an understanding that he would see Dolly and Liz frequently. But there was the rub—he needed to see his daughters all the time, he needed someone to love and with whom he could express love in words and caresses. The same old ideas began to chase each other monotonously round and round in his brain.

CHAPTER THIRTEEN

'That stuff about the early bird getting the worm ...' Mickey Harland paused, unsure whether he had Dr Arbeit's attention which often seemed to stray, '... is strictly—for the birds.'

Max Arbeit was a small man with rounded, narrow shoulders, thin, dark hair that had retreated a good deal and a badly broken nose. His large eyes were his best feature, dark brown and very expressive, often conveying kindness or sympathy. His eyes responded to Harland's little joke though his mobile mouth did not move.

'I mean, you and me, Max, we were the early birds here today. And what shall we get? A few measly crumbs, if we're lucky, thrown to us by the ghostly Victor.'

'That's right, my dear, but what to do?'

The two men stood half way along the rose-arbour, nearly out of earshot of the greenhouse. Harland was of average height but he felt quite tall standing next to the diminutive Arbeit, whose lack of inches was somewhat exaggerated by his wearing a dark grey suit that was a little too large for him. From the open greenhouse door they caught the odd word of an argument between Peter Rawlins and Victor Sorensen about having to wait till teatime for 'the knockout'. They had been glad to escape from the pugnacious Rawlins and the Ancient-Mariner grip of Eric Willert who was on his hobby-horse about life in general and business in particular becoming worse and worse. But having escaped they appeared irresolute.

Harland was thinking that he was probably the only dealer at Broomhill Park who knew that the name Arbeit was not the one that had been given to Max at his birth, but a joke with a bitter edge, for Max was a Jew who had been liberated from Auschwitz by the Russians early in 1945. On coming to

125

England, where his only surviving relatives lived, he had found that hardly anyone could pronounce his Polish Jewish name and that he would not be allowed to practise as a doctor. So he made a second career out of his passion for books and invented a name for himself that commented on his change of profession and the slogan, *Arbeit mach-frei*, to be found over the gates of some concentration camps, for 'arbeit' is the German word for 'work'. But now there was a generation of dealers who had no idea that the name was in fact a wry joke.

'Fancy a drink, Max?' Harland said. 'I'm told they do very good snacks down at the local.'

Before Arbeit could reply they heard Rawlins shout out, 'Can I just say one word without starting an argument?'

The men in the rose-arbour smiled together like conspirators. Arbeit shook his head. His eyes had a particularly intense expression as if he was giving some matter a lot of thought. 'Thanks, Mickey, but no. My sinus trouble is rather bad today and alcohol is not good for it. Do you ...' He paused as if in doubt whether to proceed with another idea. 'I thought young Sylvester seemed to be in an extremely nervous state today. Usually he's such a cheerful fellow. Do you know the French word *traqué*? Not quite "hunted", but something like that.'

126

'He seemed rather irritable.'

'No, more than that. I thought he looked frightened and I've seen enough fear in my time to be an expert on the subject. There was fear in his eyes. Why should that be? It couldn't just be disappointment about the sale.'

In turn Harland gave the matter some thought. He knew that Arbeit was unusually perceptive and had a doctor's habit of becoming interested not in what a patient was saying but in his manner, or in what lay behind what was being said.

'Perhaps all's not well at home?'

'But fear! Why should young Rupert be *afraid*?' Arbeit mused aloud. 'You see, my dear, I *know* that when one is obsessed with fear, then everything else is just sham, mere acting.'

Harland shrugged. 'I don't know, but I shall be seeing him later. He said he'd join me at the Crossed Keys. And if you should change your mind, it's only a short walk. Down to the main lodge, turn left and along the main road. It bears round to the left, so you can't see the pub from the lodge, but it's only—oh, two hundred yards, say.'

Arbeit nodded. 'Yes, I may do that. Enjoy your drink, Mickey.'

The two men walked to the end of the rose-arbour. With a wave Arbeit turned to the right on to the gravel path leading round to the main entrance of the house and the refreshments tent.

Harland stopped for a minute to smell one of the white roses. From the direction of the tent he heard Trevor Wynant's loud, jeering voice. He turned left along the path, but strayed from it to inspect a stone chapel which stood near to a fine walnut tree. He walked up close to the tree in order to touch its grey, ribbed bark which had a silvery sheen. Walnuts were already present in the form of small, green, plum-like husks that weighed down the long branches. It was a superb tree, one to inspire wonder in the Faithful on their way to Mass.

From the catalogue Harland understood that there had been a Catholic chapel at Broomhill Park for over three hundred years. The existing one was an example of the Gothic Revival, built in 1770. He could see that it was badly neglected. Damp had been at work for years, insidiously damaging the structure which was in the process of losing part of its roof. In places on the walls there were bobbly eruptions like a skin disease; other sections looked as if they had been bruised or scorched. Nettles in front of the heavy oak door and a spider-web strung across it showed that Sylvester had not acted on his suggestion and visited the chapel.

When Harland pushed the door it opened reluctantly with a creaking sigh and he was greeted by a dank, mushroomy smell. Stepping inside he had to pause, as it was so dim that he needed a few moments before he could see to the end of the small building. Neglect was obvious there too, with cobwebs on the beams and flaked plaster from the walls. Close at hand he saw a wooden board on which notices with black and purple edges were pinned or pasted. One solicited prayers for Bernard, 16th Duke of Norfolk, another celebrated the martyrdom of St Edmund Campion. There was a painted plaster cast of the Madonna in a dusty niche. A spray of withered carnations stood in a vase of stinking water. Crucifixes, missals, cards and relics of visits to Catholic shrines were mixed up in a jumble on a mahogany table. Harland felt as if he had stumbled into a forgotten cave where the strange rites of a vanished tribe had once taken place. I'm nearly sixty, he thought, and should be at my prayers but I can't think of a word to say. He shivered in the dank air; he felt as if he had been embraced by Death.

Out in the sun Harland took a deep breath of fresh air and stared up at the blue sky against the walnut tree's graceful branches. He walked along the path leading to the terrace which he had been told looked down to the lake. It was good to be alive and feel the warmth of the sun. Swallows were twittering and flying overhead, doing casual aerobatics about the park: a beautiful, immemorial scene that might well have taken Edmund Campion's eye, or that of the Roundhead Captain riding in to capture the house.

Leaning on the wall at the edge of the terrace, Harland said to himself, 'Well, surprise, surprise!' On the grass lay the usually restless Rupert Sylvester, apparently flaked out, supine, unmoving. His face was not visible but there was no mistaking that jet black hair, as glossy as an Italian's, or the duck-egg blue tie worn with a cream silk shirt and cream linen trousers. For a moment he considered waking Sylvester in order that they might walk down to the pub together, but decided not to. It looked as if the perceptive Max was right and that Sylvester was under some unusual emotional strain. Automatically he thought of the delectable Polly Sylvester and visualised her retroussée nose, open expression, charming smile and the blonde hair that appeared particularly fetching when it was pinned up at the back. But Polly was diffident, shy, somewhat elusive—Harland could not see her in the rôle of either adulteress or shrew. He retraced his steps, thinking to himself that Rupert was something of an odd-ball even though he worked hard at projecting the image of a nice, ordinary chap. His own wife Joan, who was perceptive like the Doctor, had said of

130

Sylvester, 'He's nearly too good-looking to be true, but why is he such a fidget?' Apart from the restlessness there were other glimpses of stress, as though a lot went on below the surface and there was also that over-scrupulousness, the locking of doors followed by the checking that they were in fact locked and other rituals. And all that doodling—the drawings of pin-men suspended on tightropes, the arrows aimed at targets, the crossed swords—they must indicate some inner tension ... Unsought, a quotation from Shakespeare slipped into Harland's mind: 'one may smile, and smile, and be a villain', but he dismissed it as inappropriate. How could young Rupert be a villain? Nonsense! he thought.

By the refreshments tent Harland again heard Wynant's voice, the half bullying, half humorous banter he particularly disliked and he quickened his step to get away from the sound. He thought that more and more he and his wife were becoming watchers of life rather than participants. Since their children had grown up and left home they seemed to live mainly by proxy. He knew that when he got home Joan would be eager for all that he could tell her about the sale and especially any gossip concerning the dealers she knew, the argumentative Peter Rawlins, the Doctor, young Sylvester and Jack Quinn. Hurrying down the drive, he contrasted the latter pair.

In some ways they were similar—both in their late thirties, both happily married to attractive women, both successful and unusually hardworking. But they were also dissimilar in that Sylvester's good qualities, such as his amiability, liveliness and charm, were all on the surface. Quinn did not appear amiable at first or seem to know what charm was. It was only after a time that you got to know that Jack was kind and could be a loyal friend; it took even longer to discover that he had a genuine passion for poetry and music. The differing qualities of the two men were demonstrated in the ways they operated their businesses. Rupert's double-fronted, handsome shop on a main road, the windows gleaming with goods that were often not quite what they seemed; whereas to buy a book from Jack you had to search out his office on the third floor and knock on a closed door. Sylvester was an excellent salesman even if sometimes over-pressing, like a vendor in a Middle-Eastern bazaar. Quinn was a terrible salesman, his method being to hand over a book silently and leave you to decide whether you wanted it.

A drink, Harland thought, I could do with a drink. For no reason at all, since he had spent most of the morning standing around doing nothing, he suddenly felt tired and in need of a little pick-me-up. As he walked along the road to Stony Stratford he looked round at the fields and woods, trying to get his bearings. He knew the area well, having spent four years there during the war. Serving with a secret, army wireless unit, he had finally been promoted to Staff Sergeant, but in effect that had only been a position like a trusted clerk in an office, travelling round to the wireless stations at Wing, Hanslope, Winslow and Bletchley, dishing out passes and pay. At the time he had felt he was doing the job he had been given; it was only subsequently, at the end of the war, when the revelations about the concentration camps came out, that he had felt guilty. When these outrageous events were made more real for him by Max Arbeit he felt doubly guilty. While he was travelling around these roads on a motor-bike, the Doctor had been strung up on a wall by his wrists and thrown into a cess-pit.

At a bend in the road Harland spotted the pub and his step became lighter again. Entering the garden, he saw that six or seven of the benches were occupied. A group of young people was laughing hilariously and he wondered what the joke had been. Under a cherry tree Jack Quinn was stretched out on a bench behind a table with an empty plate and glass.

Harland walked over quietly and lifted up the glass, saying, 'Ah well, the tide's out here.'

'*Juno and the Paycock.*'

'That's right, that's right. Give that man a small prize.'

'Right. I'll have a half. Bitter, please.'

Harland took Quinn's empty glass into the pub and ordered half a pint of bitter, a glass of red wine and an egg and anchovy sandwich. As he emerged there was another burst of laughter from the young and attractive group. Fleetingly he envied them.

Quinn took the glass of beer and raised it, saying, 'Thanks, Mickey, cheers. I say, you won't get fat on that.'

'No, but I may have another sandwich when Rupert gets here. If he does. I spotted him lying on the grass, out to the wide.'

'Yes, I saw his precious Bentley. He probably gets tired just polishing it.'

'Anything wrong between you and Sylvester?'

'Not really. Why?'

'Oh, he said something about you being an Irish idiot.'

Quinn laughed. 'He's not far wrong there. In fact if he had said an Anglo-Irish idiot I couldn't argue with that.'

'But something must have happened. You used to call in there quite a bit.'

Quinn drank some beer. 'Yes, from time to time. He liked me to look through his bindings. Of course, he knows bugger-all about books.'

'He's a quick learner.'

'Yes, I know, but he lacks any feeling for books. Always chooses the flashy things. Anyway, I rather enjoyed my teatime visits. I'd stop on the way back from Brighton or wherever. That nice woman Adele used to make me a pot of tea. Then, a month or two ago, Sylvester called a good friend of mine "a Cockney oiyck". I didn't say "Piss off Rupert" but I thought it, and he probably guessed. I haven't been back.'

'Will you go there again?'

'I don't know. Possibly ... oh probably yes. Life's too short. You know what the song says: "From cradle to tomb, it's only a short, short time." If he can put up with me being an Irish idiot I'll have to put up with his gaffes. Anyway I've always enjoyed the odd glimpse of his charming missus.'

'I thought something was up. Last time he mentioned you he was saying what a clever, helpful bloke you were. Today he says you're an Irish idiot and that you pushed two coppers through a plate-glass window. Now that wasn't the story I heard from Max.'

Quinn shook his head. 'There's no way I can tell that story without sounding like an Irish idiot.'

'Tell me anyway.'

'Well, once upon a time there was this Irish idiot who went to have supper with a friend of his, an old lady living in the East End. So I had a pleasant evening in Limehouse, with a glass or two of Guinness, then I drove home. I got lost in that maze of tiny streets round Wapping, changed my mind about which way to turn and banged into a bollard. Immediately a police car appeared, as if by magic. Two young coppers, very keen and not averse to the odd spot of trouble, you know the type. They told me to get out of the car in order to be breathalysed. I slipped as I was getting out and one of them pushed me up against the car. I pushed him back so hard he went over. Next moment we were all scrimmaging on the pavement. Eventually we fell through a shop window. I went first so I got all the cuts.'

'You're right', Harland said. 'It doesn't come out too good.'

'Yes, I do know that. It's what I've told myself about a hundred times.'

'And then?'

'When they got me back to the police station I think they would have liked to do me for starting an affray, arson, you name it. Trouble was from their point of view the coppers only had the odd bruise. I had all these cuts. Then they had to get their doctor to look at me and I insisted on being breathalysed. Now that wasn't quite so stupid.'

'You got off?'

'I passed the breathalyser so they couldn't

get me on that. And when I came up before the bench I suppose they thought I'd paid for my stupidity. So they fined me twenty-five pounds for driving without due care.'

Quinn finished his last drop of beer and stood up, looked round the garden and sat down again heavily. 'I ought to get back. Today's been a total washout money-wise. But, oh I'm browned off working in London in this heat. And my family's away. And I'm extremely tired of my own cooking.'

'Yes, I heard. The Doctor said Madeleine was in America. That right?'

'That's right. Her sister rented a lakeside cabin in Vermont for a month. Swimming, canoeing, riding. They're having a fine old time.'

'You didn't fancy it?'

'I couldn't afford to take the time off at the moment. And there are only two bedrooms. Just right for the four of them.'

'Have a meal with us then. Sunday lunch? I'll get Joan to phone you.'

'Fine. Great! I shall look forward to that.' Quinn stood up again, pointing to Harland's empty glass. 'Can I get you another of those before I go?'

'No, thanks Jack. I'll wait till Sylvester arrives.'

Quinn looked at his watch. 'Quarter to two. He's leaving it a bit late. Funny, I didn't think of him as the kind of bloke to have a

137

snooze during the day.'

'Nor did I. But he'll probably turn up soon. And it's a pleasant enough place to wait.'

'Well, I must depart. Reluctantly . . .' Quinn walked off, waving his hand.

Harland watched him go, then sat back and closed his eyes. The sunlight seemed to him particularly bright, or perhaps his single glass of wine was making him lethargic. He felt he might doze off himself, but kept hearing the odd sentence spoken by the group of young people or a burst of their laughter. A male voice commented on, 'This fad for drinking mineral water. It came from the States, like a lot of other nonsense. What's wrong with tap water?' A girl said, 'Yes, they're even taking the waters at Sainsbury's now.' Another girl, with a Knightsbridge voice, said, 'Abso*lootly*. *Tote*ally over the top.'

An image of Sylvester stretched out on the grass with his head pillowed on his arms came into Harland's mind. It did seem odd that a comparative youngster, known for his restless energy, should lie down on a lawn and sleep for an hour or more. He visualised Sylvester as he had been that morning in the greenhouse, doing some of his inevitable doodling on a dusty pane of glass and then irritably erasing it.

Hearing a car horn, Harland looked up to see Jack Quinn driving past slowly in his old

Mercedes and waving. He stood up to wave back before making his way to the pub's outside lavatory. He studied minutely written graffiti on the white-washed wall of the urinal but discovered it was only the usual kind of confession of some nut. He also realised that he could hear the young voices outside quite clearly. They were talking about items included in the afternoon session of the auction sale. The girl with the Knightsbridge voice was gushing over something. 'Rair-ly, rair-ly lovely.' Then he heard them mention the William Hallett mahogany cabinet which was described in Knightsbridge tones as. 'Abso*lootly* fantastic.' They'll be lucky, Harland thought. The architectural cabinet by Hallett was considered to be the prize item in the furniture section of the sale and he knew that all the top London dealers would be battling for it. He decided to look in on the auction after he had contacted Sylvester.

Outside in the sun again Harland saw that the young group were leaving the garden. He hurried over to collect his catalogue and followed the last couple who were walking arm in arm talking animatedly. The girl was the tall brunette with the unaffected voice and merry glance who had inspired most of the laughter.

Quite a number of people were walking along the road in the direction of Broomhill Park, strung out in twos and threes.

139

Harland's eyes had been taken by a magpie flying out from a copse when he heard a disturbing sequence of noises. A squeal of car tyres, a loud thud, screaming tyres again and a girl calling out in a frightened voice. Then he saw that the young couple he had followed were jumping up on to the grass bank and that a silver car was speeding towards him. Harland also jumped up on the bank, half falling in his anxiety to get out of the way. He shouted out, 'Maniac!' and turned to look at the car. He had a fleeting impression of the driver, a middle-aged man with a large face and protruding eyes. The car was a semi-sports model being driven at perhaps sixty or seventy miles an hour.

The disturbing noises continued: cries and shouts. The young couple in front were running along the road at full pelt. Cars travelling in the same direction were braking sharply beyond the bend. Harland's heart was thumping but he ran as fast as he could. When he turned the bend he came upon a confused scene. Cars had pulled up in a queue on the left of a crowd of people, many of whom were shouting and pointing. He heard voices calling for an ambulance and the police. A boy with a pale face and disturbed expression stood high up on the bank peering down at something. A stout man was saying in an angry voice, 'For God's sake get an ambulance! I mean, for God's sake!'

Harland pushed past the tall brunette, who exclaimed, 'Oh Jesus! No!' and saw that Max Arbeit was seated at the edge of the road, cradling Rupert Sylvester's body in his arms. Sylvester's handsome face was ashen and his head had fallen right back like that of a puppet whose strings had been cut. His cream suit was splattered with blood. There was more blood on Max's suit and shirt. The Doctor wore a woebegone mask, his eyes glazed as if he was absorbing pain. The sight struck Harland with the force of an hallucination. Momentarily his legs felt wooden and his heart pounded.

Arbeit looked up and caught Harland's eyes. 'The poor boy's dead, Mickey,' he said. 'I could do nothing.'

A blonde, middle-aged woman pushed purposefully through the crowd, saying, 'Can I help? I'm a nurse.'

'I'm afraid not,' Arbeit said with quiet dignity. 'I'm a doctor. He's gone. Our young friend is dead.'

Harland stirred himself from the strange numbness that seemed to hold him spell-bound and approached the Doctor who was awkwardly trying to get Sylvester's body on to the bank. Harland helped him and felt Sylvester's limp, damp hand. Sylvester's left arm had been broken and his elbow stuck out of a tear in his sleeve.

'I'll get a blanket,' the blonde nurse said.

141

'I've got one in the car.'

'I saw it,' the stout man said. 'Only a bloody lunatic would drive like that. Talk about hit and run. That was manslaughter.'

'Manslaughter,' Arbeit echoed doubtfully as he slowly got up on his knees and then stood, swaying a little. With shaking hands he tried to brush some of the dust from his trousers.

'Has anyone sent for the police? Did anyone get the car number?' the stout man asked.

A girl said, 'Yes, my husband's gone to phone for an ambulance and the police. I didn't get the number but the car was definitely a Volkswagen. A silver Scirocco.'

'I think it was a foreign number. Just DA and several numbers,' the boy on the bank said.

While the nurse covered Sylvester's body with a blanket Arbeit turned to Harland. 'Have you got a pen, Mickey?' he said. 'Can you write something down for me? Rupert said some words just before he died. It sounded like nonsense but we should write it down.'

'Yes, I've got a pen.' Harland fumbled for the biro in his jacket pocket and bent down to pick up a Broomhill Park catalogue that was lying on the bank.

'The boy was killed deliberately, my dear,' Arbeit whispered. 'I'm sure it was not an

142

accident. Write: "General pig boil". I know it sounds like gibberish but write it down anyway.'

CHAPTER FOURTEEN

Frank Shields sat outside the Kings Head pub in Westmoreland Street; he appeared very relaxed, without a care in the world, enjoying the summer evening twilight. Marylebone was not a part of London that he knew well but the pub was like a Cockney oasis in that rather formal area, with a free and easy atmosphere in which he was very much at home. Popular songs were being belted out in the public bar. It was also the kind of place where Frank was liable to be recognised, but he had changed his appearance enough to take care of that eventuality. He had rubbed a little vaseline and dust into his six o'clock shadow and that gave him a grubby, raffish look. He was dressed in a crumpled wind-cheater, beige T-shirt and dark blue trousers, all items from a special wardrobe for odd jobs which he kept in a filing cabinet in his Silver Street office. He also wore dark glasses and a brown corduroy cap, not at a rakish angle but straight on and jammed well down on his forehead, in the style sometimes affected by balding men.

Nursing a pint of Charrington's bitter, Frank sat by himself in the gloaming at a white round table in a narrow area divided from the pavement by black iron railings. He was in a perfect position to keep watch on the entrance to Woodstock Mews tucked away at the end of the National Heart Hospital. In a buttoned pocket of his wind-cheater he had a snippet from a letter in the bold handwriting of Alfred Thursby, the notorious 'Wild Man of the Left' as he was described in newspapers, and a new lipstick. Thursby had started a sentence with the word 'Sorry' and Frank had practised writing that word until he was satisfied that he could reproduce it satisfactorily.

In his left trouser pocket Frank had a stainless steel flick-knife, manufactured in Germany and the best to be had in the under-the-counter market that trafficked in such illegal items. His invaluable, colourless rubber gloves were in the other trouser pocket.

Though his eyes kept the corner of the Mews under careful surveillance and his ears were alert to the sounds of traffic so that he always picked up the diesel engine of a taxi before it came into view, his mind was not entirely concentrated on the job in hand. For no reason that he could think of his thoughts were inclined to wander off to another evening in London, a dreary winter one when he had disposed of a maniac called Eddie Bannister.

In some ways it had been one of his oddest jobs. Bannister was a tough guy whose days of usefulness to the corporation had run out and he was reckoned too dangerous to be left alive. It had been a bitterly cold January evening when Frank thought he had killed Bannister with two blows from a hammer in a warehouse in Duck Lane, Soho. That was before he had acquired the Volvo station wagon, so he had bundled Bannister's body up in a carpet and transported him out of London in the capacious boot of his old Rover.

Traffic on that mid-winter evening had been light and he had made good time driving to Dartford and Gravesend before taking a minor road into the unfrequented Thames marsh area which he knew extremely well. From Church Street he had taken successively smaller roads and then a meandering muddy lane which eventually led to a particularly desolate and remote creek in the Halstow Marshes where he kept his boat. Frank remembered vividly the bizarre moment when he had unlocked the car boot by torchlight to discover that the maniac Bannister had somehow got out of the carpet and was staring up at him with the blind, unfocused eyes of the dead...

The sound of an ambulance's siren brought Frank Shields back from strange memories of yesteryear. He watched the ambulance take the corner from Weymouth Street at speed and screech to a halt outside the hospital. There was a flurry of tense movement as the emergency patient was taken inside the premises. Frank was sitting close enough to the entrance to hear some of the comments made about the unconscious patient. He said quietly, 'You're going down the pan, John.'

Once the excitement of the ambulance delivery was over, Frank spied a taxi coming down Beaumont Street. Immediately his concentration became one hundred per cent, but the taxi sped past the corner of Woodstock Mews and the hospital to turn into New Cavendish Street. He sipped a little of his beer and thought how well he was served with essential information for carrying out his odd jobs. Phil might look a bit dolly dimple at times, but everything he said about a job turned out to be gospel and right to the point. About Alfred Thursby, Frank had been told only a handful of facts. One: although Thursby was always jabbering away about being a man of the people who lived in a council house in Yorkshire, he also had a small flat in Woodstock Mews, London W.1. Two: he was in the habit of phoning a brothel in Shepherd's Market on a Saturday evening and having a tart sent round to his bachelor pad. Three: the tart always arrived and departed by taxi, with approximately a two-hour interval between the two trips. Four: the fragment of Thursby's autograph letter showed how he wrote the word 'Sorry', with an extra large capital S and a big loop under the Y.

Frank had given the disposal of Alfred Thursby careful thought. A brief reconnaissance of the entrance to the mews had shown that the small area was lit by a lamp on the corner and that Thursby's flat was very close to the hospital, so noise was an important factor. He had seen the taxi plus blonde tart enter Woodstock Mews and had waited just over two hours since she was delivered. He was not impatient but it was a longish time to nurse one drink. Fortunately it was an extremely busy evening at the Kings Head: the bars were full and the customers all appeared to be in a jolly mood and unlikely therefore to ponder on the lonely figure sitting in the dusk outside.

As if on cue, because slightly more than two hours had passed, another taxi came round the corner from Weymouth Street and halted momentarily before taking the sharp left-turn into the mews. Excitement mounted in Frank when it disappeared from view—once more he was going up on the high wire without a safety net. He made an unobtrusive exit from the railed-off pavement area and crossed the road, hugging the shadow by the hospital; waiting at the corner of the mews he put on his rubber gloves. He smiled to himself at the thought that Alfred Thursby no doubt considered his evening's excitement was over, whereas in fact it was just about to commence.

Frank heard voices, the taxi's throbbing engine and a snickering male laugh. Some shouted comment followed the taxi as it reversed and manoeuvred to leave the mews. He pressed himself flat against the wall of the hospital in a deep patch of shadow and waited there for a few minutes before walking towards Thursby's flat which was over two garages. Lights were on behind the closed curtains of both its windows. When he was standing below the larger window he could hear a Sinatra recording of 'Night and Day'. He rang the bell but there was no response. Sinatra stopped singing and then began another song, 'I Wish I Were in Love Again'. Frank rat-tatted hard on an unusually large doorknocker and heard a voice calling out from upstairs. Through the mottled glass set in the top half of the door he glimpsed a shadowy figure. When the door opened a thick-set man with thin, brown hair and dark eyes regarded him with obvious irritation, asking, 'Yes?'

Alfred Thursby was dressed in dark trousers and a white, short-sleeved shirt; his feet were bare. Frank listened intently for any sounds from the flat apart from Sinatra who was still singing away gaily. There was just the chance that Thursby's sexual tastes ran to three-people encounters. The stairway stank of a heavy, musky perfume.

Frank grinned, saying two words so quietly that they could not be heard. He shook his head and repeated them after taking a step forward, placing his right foot on the tiled sill of the doorway. 'Cabby, guv.'

Thursby repeated 'Yes?' in an irritable tone, twitching his narrow head to one side. He had a long, thin face with deeply etched lines around the mouth; his eyes were bloodshot. There was a strong smell of whisky about him but he did not seem to be much affected by drink; he was alert and suspicious. Watch this one, thought Frank.

Frank cleared his throat noisily before saying confidentially, 'The young lady, guv . . .' He nodded knowingly. 'The young lady in the cab, like. She thinks she might have left her purse here. In the bathroom.'

Thursby looked puzzled but made the fatal mistake of half turning to look back up the stairs as he said, 'But she couldn't . . .'

Frank stepped through the doorway and with a quickness-of-the-hand-deceives-the-eye movement of his left hand produced and flicked open his knife. He shut the door behind him with his right elbow.

Thursby's dark eyes were large with excitement but he looked more angry than afraid. Frank's brain repeated the warning: Watch this one!

'What the fuck!' Thursby exclaimed.

Frank made a little movement with the flick-knife so that light glinted on the blade. He said quietly, 'It's a good 'un, John. You could cut cable with this.'

'For Christ's sake! What do you want? There's nothing here worth stealing.'

Frank grinned again, deftly transferring the switch-blade to his right hand. 'Let me worry about that, John,' he said.

'Look, I've got a few quid. You can have that. Otherwise, what? You going to take the furniture?'

'I'll see. I'm not that choosey. Now up the stairs, Chief. Careful and quiet, and neither of us will get hurt.'

Alfred Thursby made no immediate movement, looking silently at Frank, plainly weighing his chances against a man who was so fast with his hands. Turning on his heel he walked up the short flight of stairs quickly, but paused where they turned left. Frank followed him closely and saw Thursby flick a glance at an open, white-painted door; it was steel-backed as a fire precaution because of the garages below. Frank thought, Yes, Alfred, you should have taken that chance, slammed the door against me. Thursby hovered on the tiny landing from which doorways opened on to three small rooms. The smell of perfume was heavy and cloying. Thursby gave him another cold, judging look; there was no fear in his eyes. 'What now?' he asked.

'I might just have a little snort of your whisky and see what's worth nicking.'

'Listen, there's nothing here. I've got twenty-five quid on me. Take it! Otherwise there's nothing. We don't go in for gold chains and such where I come from.' When he spoke angrily Thursby's Yorkshire accent was stronger and he sounded more like the man Frank had heard in television interviews. Very quickly, in the circumstances, Thursby had got control of himself.

'Let's just have a quick dekko in the bedroom.' Frank spoke quietly, persuasively, as if he were selling something. 'You see, John, I'll have to tie you up even if I only take the cash.'

Thursby gave him a look that was as good as a threat. 'I don't like that idea.'

''Course you don't. But I can't run out of here and have you on the blower the moment I'm gone. You're sensible, do what I say, I'll give the old Bill a call myself, let them know how you've been inconvenienced.'

Thursby said nothing but moved his heavy shoulders irritably, before stepping into a feebly lit room on his right. The bedroom had

151

no windows, but a large sky-light displayed an oblong fragment of dark sky. A table-lamp shone a circle of light on to a counterpane, pillows and sheets all tangled up on a large double bed. A man's pants and socks lay on the carpet with two smeared, empty glasses. The white walls of the room were bare apart from a painting of a nude girl with long red hair, curled up like a foetus against purple and gold draperies. A suit, jackets and trousers hung from a brass rail suspended between two closed cupboards at the end of the room.

'What about them cupboards, John?' Frank asked. 'Any little treasures tucked away there, maybe?'

Thursby shook his head from side to side. 'Cupboards? You steal underclothes? I told you, there's nothing.' Suddenly he leaned forward and swung round wildly with something glinting in his right hand. Frank raised his right hand, which was holding the knife, to ward off the blow and punched Thursby in the head with his left. Thursby stumbled forward and Frank punched him twice more. Thursby collapsed, half on the rumpled bed and half on the floor; a brass ashtray fell from his hand. His eyes were open but asquint and seeing nothing. Frank glanced at his right wrist which had taken the blow from the ashtray; it ached but was not bleeding. He pushed Thursby into a sitting position and delivered a rabbit punch with his left hand which a boxing critic had once called 'the best in the business.'

Frank pocketed his flick-knife and dragged Thursby into the sitting-room where a disc was still revolving on the record-player. Sinatra was singing 'Stars Fell on Alabama'. A pair of shoes lay on the floor with some used tissues and two cushions. Open bottles of red vermouth and whisky stood on a small round table. He sat Thursby in an armchair, opened his mouth and poured whisky into him from the bottle that was three-quarters full. Frank took his time over this, treating it as a matter that merited great care, at pains not to pour too quickly or spill any of the liquid. When the bottle was only a quarter full he replaced it on the table and dragged Thursby's inert body through to the bathroom. He held Thursby up by the washbasin and used the unconscious man's fingers to hold the new lipstick as he wrote just one word on the mirror over the basin: Sorry. He also did this with great care, remembering the extra large S and the flourished loop under the Y.

There was a gas water-boiler by the bath and Frank gave it a thoughtful stare before throwing the lipstick on the floor and dragging Thursby across the landing into the kitchen. Sinatra was singing 'No one Ever Tells You' as Frank opened the gas oven and

153

pushed Thursby's head into it. After turning the gas full on he stood for two minutes with a foot on Thursby's back, but the 'Wild Man of the Left' appeared tamed at last and showed no sign of regaining consciousness.

After shutting the kitchen door, Frank looked quickly into each room. In the sitting-room Sinatra had stopped singing 'I Won't Dance' and the machine clicked off into silence. Frank pulled the steel-backed door tight behind him and turned off the light before descending the stairs. He peered through the mottled glass of the front door and opened it an inch and then another before leaving the premises. Once more he hugged the shadow of the hospital. Just before he walked into Westmoreland Street he paused long enough to remove and pocket his rubber gloves. As he did so he gave a moment's thought to a possible gas explosion so close to the National Heart Hospital, but consoled himself with the fact that many of the patients were halfway down the pan already. 'Nice one, Frank,' he said quietly, and walked briskly out of the mews.

CHAPTER FIFTEEN

A magnificent statue of the first Duke of Wellington confronts the busiest crossroads in the City. The Iron Duke is portrayed, high in the air, mounted on his charger, Copenhagen, and looking down on the unending traffic in Princes Street, Poultry, Queen Victoria Street, Cheapside and King William Street. He does so with a calm, thoughtful expression, probably much as he once confronted the rampaging mobs outside his residence at Hyde Park Corner, known as Apsley House or Number One, London. It is a superb site for the statue because Wellington thus appears to guard the Royal Exchange and the Bank of England. The statue stands on a massive stone block; letters boldly engraved in the stone proclaim WELLINGTON on both sides, and ERECTED JUNE 18 1844 on the back and front. It is protected by heavily spiked, stout iron railings but that does not prevent it from receiving a tithe of collapsed beer cans, broken bottles and potato crisp bags from modern barbarians.

On a cool, cloudy June morning three City men met by the statue where ancient Threadneedle Street joins venerable Cornhill. In fact, the men first saw each other just in front of the Royal Exchange by the War Memorial and then walked together by the great equestrian statue that dominates the area.

Their meeting by the statue had not been arranged, but was not altogether surprising as they were all men of fixed habits and each Monday morning they walked to Jope's dining-club just as the church bells struck one. They always took the corner table at Jope's at ten past one and the oldest waiter there said that, 'You could set your watch by them.'

All three men wore sober City garb without those touches of exoticism that mark out the buccaneers among the stockbrokers and the men from Lloyds. They did not attract any attention from the milling crowds whose minds were mainly concerned with their own lunches and yet they were all unusual, indeed remarkable men.

The oldest of the three friends, a stocky man with a Punch-like chin and nose, was Admiral Cornwallis-Burlace, once in the newspaper headlines for wartime Naval exploits but more latterly on the front pages for intrepid single-handed yachting trips. The comparatively young, slim man was Anthony Vallance who for a short period was regarded as the Golden Boy of the Conservative Party before being mysteriously dropped by the Tories, only to reappear as the thrusting head of a great property firm. The giant of a man with a bronzed bald head and striking profile, somewhat resembling a bust of Julius Caesar, was the fabulously wealthy Piers Mortain who could trace his ancestors back to William the Conqueror's half-brother Robert, Count of

Mortain, the owner in antiquity of the Cornish parts of Macretone. Piers Mortain was himself a substantial landowner in Cornwall, but chose to live mainly in Grosvenor Square.

The trio, who met without exchanging a word, had a good deal in common. They had all once been new boys, in bumfreezers and Tweedledum collars, at Eton and had all graduated to the coloured silk waistcoats and sponge-bag trousers of Pop. Vallance was more inclined to small talk than the other two and would occasionally reminisce about his relatively recent days at Eton when there had been an outsize Cockney cook, Mrs Renkas, famous for wearing size ten men's leather brogues; and a daring youth, Ranulph Twisleton-Wykeham-Fiennes, dressed in a frogman's outfit, had sabotaged the floodlit Procession of Boats on the Fourth of June. The Admiral and Piers Mortain never spoke of their earlier epochs at the famous school.

As well as being old Etonians the men had similar backgrounds and many shared interests. They also had friends in common and Anthony Vallance had married Piers Mortain's niece. They had belonged to Jope's dining-club for over twenty years and had been extremely successful in their City careers. But personal achievements and financial gain had not been mentioned at their recent luncheons, for they also shared a

157

profound concern about the future of their country which they always referred to as England rather than Britain. They believed that a bloodless revolution had already taken place in England over a period of sixty years, whereby power had been largely transferred to what they called 'the Union stormtroopers'; they accepted this as a *fait accompli*, but were united in a stern resolve to resist 'a bloody insurrection by the lunatic left'.

The trio waited in silence for the traffic lights to change and crossed over the road to the ancient site of the 'Stocks Market', turned left by the Bank of New Zealand and left again by the Mansion House. Jope's dining-club was tucked away in St Stephen's Row, close to the Mansion House and the Church of Saint Stephen Walbrook. The proximity of the rear of the Mansion House meant that Jope's narrow eighteenth-century premises always had to be artificially lit, and the only view from the front windows was of a blank wall. But it also meant that, two minutes walk away from ceaseless traffic, Jope's members found themselves in a quiet backwater; and there was a view from the side windows of the graceful trees in the churchyard where Sir John Vanbrugh was buried in 1726.

Anthony Vallance's secretary had telephoned to arrange the simple menu for the luncheon, as was often done by members. Bills were rendered quarterly and it was the custom to add something to the cheque as a tip to be shared out amongst the staff, so it was quite feasible to enter the old premises, to eat and drink and leave without saying a word other than 'Morning' to Smithers in the cloakroom and the waiters.

Vallance had once been a man accustomed to gossip, but over the years he had become more reserved like his two friends and had taken on something of their neutral colouring. The men deposited umbrellas and bowler hats with Smithers but, exceptionally, Piers Mortain kept his crisp copy of *The Times* as they hurried in silence along the hall. They passed the panelled room with the celebrated sycamore and shagreen furniture, where some members were drinking sherry. On the dimly lit stairs Vallance enquired about Mortain's train journey from Plymouth but the reply was mumbled and unsatisfactory.

The trio took their corner table, which looked directly down on the old gravestones of Saint Stephen Walbrook, at precisely ten minutes past one. Once seated, they visibly relaxed. Their table was the most sought after at Jope's, secluded and positioned so that Mortain had room to stretch out his unusually long legs. 'Paddington was like a scene in a rather bad dream,' he said to Vallance. 'So many people on the move. All milling about

159

as if they didn't know where they were going. And such extraordinary luggage! Like refugees.'

'Everything is changing. The whole country is chaotic,' Vallance said. He made a neat gesture with his elegant hands to express the chaos and his desire to compress it into order.

The ambience in the dining-room was pleasant; the lofty ceiling and dark panelled walls seemed like repositories of ancient secrets. A slight breeze stirred the brocade curtains; the white linen tablecloths and silver cutlery were immaculate; quiet conversations were going on at two other, well-spaced tables; there was a faint scent of melons in the air.

Jope's menu only existed in verbal form and was simplicity itself. Basically the establishment continued to offer what it had supplied for over two hundred years—the best Welsh lamb and the finest Scotch beef in London; in season, lobsters, oysters and Scotch salmon were served; grilled soles were usually available; the chef had been congratulated on his Turbot Bonne Femme. Other reasonable requests were met, but new members who had often waited ten years to join the club were informed that it did not set out to cater for exotic tastes.

Brown, the oldest waiter, placed a well-chilled bottle of Meursault, Cuvée

Goureau, on the table, brought them each an Ogen melon and retired to a position near the door where he was out of earshot but could watch the three friends.

The Admiral poured the wine, giving Mortain only a meagre amount. He said, 'Wellington predicted our position today. He said that when the man in the street started to question established political and religious ideas Europe would go through "a very bad half hour indeed".'

Vallance nodded. 'That half hour has started.' He fished in his waistcoat pocket and produced a press cutting. 'This is about one of those Militant Tendency documents, headed "British Perspectives", predicting a full-scale confrontation and civil war.'

Neither of his companions made a comment so Vallance followed their lead in eating and drinking in silence. Brown removed their plates and brought Mortain a cutlet of cold salmon and placed a tureen of new potatoes and one of green peas on the table. He served the Admiral with a grilled plaice and Vallance a grilled sole, both on the bone. He inclined his head towards the bottle of white burgundy which was only a quarter full and caught the Admiral's eye. The Admiral nodded.

The three men continued their meal in silence until Brown had brought another bottle of the white burgundy. When the

161

waiter was again out of earshot, Mortain took his first sip of wine. 'Too much to hope that the fellow who cheerfully predicted civil war was the chap who fell out of that tower block?'

'Alas, you're right,' Vallance said.

'Ah well,' the Admiral muttered. His prognathous chin rose. 'His time will come. Fortunately these fellows seem to have forgotten that old rhyme: "Twice armed is he whose cause is just. Thrice armed is he who gets his blow in fust".'

Mortain nodded before picking up his copy of *The Times* from the floor. He opened it at page three and flourished it above the table. 'I see that Alfred Thursby's been found dead in a gas-filled flat.' He glanced round the room before adding very quietly, 'I presume that is Starr's work.'

Vallance spoke equally quietly. 'Only at a remove, as it were. He's working through friends of friends. The chain of command is quite a long one, but Starr gave the order.'

'Is that a good idea, a long chain of command?' the Admiral asked. 'I should have thought the fewer people involved the better.'

Vallance replied quickly, 'No, it's quite secure. The nuts and bolts of the affair are being dealt with by a mechanic who's been described as "torture proof".'

'A mechanic?' the Admiral queried. 'You mean a mercenary?'

'Not exactly,' Vallance replied. 'I mean a professional killer.'

'Really? There are such people?' Mortain said.

'This one is considered the best there is. Someone intelligent enough always to cover his tracks.'

Mortain said, 'An intelligent professional killer sounds like a contradiction in terms.'

The Admiral shook his head. 'We may not like the idea of using such a man but if we can head off a possible civil war...'

'Starr went into the matter with great care,' Vallance said.

Mortain made an impatient gesture. 'I've heard Roscoe Starr described as a dangerous man.'

The Admiral shook his head again. 'Only to his enemies. And remember, there may well come a time when we need a dangerous man.'

'Roscoe does exactly what the General tells him,' Vallance said. 'He's not going to embark on any adventures. The General will see to that.'

Mortain frowned doubtfully. 'Yes, but can the General control him?'

The Admiral replied firmly, with a hint of fierceness, 'Yes, of course, the General can control him. I must remind you, Piers, that only the General and Roscoe know of our own involvement in this matter. We have to rely on them. If we don't trust them we shouldn't be involved at all.'

CHAPTER SIXTEEN

The death of Rupert Sylvester was much lamented in the Surrey village of Alderbury and it affected most of the people who lived there to some degree, for at one stroke the villagers had lost the energetic chairman of their Council, the captain of their cricket team, a fine baritone in the church choir, a member of the bell-ringers and last but not least the proprietor of a prestigious local business, one that stopped motorists on their journeys to and from the south coast.

In both the local pubs, in the tiny village post-office, while queuing at the butcher's shop, or leaving the church, there was a buzz of comment on 'the tragedy': 'What was he—late thirties?'; 'Extraordinary that a spry young chap like that should be knocked down by a car'; 'It makes you think'; 'I still can't credit it'.

Even Sylvester's sole enemy in the village, the Trotskyite Judy Browning, found his violent death rather depressing though she could not understand exactly why it should have that effect on her. She tried to explain it in a telephone call to her friend, Sarah Levey, by saying, 'It seems to have cast rather a blight on the local people. The village postmistress was in tears! Of course he was very active here—had a finger in every pie . . .' Outwardly Judy Browning gave no sign of her feelings, but it was different with several other people in the village. Adele Rogers, on her infrequent appearances in public, looked distinctly pale, Pamela Stratton-Smith was plainly unhappy and Brigadier Bealby seemed particularly thoughtful as if he were pondering some aspect of the affair which others had overlooked.

Polly Sylvester was pale too, with dark shadows beneath her eyes, but she kept much to her usual routine and took to exercising the black mare, Night, although she was not a good horsewoman. It was noticed that she and Louise Simpson met one day by the Alder Pool and silently embraced each other, an unusual act which caused some significant looks among the village gossips.

So Sylvester's death had a far-reaching effect on village matters, like a stone being dropped into a pond and sending out ripples. The people of Alderbury also maintained that the weather changed drastically the day 'the Captain' died. Before his sudden decease they had been complaining about the period of hot, humid days: 'Terrible sticky, ain't it?'; 'So close you don't feel a bit like work';

'Awful stuffy'. Afterwards their complaints were in the normal summer vein: 'Isn't it cold?' 'What a wind, eh?'; 'What happened to our summer, then?' The truth was that the weather had reverted to the usual English mixture of fair days and foul. Families on seaside holidays would sally forth with bathing costumes and towels after breakfast but have to return from the beach before lunch in order to seek shelter from rain or a cold east wind. Many people staying at south coast resorts cut short their holidays and sped back on the A281 to Guildford; but the Court Antiques shop did not beckon or beguile them with its glittering display of highly polished objects since the blinds were down and a 'Closed' notice on the door gave no indication as to when it might re-open.

On the day of Sylvester's funeral at the local church Alice Prince, the wife of the butcher, left her cashier's cubicle to walk out of the shop and see what the weather was like. The forecast had not been promising and standing in the pale sunshine under a watery sky she called out to her husband, 'It don't know whether to laugh or cry, Stan! Oh, I hope it won't rain and spoil everything.'

The moment Alice made her last comment she realised it was a stupid thing to say, but she could see that her husband had not taken it in. Stanley Prince was methodically mincing pork for sausages with a gloomy, abstracted expression that showed his mind was not on the business in hand. Alice knew that he would be thinking about Sylvester in his role as captain of the cricket team, for her husband was also a keen member of the eleven.

When Alice Prince first encountered Rupert Sylvester she had been favourably impressed and to a close friend she confided that he had, 'The kind of film-star good looks that make you feel a bit weak at the knees.' She had also been much taken by his charm and what she called his 'old-fashioned gallantry'. In the early days of his being in the village she was under the impression that he was flirting with her, which made a change as her husband seemed to have lost all interest in romance. But gradually it dawned on her that such charm was automatic with Sylvester and that he turned it on equally with old Miss Pringle and little Mrs Watterson. And as for flirting, he went right over the top when it came to that snobbish, conceited Miss Louise Simpson. So Alice had turned against Sylvester, particularly since her husband was always going on about what a fine chap he was. To her confidant she said she thought that Sylvester was 'too good to be true' and 'There's more to him than meets the eye'. In a way, therefore, Sylvester's accident had not come as such a shock to her, since she was half expecting some revelation about

167

him—that he would be unmasked as a
confidence trickster or even a Russian spy.

'I'm going home to change, Stan,' she said.
'Now, don't you leave it too late! I've pressed
your navy suit and I found that black tie.
D'you hear?'

Stanley Prince nodded but said nothing,
just lifting his left hand in acknowledgement
as she hurried away. He was a stocky man
with large biceps and was considered the best
batsman in the Alderbury cricket team after
Sylvester. He lacked Sylvester's skill but was
capable, on occasion, of hitting a cricket ball
right out of the ground. For the past few
years he and Sylvester had always opened the
batting, and they had made a formidable pair.

Prince took the pan of minced pork and
put it in the refrigerator and put the mincer in
the sink. His movements round the shop as
he tidied things away were automatic, his
mind being full of memories of cricket and
Sylvester. Long summer evenings when it
would be dusk before stumps were finally
drawn and Rupert would take the whole team
for a drink at the White Rose. Sylvester
encouraging the team in his pleasantly deep
voice. He had the habit of saying things that
sounded very old fashioned, and yet seemed
right from him: 'Good shot, old sport';
'Tophole!'; 'Well done, that man'; 'Bai Jove,
Stan!' If anyone else had said 'Bai Jove' it
would have been a joke but it seemed natural

with Rupert whose enthusiasm had always kept the team on its toes. Prince felt that cricket would seem tame without him and he viewed the prospect of the next match with dismay. He went through his final chores like an automaton, looked round the shop with eyes that did not really take in details and put the 'Closed' sign on the door. Glancing at his watch he realised he had cut it fine, walked very quickly to the end of the lane leading to his cottage and then broke into a run. He cursed himself for bothering with that last-minute mincing.

Mickey Harland drove up by the butcher's shop in Alderbury just in time to see the front door being closed and a burly man turning away from it and scurrying down the lane. Harland decided to leave his Austin Princess close to the shop, facing the village green, as he could see a long line of cars by the church and disliked any complication about parking.

The extent of the village had come as a surprise to Harland, for he had presumed from his infrequent visits to Sylvester's shop that there was not much more to Alderbury than the cluster of old buildings on the main road. Instead, he found that it was a sizeable village grouped round a river and a pond, the houses straggling off in all directions. It was another surprise to see how attractive it was, with a white-painted footbridge across the river and white picket fence round most of the pond. The third surprise was the sight of so many people making their way to the church on foot—it was obvious that Sylvester's funeral was considered an important event locally.

Harland extricated a bunch of carnations and locked his car with a heartfelt sigh, sounding much put upon. It was a sad event to attend for he had liked Rupert and had also admired his vitality; he found it depressing that such a vital young life could be snuffed out so easily, like a fly being swatted. But he also sighed because he was aware of his own inadequacy in such situations; he could never think of suitable things to say, any words that came into his head seemed trite and pointless. He bent down with another sigh and brushed the legs of his rarely worn, clerical-grey suit which seemed to have picked up a lot of fluff on the drive from London. He was conscious that the suit had a musty smell with just a hint of mothballs.

Looking along the road leading to the church, Harland noticed an old woman locking the door of an ancient Daimler limousine and then walking along by the line of cars, making agonisingly slow progress with the aid of two sticks. Harland followed in her path, undecided whether to offer her his arm. The decision was made for him when he saw Max Arbeit half in and half out of his green Mini, fussing with something on the back seat. Harland was glad to see someone he knew because he had begun to wonder whether any other dealers would turn up for Sylvester's funeral.

'What's wrong, Max? Anything I can do?'

Arbeit extricated himself awkwardly and turned with an unhappy grin. 'No, Mickey, thanks. It's just that this spray of flowers ... It looked so nice when I collected it from the florist.'

'It looks fine.'

They walked slowly towards the crowd of people that had formed by the lich-gate.

'I wonder why the hold-up?' Harland said.

'The coffin is there, Mickey, by the gate. It waits there apparently till the clergyman arrives. Or so I was told.'

'Really? Well, you'll have to tell me if I put a foot wrong. I'm not at all religious and I haven't been inside a church for years.'

'That will be a case of the blind leading the lame, my dear. I'm a non-religious Jew. But I don't think that matters at all. We've just come here as a sign of respect for Rupert. Poor boy!'

'You're right of course.' Harland fished out an assortment of cards and pieces of paper from his trouser pocket. He did not possess a notebook or diary, and kept a collection of such scraps which he daily transferred from pocket to pocket until their significance had elapsed. 'Look, I've still got the note I made

171

that day. What a rotten shock it must have been for you, being just behind him! Do you think the police made anything of that strange phrase, those words he said to you?'

'Who can say? Of course I told that sergeant, the first one to turn up and then I repeated it to the C.I.D. man when I went to the police station at Buckingham. And again when a detective came to see me. But the sergeant seemed to think that the car might just have got out of control. And he made a big thing about the bank being very narrow at that point. But I'm still convinced it was deliberate.'

Harland could not think of a meaningful comment to make. A deliberate intent to murder Rupert Sylvester seemed highly unlikely, even fantastic, but Arbeit had been the main witness to the event, positioned only a matter of fifty feet from where it had happened.

There was no movement in the crowd gathered by the lich-gate. People stood silently, so Harland followed suit, looking at the carved lettering on the arches of the oak gate which proclaimed that it had been erected 'To the Memory of Felicity Bealby' in 1902. He looked too at the tower, which was plainly of an earlier epoch than the rest of the church, a massive structure with twin gables, rising perhaps sixty feet. Then he noticed how wreaths and sprays of flowers lined both sides of the gravel path that wound up through the churchyard. There appeared to be an extraordinary number of them. The sky had darkened with a threat of rain and what light there was seemed to be absorbed by the old gravestones, the yew trees and blackberry bushes. A crooked shaft of sunlight fell on a large tomb with black iron railings and then was extinguished.

Harland felt a hand on his sleeve and looked round into Arbeit's worried eyes. 'I also mentioned it to Mrs Sylvester when I came to tell her about—what happened,' Arbeit said. 'I don't know if I did right, Mickey, but I felt I had to.'

Harland nodded, but a chance to reply was lost as the crowd moved forward behind the uplifted coffin on which lay two wreaths and a large spray of roses. A tall clergyman with a lot of wavy silver hair led the procession, saying in a lilting, tremulous voice, 'I am the resurrection and the life, saith the Lord: he that believeth in me, though he were dead, yet shall he live...'

There was such a press of people on the narrow path, all seemingly impatient, like a silent but excited theatre queue, that Harland found it impossible to be selective about where to lay his small bunch of white carnations. Max Arbeit had become lost in the crowd and Harland's partner on the path was a wheezing, fat woman who took up a lot

173

of room and had surprisingly sharp elbows. He let his flowers drop between a formal wreath and a much larger bunch of carnations which made his own appear insignificant.

Harland felt ill at ease, like an interloper or impostor, as he had done before on his rare attendances at church. Not for the first time he felt that those who did not believe should keep away from religious services. Gloom was setting in steadily as the sky darkened and a rising wind made a mournful sound as it stirred the old yew trees. He noticed the neatly cut turves and the large pile of clay which marked the area for a new grave, in what seemed a favoured spot, close to the door of the church.

His doubts about the wisdom of his attending the funeral were suddenly dissipated and his spirits rose as he passed through the oak porch that sheltered the church doorway. This was caused simply by the unusually strong, indeed nearly overwhelming, fragrance of flowers wafting out from the church, like the sweetest possible exhalation. It was something unique in his experience—so strong yet delicate, without any of the cloying quality of a heavy perfume. Stepping into the church, he could see the source: so many flowers festooned the old building that it looked as if a hothouse and a garden had been stripped to make a wonderful floral tribute to the memory of

Rupert Sylvester.

For a moment he was taken aback by the unusual sight. Love, he thought, this is love. He experienced the odd sensation called 'a lump in the throat', not because Sylvester was dead but because someone had been so moved by his death. He felt for all human beings because they were all, willy nilly, in the same boat—all loving relationships were finally doomed and there could be no happy endings.

As he walked slowly down the aisle, Harland wondered whether all the delightful decoration could be the work of Polly Sylvester. He had to admit there was a touch of envy in his thoughts; he never envied others their fine possessions, but envy did come into his mind occasionally when he saw a young couple who were much in love. Yes, he thought, I should like to be adored as Rupert quite plainly was adored.

Far behind in the queue Harland heard Max Arbeit's hacking cough, deriving from his broken nose but probably triggered off by encountering the strong, sweet odour. The scent and sight of the flowers had an audible effect on many people, for he kept hearing gasps and stifled exclamations. He also overheard a whispered, repeated name with a sibilant sound: 'Louise Simpson, Mrs Simpson—Simpson.'

Looking for an empty place in the pews,

Harland noticed two faces he had not expected to see there. The usually cynical Peter Rawlins who could be sharp or spread innuendo when he was bored, the man who had welcomed Sylvester's vacating the greenhouse with a tart comment, was staring towards the coffin with a stony expression. And Jack Quinn was in the middle of a crowded pew, towering over his neighbours; the scars on Quinn's face were becoming less noticeable and he was well dressed for once in a dark blue suit and white shirt.

'Louise Simpson.' Harland heard the name whispered twice as he squeezed past several people to take an empty space by a pillar at the side of the church. The second time it was said by a middle-aged woman with a peevish expression who nodded towards the flowers as she commented *sotto voce* to a younger woman: 'It's that Louise Simpson—her father's gardener told me.'

Harland stared round the church, noticing with what care each spray and vase had been placed—it must have been the work of hours to achieve what could only be an ephemeral effect, however glorious. The refrain of an old song tinkled in his head: 'Say it with music'. Louise Simpson, he thought, you have not laboured in vain—you have said it with flowers.

Gradually the surprisingly large congregation settled into silence. People were standing all round the sides and the back of the church. They began to sing the hymn 'The day Thou gavest Lord has ended', and Harland pretended to sing too, mouthing the words as his singing voice was flat.

When the hymn came to an end, a slightly built man dressed in a black suit began to read the psalm: 'The Lord is my shepherd: therefore can I lack nothing ...' He had startlingly blue eyes and a commanding presence as if he was used to being listened to in silence; he read well in a voice that gave each word its due weight, but Harland's mind shied away from the simple, majestic message. His mind was always restless; his wife aptly compared it to a butterfly, flitting from one thing to another. He looked up at the ancient woodwork of the nave and then at an alabaster effigy of a knight reclining on a stone tomb.

It was the same even when the Vicar spoke about Sylvester. The address dealt with Sylvester's good works in Alderbury, which was something new to Harland, but he found himself unable to concentrate on the sonorous sentences. The Vicar was plainly of Welsh origin and he spoke in a stagey fashion, like an actor in an amateur play, with unnecessary flourishes; and he had the irritating habit of pushing back a strand of wavy hair.

Instead of listening attentively Harland studied the people in the front pew. The owner of the very blonde hair pinned up at the back was Polly Sylvester. Sitting next to her was a young woman very similar in appearance and then two older people who were probably her parents. He looked at other backs and side views, trying to guess which couple could be Sylvester's parents. And then his attention lapsed again and he stared at the faded gilt lettering on a black marble plaque, deciphering the name 'Bealby' which had also been engraved on the lich-gate.

Simpson—Simpson. The sibilant name echoed in Harland's brain. He quickly formulated an idea for a scenario in which the handsome Sylvester had been conducting an affair with Mrs Louise Simpson. The affair had been discovered by Mrs Simpson's husband who had then murdered the adulterer. But as soon as he had finished building up the shaky theory, another part of his brain demolished it. To have killed Sylvester by running him over on the road to Stony Stratford would have required a lot of planning and more than one person would necessarily have been involved. Someone would have had to follow Sylvester or know his plans for that day and someone would have had to have watched him and give the tip to the driver of the silver car. The more he thought about it, the more people were required to carry out such a plan. The idea of a jealous husband working with collaborators was nonsense and so was the idea of there being a group of people anxious to kill the owner of a small antiques shop. It was obvious that Arbeit was mistaken.

The Vicar said, 'Let us pray,' and these words and the movement of the congregation stopped Harland's idle daydreaming. Kneeling down made him feel even more of an impostor since he could not bring himself to pray; instead he said to himself that he was sorry for Polly and anyone else who had loved the dead man.

There was another hymn and then the congregation began to file out, following the coffin. The young woman who had been sitting next to Polly Sylvester was plainly her sister, with hair that was nearly as blonde, similar eyes and tip-tilted nose. And the next woman was just as obviously Polly's mother. Harland was not sure of the identity of the man following them, who was about his own age; he was of average height but heavily built with a weathered complexion and a partly bald, freckled head. He did not look like either Polly or Rupert.

Peter Rawlins went past deep in thought, apparently oblivious of those around him. Jack Quinn followed shortly after, pulling a funny face and looking impatient, probably anxious to get to one of the pubs on the main road for a drink. Harland surreptitiously glanced at his watch to see that it was a quarter past twelve and the pubs would be open.

When it was his turn to file along the aisle, Harland found himself close to Max Arbeit who turned to whisper, 'Polly said that she hoped any dealers who came from a distance would go back to Vine Cottage afterwards. What do you think?'

'I don't know.' Harland knew he disliked attending wakes that often degenerated into parties at which the dead person seemed happily forgotten—they seemed macabre to him; but he didn't know how he would frame an excuse for not going to Sylvester's house.

Outside he found the clouds had largely cleared and the sun was shining weakly from a hazy sky. There was already a crowd filling the path along the front of the church by the open grave, so Harland stood at some distance from it by a gravestone on which he could read, in fine eighteenth-century lettering, 'Here lyeth Sarah Bealby'.

In the open air the Vicar's delivery seemed even more theatrical as he spoke the simple, moving words of the committal with unnecessary crescendoes and diminuendoes: 'Man that is born of a woman hath but a short time to live, and is full of misery. He cometh up, and is cut down, like a flower; he fleeth as it were a shadow, and never continueth in one stay. In the midst of life we are in death . . .'

180

Harland looked round at the people standing a little apart from the main crowd, noticing that Jack Quinn was on the very edge of the gathering, halfway down the path, looking as if he were ready to make a swift retreat. Max Arbeit was positioned like himself but, due to his dimunitive stature, was quite unable to see what was happening as the coffin was lowered into the grave. This final event led to some of the women crying quietly; but one pale, rather striking girl gave way to her pent-up emotion, sobbing so that her body shook with inimitable, genuine grief.

Earth was being thrown into the grave as the Vicar said, 'The soul of this our dear brother departed, and we therefore commit his body to the ground; earth to earth, ashes to ashes, dust to dust...'

Harland wondered again at the size of the crowd in the churchyard, many of whom were obviously moved by the ceremony. He felt sure that not a quarter as many would attend his own funeral and decided it must be partly due to Sylvester having lived in a village where presumably everyone knew everyone. And from what the Vicar had said it appeared that Rupert had been much involved in local affairs and church matters. He was struck once more by the extraordinary energy of Sylvester in building a thriving business while finding time for so

181

many other activities.

'What do you think, Mickey? Should we be intruding at Vine Cottage?' Arbeit had moved next to him as the burial ceremony ended and the crowd began to disperse. 'I'm in two minds about it myself. What is the done thing?'

'I really don't know. The people there will be mainly relatives and close friends. I don't think . . .'

'Doctor. Mr Harland. I'm sorry.'

Harland turned round to see that Adele Rogers had come up by the Bealby gravestone and was holding on to it as she leaned towards him. She wore a black frock and black velvet jacket. Grief had affected her looks. Her complexion was pasty and there were dark shadows beneath her eyes; her faded blonde hair looked skimpy and lifeless.

'I'm sorry to bother you but I have to say something.'

There was a pause as a knot of people talking quietly together went past. Harland was particularly sorry for Adele as he felt sure that the death would have quite a big effect on her life; he thought that she would find it difficult to find a congenial job if Polly decided to close Court Antiques.

'Yes, what is it, Adele? Can we help?'

'Mrs Sylvester told me that you were there—that day. At the Broomhill Park sale—and afterwards—on the road when he

182

was killed.'

'That's right.'

'We were very close, my dear,' Arbeit said. 'I can assure you it was all over quickly, painlessly—he did not suffer. A minute or two and he was gone.'

Adele Rogers shivered. 'I know. But Polly also told me that you heard Rupert say something. The name Boyle?'

Arbeit looked a little puzzled but nodded gravely. 'Yes.'

'I'm mystified that he should have mentioned that name just then. But he *did* know a man called Boyle. I met him myself. He came to the shop twice that I know of. A big, burly man. But I don't think he was a customer, I had the impression that it was some private matter. Each time Rupert asked me to show him into the back office. And Rupert seemed nervous when he came.'

'A man called Boyle,' Arbeit repeated. He nodded away like a mechanical doll as he gave the name much thought.

CHAPTER SEVENTEEN

'Young Frank' was pleasure bound. His pleasures were many and varied but those at the top of the list had something in common, to do with imposing his will on the world, changing the status quo, leaving his mark on life. He liked to shoot a cock pheasant in its full glory—to stop its 'korr-kok' sound and see the vigorous, multi-coloured bird crumple into a heap of feathers; he enjoyed pulling a massive conger eel from its lair in the rocks and hauling it into his boat while it was still full of fight and danger; but more than these he liked to make a lovely woman stoop to folly. With his carefully chosen women he showed a veiled and taunting sadism that his wife, Doreen, had never experienced.

Frank picked his way carefully along Shelton Street. The little shops there, at the end by St Martin's Lane, were all closed and due to be demolished; the pavements were covered with rubbish and Frank was always careful about where he trod. Despite the rubbish he liked the atmosphere of the semi-derelict street. The faded façades, broken doors, makeshift shutters and barricaded windows looked odd and mysterious under the evening sky. He paused to read some of the peeling façades and imagined the shops being opened years before with enthusiasm and high hopes. 'All gone down the pan, Frank,' he said to himself with a lopsided grin.

It had been a cloudy, hot and humid day. But the sky had cleared in time for a magnificent sunset and that was rivalled by an exotic, violet sky. Then a cool breeze had

184

sprung up from the east: Frank was glad about the fall in temperature as he disliked the contact of sweating bodies.

When he left his house in Chelsea there had been a definite 'atmosphere', for Doreen had been complaining about his going out again in the evening. 'But it isn't a nine to five job, girl! Definitely not,' he had patiently explained. Doreen had accepted that in sulky silence and Frank had got out 'smartish'. Perhaps Doreen's suspicions were stronger than usual because he was not dressed for business but for relaxation, in brown silk and mohair trousers and a dark brown suede jacket both of which had been lovingly tailored for him by an old boxing fan.

Despite the perfectly clear sky Frank could hear the faint roar of distant thunder and see the occasional flash of lightning far away in the south. He hoped the storm would come closer, preferably right over Covent Garden, for he knew that Betty Rosalie Gibbons was terrified of thunderstorms.

As his footsteps echoed in the empty street Frank asked himself a question in his give-nothing-away voice, spacing out the words: 'Now—Frank—do you fancy—a nice cup of Rosie Lee? Yes—Frank—thank you—I would like a nice, strong cup of Rosie Lee.'

Sessions of sex with Betty Rosalie Gibbons appealed to Frank Shields in several ways.

185

First of all she was a very good-looking doll with the creamiest skin he had ever seen. 'Nearly good enough to eat' was how he described it and he had nibbled at it a few times. He could testify that she was a natural blonde and she had big, green eyes that readily filled with tears. Betty was a very sensitive, emotional woman and Frank, being rather short on emotions himself, liked dallying with someone whose feelings were intense. Also the fact that Betty Gibbons was supposed to be his wife's best friend had a definite attraction for him. Then again, Betty was wild for the kind of teasing, semi-sadistic sex in which he specialised and when she had been deprived of it for a week or two she became 'a right little raver'. Finally, Frank despised her husband, Geoffrey Palmer Gibbons, and that added a certain piquancy when he was screwing Betty into the ground.

Frank felt on his best form, up on his toes as if waiting for a first round to commence and very much aware of everything going on around him. Turning into James Street, he stopped to look round before opening a door painted billiard-table green. He smiled to himself, acknowledging that the caution he showed in carrying out his odd jobs was beginning to rub off on his everyday life, but he could hardly grumble at that seeing he was being paid five grand in cash, in advance, each time he disposed of a red toe-rag. The tea-jobber with the office in Silver Street had been complaining that morning about escalating costs and the punitive rate of interest charged on overdrafts. Frank had listened patiently, interposing the odd phrase such as 'Yes, it's murder' or 'A diabolical liberty', while he was thinking that his main problem was in knowing what to do with so much cash.

Frank walked up a flight of stone steps that was very familiar to him. Geoffrey Palmer Gibbons was a minor executive in a cat food firm who was obsessed with his job to the exclusion of everything else. The cat food business was a constant source of humour to Frank but he only expressed it obliquely and Betty rarely got the drift of what he was saying. Gibbons was often away travelling to inspect supplies of offal, fish and meat unfit for human consumption, so that it would have been possible for Frank to visit the James Street flat regularly twice a week if he had wanted to. That would have pleased Betty but Frank was not interested in pleasing anyone apart from himself. It suited his purposes best to keep her on edge and uncertain whether he would ever be knocking on her door again.

Frank ran up the next flight of steps, rapping out some left jabs as he did so. But he paused, not for the first time, at a door coloured a faded azure like an old tattoo;

there was an extra large brass knocker on it, in the form of a terrified cat with an arched back on which the hair stood on end. Frank was intrigued by the combination of the colour of the door and the petrified cat and for a moment was tempted to knock and see what happened.

The Gibbons' door, on the top floor of the building, was painted black and was particularly glossy, with a brass plate engraved: 'G. Palmer Gibbons'. The highly polished brass knocker was in the form of a bird with outstretched wings which Betty declared to be an albatross, but Frank did not put much faith in what she said.

He banged on the knocker and soon heard footsteps click-clacking on the parquet floor of the hall. The door opened and Betty stood before him in a long dress made of green Indian silk. The next moment she fell into his arms, saying, 'Darling!' in a tremulous voice. He could feel the warmth of her body through the thin material and knew that already she was half aroused; a few touches and kisses would have her writhing and moaning for sexual release.

He held her waist very lightly with half open hands, as he would his mother-in-law, and gave her warm cheek a brotherly peck.

'Hello doll.'

'Darling'—Betty drew out the endearment in a way she had, so that it sounded full of

188

longing—'Darling—I was expecting you *last* week. I waited and waited. You said you would . . .'

'I said I would if I could, but I couldn't. Something came up sudden. Business.'

'Not another woman?'

Frank did not bother to reply to this question which was bang on target. He moved past her quickly, walking across the hall and into the living-room which was bright with primary colours. His two favourite objects in the room were both photographs of Geoffrey Palmer Gibbons of cat food fame. One, on the white wall, showed him on his wedding day, with Betty, a bridesmaid and the best man. Gibbons and his best man were dressed in pale grey morning suits with grey top hats and Frank thought they looked ludicrous. He moved over to the other photograph, a portrait of Gibbons in a silver frame, on top of the television set. Gibbons was blond like his wife but verged on the albino and Frank had made oblique references to this lack of colour by asking Betty if the photographer had got the lighting quite right. Gibbons, with his large pale eyes and silly smile, surveyed what went on in the room and Frank always tried to give him an eyeful.

A couch, covered in bright green linen, faced the washed-out Gibbons portrait. Frank sat in the middle of the couch, smiling back at

189

it. Betty came into the room. 'Would you like a drink, darling?' she asked.

'No drink. Take your shoes off.'

Betty took off her dark green sandals while remaining standing, pulling up her long dress as she did so, and displaying a lot of white leg.

Frank looked at her attentively as he asked, 'Are you all right?'

Betty nodded. She had a strange, humble expression into which Frank read all kinds of things. He knew that she was desperate to have a child but that G. Palmer Gibbons was unable to oblige in that direction. Frank, on the other hand, was keen that there should be no new addition to the Gibbons family and certainly not one with dark brown eyes and quick hands. Geoffrey Gibbons appeared healthy enough but Betty said that he found it extremely difficult to manage an erection and impossible to keep one for more than a few seconds; whereas Frank had never experienced any problems in that area and his ability to be 'ready again so soon', as Betty euphemistically described it, was a source of wonder and delight to her.

'Well, what *do* you want?' she asked coquettishly.

Frank held out his hands clenched into fists. 'Open the right one and you can have what's in the left.'

Betty knew that it would take a chisel to do

the job if Frank wanted to keep his hand clenched, but she also knew him well enough to pander to his whims. First, however, she pointed to the dark bruise that half circled his wrist where he had taken the blow from the ashtray wielded by Alfred Thursby.

'What's that Frank? How did you do it?'

Frank gave her one of his lopsided grins, thinking, Don't ask too many questions, doll, or I shan't be calling in here again. 'Leave it out, girl. It's nothing,' he said.

Betty tugged hard at his right fist with her white, soft hands, striving to move his thumb, making a good pretence of a real struggle, ending up half on his lap, with her full breasts close to his face.

Frank pushed her back on her feet, opening his right hand to disclose a very thin gold chain with a heart-shaped lock.

He leant down and encircled her right ankle with his left hand. 'It's to go round there, to show that you're my slave.'

'Oh darling, it's lovely! But I couldn't wear it. Because of Geoffrey.'

Frank grinned again. 'You put it on, doll, and keep it on. Otherwise I'm off right now and I shan't be back.'

She looked at him without saying anything, weighing things up; she knew that he never made an empty threat. Then she put her right foot on the couch, between his legs, saying, 'You put it on then, darling.'

He held her ankle, moved by a whim to jerk it suddenly so that she would be thrown off balance, and to ill-treat her, but thought: All in good time. As he put on the anklet he nodded towards the portrait of G. Palmer Gibbons, implying that he would get his eyeful later.

'Take everything off, doll,' Frank said. 'Slaves only wear a chain.'

She undressed with the confidence of a woman who knows she has a good figure. Her breasts were full but they did not droop like Doreen's; her nipples were small, pink and hard at that moment. Without her dress she gave off a heady smell of lilies-of-the-valley.

'Into the bedroom girl. All slaves have to be punished from time to time, you know!'

Betty dropped her green silk camiknickers and walked out of the room, turning off the light in the hall as she did so.

Frank undressed quickly, demonstrating to the Gibbons portrait that getting an erection was no problem for a normal man. He padded along the hall which was only indirectly lit by a table-lamp in the bedroom. Betty lay face down, half crouched over the foot of the bed. He put his cold hands on her warm waist and entered her from behind. She shuddered and sighed. 'Oh, sweetheart, that's so lovely! Darling! Darling!'

Just a few strokes brought her to a state of tension where she writhed and moaned. She was so wet that he could hardly feel her. As she began to girate in a familiar fashion Frank withdrew and she groaned. He left the room, ignoring her pleas.

Frank padded back to the well-lit living-room and took his seat in the middle of the green couch, giving G. Palmer Gibbons a wink as he did so.

After a minute or two Betty stood in the passage. In the dark she had the jewel-like eyes of a cat.

'Here, pussy. Here, pussy,' Frank called to her. She stared at him with a half-rebellious look. 'Down on your hands and knees then,' Frank said. 'Pussies don't walk like that.'

Betty got down on her hands and knees and Frank said, 'That's right. Now, you crawl over here. I've got something for you.'

CHAPTER EIGHTEEN

On a fine afternoon in late June, Jack Quinn drove through Guildford following the circuitous route that leads motorists bound for the south coast round the city and out on to the A281. He covered so many miles every week in his old Mercedes, quartering the country to attend auction sales and buying from other dealers, that driving was a semi-automatic process for him, leaving his mind free to range over various matters but usually those concerning his family or business.

Speeding along the A3 to Guildford, his thoughts had been centred happily on his young daughters. He had been bombarded with picture postcards from them so he was able to visualise the cabin in Vermont, his daughter, Dolly, on horseback, his daughter, Liz, fishing and both of them in a canoe on the lake.

But in the crowded High Street of the always busy cathedral city Quinn had become angry when another motorist drove dangerously close to an old woman hobbling across the road; in fact he had to restrain himself from getting out and tapping on the windscreen of the car which had nearly bumped into the woman. For a moment or two he felt like a ticking bomb: tension born mainly of sexual frustration and the impasse over his hollow marriage had brought him to a state where he was seeking an outlet for pent-up aggression. It was this that had contributed to his trouble with the police and he knew that he had to be on guard.

But once out of the city and on the comparatively open road leading to Alderbury, Quinn was able to forget his own problems by thinking about Polly Sylvester and the Court Antiques shop. He had been surprised when she phoned him saying that

194

she wanted his advice on a business matter, but he welcomed the opportunity to get out of his office and away from London. He was a Londoner who had never lived anywhere else, but the charms of the metropolis had become somewhat tarnished for him and it was the time of year when the countryside looked at its best.

Quinn could not remember exchanging more than a dozen words with Polly Sylvester, though he had always enjoyed glimpsing her at the shop. It seemed odd that she should turn to him for advice, but he was reasonably well equipped to give it because he had been born over a second-hand shop in Hammersmith and most of his life had been spent amongst dealers. He imagined that Polly would ask him about selling the shop in Alderbury and he was going to advise her to get rid of it promptly while it still had the aura of success bestowed by Rupert's quite exceptional energy and capacity for hard work. Under another owner the shop would probably soon deteriorate into one of those lack-lustre places which motorists speed past without a second thought. At the moment he knew it was eye-catching even though the highly polished contents of the handsome bow windows were often second-rate items.

Glancing in his rear mirror, Quinn put his foot down on the accelerator and the Mercedes surged forward. There were some clear stretches on the A281 where it was possible to speed, but Quinn was particularly keen to avoid any trouble with the police, because his absurd fracas with two members of the Met would undoubtedly have led to his name being on official files.

Slowing at a sharp bend he was able to look across a vista of fields and woods without a single building in sight. Further off in the same direction lay an arboretum, marked on his map in red, which he had often meant to visit, having looked up the word in a dictionary and found that it meant a botanical garden for the growing of trees.

After passing by an attractive farmhouse and a copse of oak trees he took another bend which was long and curved back on itself, as if designed to slow motorists down just before they reached Alderbury. Seeing the village again he thought how attractive the two old pubs, Tudor cottage, bakery and the double-fronted antiques shop looked—like an oasis for tired and hungry travellers. Quinn glanced at his watch and saw that he was later than he had intended, due to the heavy holiday traffic. The pubs were open and he fancied a pint but that would have to wait until he had seen Mrs Sylvester.

The blinds were down in the windows of Court Antiques and as he parked in front of the shop he saw one of them being twitched aside. While he was locking his car Polly appeared in the shop doorway and gave him a grave smile. He approached her with a similarly grave smile and a tentative wave. He felt unsure of himself with her and a little on edge, purely because he found her very attractive, whereas he could be completely natural with Adele Rogers and Pamela Stratton-Smith who worked in the shop, having on the odd occasion even been able to make them laugh. This was no time to try for a laugh but he was aware that he would have no idea of how to go about it with Polly. She wore a blue and white cotton dress with a navy cardigan and sandals. Her blonde hair was piled up on top of her head with one or two tendrils escaping; he thought she looked particularly fetching. She held out a hand that seemed like a child's when it was enfolded in his. Her sudden grimace, both funny and sad, something like a clown's expression, encompassed a lot, including the absurdity of the accident which had obliterated her husband.

'It was terribly good of you to come. I phoned you on an impulse and then very nearly called back to tell you not to bother. I mean, I felt guilty thinking of that drive from London and the roads all chock-a-block with people going on holiday.'

'Don't give it a thought. I felt like getting out of London. I can see Berkeley Square from my office and this morning I spent some time standing at the window just looking at the trees. So—it's a nice trip for me.'

'Will your wife be expecting you back for dinner?'

'She's in America with our daughters. It was supposed to be a two-week trip, but it's been extended to three.'

'So, your girls have been missing school then?'

'Yes, but it was an unusual opportunity. My sister-in-law rented a lakeside cabin in Vermont. They've been having a splendid time there.'

They entered the shop which, empty of people and in electric light because of the drawn blinds, seemed faintly gloomy even though the floor and many of the contents gleamed with polishing. A console giltwood table with a white marble top supported by three cherubs stood close to the door, as if placed there temporarily.

'That's nice,' Quinn said. 'I like it. A new acquisition?'

'Not really.' Polly grimaced again, but this time there was more amusement in her expression. 'More of a mistake. Apparently we sold it a couple of weeks ago to a nice young chap who wanted it for his mother, a birthday present. Now it turns out to have been broken and repaired. It seems that the cherub holding the cornucopia is not original. So I had to give the chap his money back.'

'All dealers make mistakes, dozens of them, it's part of the business. I make them every week.'

'Yes, but I think we may have made more than our share, just through not knowing enough. However, would you like some tea? Or would you sooner come back to the cottage for a drink later on? Perhaps you have to rush off?'

'Not at all. I should like to see your cottage.'

'I was going to ask you to come back there with a few other people—after the funeral. I looked for you but you'd vanished.'

'Yes, I know, I'm sorry. I should have liked the opportunity just to say to you that—that I was very sorry about ... Well, you can see it's true what my wife says, that I never know what to say.'

'You came, that was enough. Rupert admired you.'

'I don't know about that but we seemed to get on all right, until the last time I called here, a month or two ago. He seemed very edgy that day.'

'You're right, he was. He did seem to be nervous, upset, for some weeks on end. I don't know why.'

'Well, how can I help you? I can't advise you about that table, though I could put you in touch with an expert.'

'Oh no, it's not that. Something much

more important. Please sit down. I know it's a bit gloomy here at the moment but I want to stay till we've talked for a few minutes . . . The point is, I wanted to know whether you would advise me to sell the shop?'

'Is that what you want to do?'

'My parents think I ought to. And they're coming down here to stay in a week or so. I know they think I should sell and perhaps get rid of Vine Cottage too, but I like it here. I love living in a village. Gradually you get to know everyone.'

'I could see that. I've never seen such a magnificent display of flowers.'

'Oh, those in the church were all put there by one person, a friend of ours called Louise Simpson. Her father owns the biggest house hereabouts and Louise just emptied his hot-house.'

'So, you don't want to move, but what do you feel about the shop? Are you interested in it yourself? That's the main factor.'

'I think I could be . . . And Pamela thinks she could do the buying. Her children have both left school now, so she could work here full-time. What do you think about that?'

'I should say that Pam's good at business. Certainly she's got a gift for selling and that's rarer than you may think. I'm a terrible salesman. Yes, I think she might be good at buying too—but after a while, in which time you would have to expect the profits to dip a bit. But she couldn't manage here with just Adele. Are you thinking of working here?'

'Ah, you've divined my secret.'

'Then my advice depends on just how keen you are. If you really want to work hard at it and read every reference book you can find, then I suggest you have a go. But you'll make heaps of mistakes.'

'Thanks, Jack. Your friend, Charlie Saunders, said you were a helpful chap. Shall we go then? I popped a bottle of white burgundy in the fridge in case you had time for a drink.'

Quinn waited for her to switch off the lights and lock the front door. Standing close to her he noticed her delicate lavender fragrance and saw how fine and clear her skin was. She blushed slightly under his intent look. 'This will be good news for Adele, that you're going to keep the shop,' he said. 'I should think she would be rather lost without it, she always seems so enthusiastic.'

'Adele is a treasure. You know, I am getting keener about the idea the more I think about it. Perhaps you can suggest some books I should read?'

'Of course. Now, shall we take the car or walk? I would sooner leave it here if that's all right.'

'Yes, let's walk. It's a beautiful day.'

CHAPTER NINETEEN

Polly stood for a few moments outside Court Antiques. 'So, the blinds will go up on Saturday,' she said. 'I shall tell Adele and Pam tomorrow that we're to have a shot at running it together. Good! I feel happier now, Jack.'

Turning down the small road by the baker's shop, they soon left the noise of traffic. On the day of the funeral Quinn had been surprised at the number of people to be seen in Alderbury; on this fine summer evening the village appeared to be deserted although he could hear the occasional distant shout and burst of muted applause. Pointing towards the source of the applause he asked, 'What's that?'

'Cricket. We have a very enthusiastic team. Rupert was keen too. In fact he was the captain . . .'

The road curved round to the right past the butcher's shop towards the church, but Polly took a footpath across the village green.

'Now, you'll get a close look at our famous River Alder. A constant source of irritation to the local lads because it's so clear that the fish seem to be immune to angling. You see them drop a baited hook right by a fish and it's studiously ignored.'

'What about the pond?'

'Oh, they're not allowed to fish in the Alder Pool, because of the swans and coots. Besides, the carp were put in the pond by the father of our butcher and Stan regards them as pets.'

They stood silently for some minutes on the white footbridge, peering down into the limpid water of the river. Quinn was aware that his tension had left him; he also felt much more at ease with Polly, no longer anxious about finding something to say and able to remain silent by her side. The Alder was fringed with reeds, meadow sweet and purple loosestrife; a few clumps of green weed were constantly tugged this way and that by the hurrying water. Whirligig beetles and water-boatmen seemed to lead a charmed existence on the surface; glinting, tiny fish darted about on the stony bottom. The river was so clear that it was like looking down into an aquarium in which every minute inhabitant of the small world below the bridge could be seen. For the first time in his life Quinn felt a twinge of envy about people who lived in the country, away from man-made horizons, constant noise and the stench of petrol fumes.

'Very occasionally,' said Polly, 'if you're lucky, you can catch a glimpse of a kingfisher here, flashing along by the shallows under those trees. They dip down after sticklebacks and minnows. But it seems we're not going to be favoured this evening.'

Quinn was aware that she was looking closely at his face and he made a move towards the end of the bridge. He was anxious not to have to explain his numerous cuts; he did not want to lie to her but equally he did not want her to think he was a brawling idiot. It would be extremely difficult to tell her what had happened and how there was something to be said in his defence, particularly as her experience of the police would be largely confined to village bobbies cycling along country lanes. He doubted whether she had ever encountered a couple of tough guys like the coppers who had been cruising round Wapping in a white Rover.

When they had crossed the village green they walked along a path by a carefully shaped lime hedge and Polly said, 'This runs the length of our garden so you can see it's quite large. Rather a problem now.'

'You mean that Rupert used to do all this?'

'Yes—with a tiny bit of help from me. Whether I shall be able to keep it at all decent is rather doubtful.'

'He really did have a phenomenal amount of energy. I always thought he looked very fit and agile—which made that accident seem . . .'

'You've been listening to Max Arbeit.'

'No, I haven't talked to Max since the day

204

of the sale.'

Polly sighed and grimaced again so that her mouth turned down at the corners. 'Well, Max seemed to think that perhaps it wasn't an accident. He was the person closest and he thought the driver did it quite deliberately.'

'But that would make the driver a maniac! No, I have a high opinion of the Doctor, but he must be mistaken. I walked along part of that road myself at lunchtime that day and I felt fairly vulnerable. The road curves sharply and the bank varies in height so that one tends to walk on it and then jump down into the road again.'

'Anyway, Max will have to give evidence at the inquest. Perhaps then I shall hear what the police really think. They were very guarded about his idea.'

Polly opened the gate in a white picket fence and gestured. 'How do you like Vine Cottage?'

To the left of the wide gravel path there was a stretch of box hedge which the craft of topiary had made to resemble a row of heraldic birds. Beyond it a low, white building with massive, black beams was set slightly at an angle to the path, facing south. It had twin gables and mullioned band windows; its roof of old tiles dropped eccentrically low at the back. There were two rose beds in the front lawn which ran up to a bank and a tall hawthorn hedge. A magnolia tree grew at one side of the cottage and honeysuckle had been trained up around the front porch.

'I must say the charms of Westminster are dwindling fairly fast. We wake up to petrol fumes. You have roses and honeysuckle.'

'Yes, but there is the winter of course. It looks fairly dreary here at the end of November. No street lights, remember. And the path tends to get flooded. Still, I shan't leave this place unless I have to.'

Quinn was surprised to see that Polly had left the front door unlocked. She twisted its circular handle and the door opened to disclose the hall paved with gleaming red bricks. A large embroidered coat of arms had pride of place on the facing wall. An attractive walnut grandfather clock with an unusually large face kept the time with a loud tick-tock. After entering the cottage Polly stood still for a moment or two, her head cocked as if she were listening for something or someone upstairs.

Looking at the attractive lettering on the clock, which showed that it had been made in Tonbridge in 1795, Quinn was silently cursing at the idea that there might be someone else in the cottage as he had been looking forward to a relaxed *tête-à-tête* with Polly. But she did not call out and he could not hear a sound from above. She smiled and led the way through the hall into a large sitting-room with a ceiling so low that he could see he would have to be wary of the heavy oak beams. She noticed his glance in their direction and said, 'Yes, do take care! Rupert used to warn anyone as tall as you—with that bit out of *Alice* about people over ten miles in height having to leave the court.'

The large room had cream walls and there were cream rugs on the old brick floor. It was simply furnished with a large sofa covered in flowered material and three matching armchairs. A low mahogany table with two bowls of flowers stood by the french windows which looked out on to the main lawn at the back of the cottage. A television set and a record player with a large collection of records in a wooden stand were ranged along one wall.

Polly turned to leave the room saying, 'Do put a record on—if you like music, that is.' She paused by the door. 'You know, we could easily have a kitchen picnic with the wine. Just some smoked ham and salad. And rather good granary bread from our local baker. What do you say?'

'Yes please. Impromptu meals are the kind I like best.'

Once again Polly stood still with her head cocked as if listening for any sound in the cottage. Quinn was puzzled that she had not mentioned the presence of anyone else in her suggestion of the meal. 'But you're sure you want me to stay?' he said.

'You're staying.' Polly left the room and Quinn crouched down by the wooden stand filled with LP records. Looking along the spines, he noticed that most of them were in his own collection. On top of the stand there was a pile of old 78s in brown paper jackets—Deanna Durbin, Jack Buchanan and a number of others whose names meant nothing to him. He selected a French disc featuring the singer Charles Trenet and soon had the song 'Que Reste-t-il de Nos Amours?' spinning round.

Polly appeared at the door holding out a glass of white wine. 'This is yours. I just have to pop upstairs a sec, then it will only be five minutes. Ah, I'm glad you like Trenet. There's a super one called "Un Photo de ma Jeunesse".'

As he sat, with the glass of wine in his hand, looking out of the french windows, listening to the faintly ghostly song, Quinn was conscious of more positive enjoyment than he had known for many months. Too pleasurable in fact, he thought—there must be a catch somewhere. He remembered that at the funeral Polly had sat in the front pew with another blonde who resembled her a good deal; possibly that was her sister who was at present lying down upstairs and would emerge just in time to spoil the intimate

208

supper for two.

'Care to open a tin?' Polly called out. 'It's supposed to be genuine *foie gras*. I don't really approve, but my sister brought it back from the Dordogne. And it will go rather well with the ham.'

The cream colour scheme also applied to the kitchen of Vine Cottage. It was large and airy with a series of windows and half-glass door opening out on to the side garden. A Dutch dresser, painted cream, stood next to a cream-coloured Aga. Bundles of dried herbs and strings of onions were suspended from the beams. Flowers in pots and bowls stood all along the window-ledges.

Quinn opened the tin of *foie gras*, noticing that the table was already laid and glad to see that there were only two sets of knives and forks.

Polly turned round from cutting something and handed him a piece of cheese of a faintly orange colour. 'Try that—as a pang-slayer. It's Ilchester, applewood smoked.' She stood with her head slightly on one side as he tasted it. 'Like it?'

Nodding, Quinn thought that he did like the taste but he liked her informality in handing it to him even more. Yes, I'm enjoying this a bit too much, he thought. After pouring some wine for Polly, he raised his glass. 'I'll propose a toast. Success—and enjoyment—with the shop. Good luck.'

Polly smiled and was just raising her own glass when Quinn heard a faint call of 'Cooee' coming from the garden. A moment later it was repeated. Then he heard a louder call, 'Cooee—Polly?' The voice was light in timbre but undoubtedly male.

Polly said, 'Oh, that will be Rex,' in a matter-of-fact voice as though she were half expecting the caller. She opened the half-glass door and shouted, 'Come round to the side, Rex. The kitchen.' After waiting a few moments she walked out of the door, saying, 'Shan't be a sec. Be a pal and pour another glass of vino.'

Murmuring, 'Sod it,' under his breath, Quinn found another glass on the dresser and poured a small amount of wine, hoping that the intruder would have the tact to depart when he saw that supper for two was being prepared.

Hearing Polly laugh, Quinn felt that his luck had changed and that the rest of the evening might not be as pleasurable as he had anticipated. Polly laughed again and appeared in the doorway holding the arm of an elderly, slightly built man with well-brushed silver hair and strikingly blue eyes. Quinn recognised him as the man who had read the lesson at Sylvester's funeral service. He limped in, looking very relaxed, blue eyes twinkling.

'Jack, I want you to meet Rex, our

neighbour from the Hall, just over the trees at the back. Rex, this is Jack Quinn, a book-dealer friend of Rupert's, who has very kindly been advising me about the business.'

Bealby smiled, showing very white teeth, and put out a thin, brown hand to be shaken. 'Ah yes, I spotted Mr Quinn in church, towering over his neighbours.'

The look Bealby gave Quinn was straight and piercing. He was dressed in gardening clothes—corduroy trousers faintly green at the knees and an old brown cardigan—but his hands were spotless, with well-kept nails. He had an indefinable air of authority, as if he were used to giving orders and having them obeyed.

'Jack lives and works in London,' Polly said. 'I'm told he has elegant premises in Berkeley Square.'

Quinn laughed. 'Change that to three and a half rooms on the top floor of a building in Davies Street. You only get a view of Berkeley Square by squinting. Not elegant.'

'Do sit down, Rex.' Quinn noticed that Polly still held Bealby's arm and that she looked at him very affectionately. 'You must join us. I absolutely insist. Only a cold snack and it's no good saying you've already eaten because I know your habits by now.'

Bealby sat down at the table, smiling and shaking his head. 'You see how it is, Jack. I'm ordered about by this formidable young woman. I could have done with her as a sergeant major during the war. Direct questions and simple orders that can't be misunderstood.'

Polly bent down to one of the cupboards under the windows and extracted a bottle. 'I'll put this in the fridge and carry on with the meal, such as it is. You two talk.'

Bealby shook his head again while looking affectionately towards Polly. 'I don't like intruding but I suppose it's hopeless to argue. I only came over here on patrol as it were, because Polly's house was broken into yesterday. Did she tell you about that?'

'Do you mean a burglary?'

Polly stopped shaking a colander at the sink and sat down at the table. She raised her glass and said, 'Cheers. No, not a burglary, more a I-don't-know-what. I went to see my doctor and when I came back to the cottage I knew someone had been inside. It was easy for them as we don't lock up round here.'

'So I noticed,' Quinn said. 'Is that wise?'

'Probably not. But people here just don't bother. There hasn't been a burglary round here for yonks. Anyway, as far as I could see nothing had been stolen. There were a few odds and ends of jewellery in the middle drawer of my dressing-table and they hadn't been touched. But someone had definitely been in Rupert's study and moved things around on his desk.'

'Did he keep any cash there?' Quinn asked. 'I do at home.'

'No. Any cash for the business is kept in a safe at the shop. And I keep my money and cheque-book in my handbag.'

'I came over here yesterday evening,' Bealby said. 'Immediately Polly told me. We made a list of valuable things and checked them all. She could not think of anything that was missing.'

'That's certainly very odd—I don't think I've ever heard of a non-burglary before.' Quinn had noticed a loving look between Polly and Bealby; he was rather surprised that some kind of a relationship had grown between a woman in her early thirties and a man probably older than her father, but he was sure that it existed. 'So what did the police make of it?' he asked.

Polly shook her head vigorously. 'I didn't tell them. What was the point? What could I tell them? Nothing was taken, nothing even damaged. It was only because I happened to know exactly where things were on Rupert's desk that I knew anyone had been in there.'

'They could have looked for fingerprints.'

Bealby nodded. 'Yes, I did suggest that to Polly, that she should give the C.I.D. people in Guildford a ring, but she made a good point when she said that no one had actually *broken* in. Ten to one they just walked in through the front door which was left unlocked—so had a crime been committed?'

'There's a bust of Wellington on the desk, positioned so that it looks directly at anyone entering the room,' Polly said. 'Walking past the study I noticed that the bust had been turned round. Then I saw that a folder of letters to do with heraldry had been moved too. Rupert only used that desk for writing letters and for work on his hobbies—heraldry and collecting material about Wellington.'

'But presumably you wouldn't know if anything had been taken from the desk?'

'That's true, but I do know that there was nothing at all valuable. Just pages of doodles, letters, his sketches of coats of arms, armorial bookplates, that sort of thing...'

'It seems hardly credible that anyone would risk entering a house just to read some letters,' Quinn said.

'Ah, I have a theory about that,' Bealby said in a voice that was a shade deeper and more emphatic than his usual throwaway delivery. 'Mind you, it's one I should find very difficult to prove and certainly I haven't been able to convince Polly as yet. But I believe that the mysterious non-burglary may have something to do with a man called Roscoe Starr.'

'Is that someone who lives in the village?' Quinn asked.

'No. The name means nothing to you?'

'Perhaps—I feel I've seen it, or read

something concerning Roscoe Starr. It's an unusual name.'

Bealby nodded. 'An unusual name for an unusual man. You may well have read it since it's a name that's been in the newspapers often, though largely before your time. Roscoe is about fifteen years younger than me but I knew him briefly during the war. We were both in the battle for the bridge at Arnhem in October, 1944. I was wounded and taken prisoner there. Nearly everyone on the bridge ended up in the bag, yet against all odds Roscoe somehow escaped. Miles behind enemy lines, surrounded by crack troops—extraordinary! And he was decorated for an unusual act of bravery at Arnhem—he actually jumped on to a Jerry tank and put it out of action with a grenade. Then the newspapers somehow got on to the fact that he was only eighteen at the time. It seems he had lied about his age in order to join the Parachute Regiment at the end of '43.'

'An unusual man indeed!' said Quinn admiringly.

'He's that *rara avis*, a man who lives for excitement, thrives on danger.' Bealby paused to muse a moment. 'I saw a good deal of action from '42 to '44 but I doubt if I knew more than two or three men like Roscoe. Invaluable in war of course; but in peacetime such a man is just an adventurer in a world where there is no legitimate place for him.'

'What did he do after the war ended?' Quinn asked.

'His army career finished in Malaya in 1949. He was a Major at the age of twenty-three and he won three decorations for valour, but they were glad to see the back of him. He left under some cloud or other, I know. A friend of mine, a professional solider, told me that Roscoe had been ordered to resign and said he was "a reckless, dangerous man". After that his name turned up in the papers from time to time, always in a dubious context. Roscoe became a mercenary in one of those Arab states and in the Congo and Angola. There were a number of unsavoury stories, but probably some of them weren't true—give a dog a bad name, you know. Then in the mid-1970s he surfaced in Northern Ireland—the newspapers said that he was training a Protestant para-military group.'

'But why do you think he might be involved here?' Quinn asked.

'I saw him in Alderbury only about six weeks ago, on a Saturday. I went to the White Rose for a beer and sandwich and I saw Roscoe in the car park talking to Rupert. Talking very animatedly too, I can picture him now...'

'Are you sure it was Mr Starr? Didn't you say you hadn't seen him for nearly forty years?' Polly wagged her finger at Bealby.

'That's an awful long while.'

'Yes, I know, dear girl, it must seem like ancient history to you, but the fact is Roscoe has changed very little in that time. He had very full, sleek black hair. There's a white streak in it now so that his thatch looks rather like a badger's. Otherwise he's much the same man, I'd swear on it. And I saw him in the village again yesterday afternoon, in a car with another man, a biggish chap. Roscoe is of medium height and build, still quite boyish looking apart from his white-streaked hair.'

'So you think the finger of suspicion points at him?' Polly asked, frowning. 'But why?'

'Ah, I can't tell you why. But the coincidence is too strong for me not to suspect him. Roscoe's presence anywhere hints at trouble, danger, intrigue. He was in Alderbury yesterday, this man who can't live without excitement. 'Nuff said I think.'

CHAPTER TWENTY

Mickey Harland was 'mooning about' in his bookshop in Cecil Court. His wife, Joan, said that he spent most of his life mooning about and Harland had to admit that there was some truth in that. He also accepted that it must be very irritating to her, Joan would be reading or working at her tapestry, both of which she did with rapt attention, while he moved restlessly about, switching through all the programmes on the television before turning it off, picking up books and putting them down again, fiddling with the wireless, trying to pick out a tune on the piano, looking out of the windows of their flat. 'My God, you're a fidget!' she would sometimes exclaim. She had found Rupert Sylvester nearly as irritating, but at least with Sylvester there was the bonus that he was good to look at.

Mea culpa, Harland thought, I am a fidget. But what Joan did not appreciate was that mooning about could occasionally be useful. From books and magazines and stray thoughts a trail would sometimes emerge that proved to be of value in his business. He remembered Max Arbeit, years before, saying something to that effect. They had been having a coffee in a half-empty café in Chancery Lane after a book sale at Hodgson's auction rooms. 'An idea, Mickey,' the Doctor had said, looking round to see if there was any chance of them being overheard. 'Just getting an idea ... Thinking something out can sometimes be of more use in this business than rushing here, there and everywhere. A lot of people never realise that, my dear.'

Harland stood near the front of his shop, gazing round and thinking how nice it looked with all the shelves freshly painted and every book dusted. There had been times during the spring when the decorations carried out by a tea-swilling, cigarette-smoking Cockney duo had been a threat to his nervous system but in the end it had all proved worthwhile and his premises appeared nearly as spick and span as Rupert Sylvester's. An image of Rupert came into his mind, looking nervous and agitated in the greenhouse while they waited for the settlement over the books in the Broomhill Park library. It was strange to think of Rupert's tension and exasperation only a matter of an hour or two before he was removed from the world of the living. Harland began again to brood on Arbeit's theory that the removal was deliberate, a murder in fact, in which a man called Boyle was somehow involved, when he realised that his assistant, Mrs Cathcart, had been saying something.

Mrs Cathcart shook her head of short brown curls which was the only sign she gave of tried patience. 'I said, do you want me to catalogue the Portolan or not?'

The Portolan on vellum was a delightful example of the chart-maker's art showing how the Mediterranean appeared to navigators circa 1550. During the thirty odd years Harland had been a book-dealer he had criticised other dealers who were also collectors, but in recent months he had shown symptoms of coming down with the collecting bug himself. Portolans very rarely came on the market and he had been tempted to keep such a fine example as the one Mrs Cathcart now held up. The coasts were outlined in green with place names in Gothic letters in red and black. The only decorations were devices of the sun and moon in umber heightened with gold and a mythical sea-monster in silver.

'Yes, I think so—yes. Say that it was probably the work of a native of the Balearic Islands by reason of the gold filling-in of Ibiza.'

'Right. No price.'

'Yes, I'll think about that. It's going to be very expensive by the time I've finished with it.'

Mrs Cathcart smiled in a way that gave no indication of her feelings on the subject. A divorcée in her mid-thirties and an ardent feminist, she seemed to find men generally irritating and that no doubt included him. But while he was mooning about doing nothing productive, she was busy at work on their annual catalogue; she was extraordinarily efficient, better than him at all aspects of the business except that she lacked his 'flair'.

Harland opened the shop door and stepped out into Cecil Court, a pedestrian way connecting Charing Cross Road with St Martin's Lane. It was cool for the end of

June, cool enough for April, but the sky was a crystalline blue and the sun was nearly directly overhead making his newly painted premises appear to glitter and gleam. He had chosen dark green paint for the façade, with lettering in gold: 'HARLAND & CO: OLD BOOKS AND ATLASES'. There were booksellers to the left and right of him, a row of booksellers facing him. People who did not understand the antiquarian book business thought that having so much competition around could not be good, but the dealers in Cecil Court were not in rivalry since their stocks varied considerably.

After walking to the end of the Court close to Leicester Square tube station, Harland turned on his heel and walked back simply for the pleasure of seeing his shop as a stranger might. Jaillot's large *Atlas Nouveau*, open at the majestic title-page, had pride of place in his window display and certainly caught the eye. On the right of it he had scattered a handful of books by the Victorian explorer, Sir Richard Burton, on the left a copy of Sir Thomas More's *Utopia* which had the first printed map of an imaginary country. In the centre of the window there was a card with a quotation written out in Mrs Cathcart's bold italic hand which he read again:

The boats panted upstream. They were going into a strange land, a land of strange

221

creeds, strange habits, unmeaning language, strange sacrifices. They went upstream in that morning of the world, upstream, holding their lives in their hands, as today our ships pant up unknown streams of an Africa not so remote: as ships will pant up unknown streams till the end of time...

Joseph Conrad *Heart of Darkness*

For a minute or two Harland stayed where he was, thinking about the very strange land for which Rupert Sylvester might have embarked. Could it be that Sylvester's spirit was now in a land so strange as to be inconceivable to the human imagination or had he in fact been blotted out like a squashed mosquito? Harland thought of all the people he had known who might also have embarked for that same strange land: his parents, his parents-in-law, seven or eight uncles and aunts, several friends, four of the boys in his form at school, probably ten of the soldiers he had served with during the war, dozens of acquaintances. Cancer, pneumonia, heart attacks, a brain tumour, one soldier crushed under a tank, two sailors drowned at sea, three suicides. The image of Sylvester's cream linen suit spattered with blood recurred in his brain with dramatic clarity. He acknowledged that he had been much

222

shaken by that sudden death—such a healthy and vital young man . . .

'Morning, Mr Harland.' He turned and saw one of his more reliable customers, Henry Aspinall, a prosperous stockbroker, with his plump hand on the handle of the shop door. He said 'Good morning' with a grin, acknowledging that he had been lost in a daydream.

Aspinall entered the shop, saying over his shoulder, 'Your colleague, Mrs Cathcart—she sent me a card about a book you've found. One I'm quite bullish about. What efficiency! We could use her in my office.'

'Yes, thanks, but she happens to be quite indispensable here.'

Aspinall smiled, waving to Mrs Cathcart who was seated at the back of the shop so that she could keep an eye on everything. She held up a tiny, morocco-bound volume.

Harland turned on the lights in his basement and descended the stone steps, knowing that Mrs Cathcart was much better at selling than he was himself and that Henry Aspinall preferred dealing with an attractive young woman rather than a man of his own age. Good God! Harland thought with a kind of delayed shock, I *am* nearly Aspinall's age, nearly as old as that plump, old buffer, nearly sixty. Most of the interesting part of my life is over—no more romance, no more provocative looks from women, never again the pleasure

223

of having a young child in the house, no more days when one feels full of energy and anxious to be bustling about like young Quinn. I shall just get older and duller and lazier and Mrs Cathcart will take over more and more of the business. He had already accepted the prospect of having her as a partner; now he visualised the façade of his shop changing from 'Harland & Co.' to 'Harland & Cathcart' and then to 'Cathcart: Feminist Books.'

The basement, exactly the same size as the shop above, had been freshly whitewashed. Some of the wall space was covered with bookshelves which were mainly used to sort and house recent acquisitions. Selected customers were sometimes allowed into the basement to inspect the new purchases, so Harland kept the large room reasonably tidy. The two desks were not so tidy, the larger one being covered with what his wife called 'a muddly jumble': letters to be answered, auction catalogues, lists, invoices, and a mass of strange oddments which he felt disinclined to throw away. Under a glass paperweight shaped like a large mushroom there were numerous scraps of paper which he had discarded from his pockets, often bearing notes the significance of which he no longer remembered.

Seated at the large desk idly looking through a pile of old catalogues with a view to disposing of them, Harland's attention was taken by the one for the Broomhill Park sale because he noticed a small tick in ink on its front cover. He remembered picking the catalogue up from the bank at the side of the road where Sylvester had been killed; he had thought at the time that it was his own copy, but the ink tick showed that it was not because he only ever pencilled in prices on a catalogue.

The end-paper had been torn out, used when he wrote down Sylvester's reported last words—'General pig boil'—which had sounded like utter gibberish until Adele Rogers said that Rupert knew a man called Boyle. Turning to the title-page he saw that it was decorated with a pen and ink sketch of the Mallalieu coat of arms and realised it must be Rupert's copy, knocked from his hand as he was hit by the silver car. This was confirmed by the sight of typical examples of Sylvester's doodling, such as a tiny man falling from a great tower. A miniature skull and cross-bones made a prophetic tail-piece at the bottom of the last page of text.

On the blank page before the back cover Harland found two names written in Rupert's large, clear hand: 'General Piggott' and 'T. Boyle'. By the side of Boyle's name there was a note: 'Phone between 9 and 10 a.m. 01-723 8888.' Given the reasonable assumption that Max Arbeit had mistaken the name 'Piggott' for 'pig', Rupert's last words now made some kind of sense. It was just possible, Harland thought, that Rupert had auction bids for the Mallalieu sale from a General Piggott and a T. Boyle, but it was also extremely unlikely that a dying man would mention them. No, those names must have been of special significance to Rupert. Harland lay back in the chair with his feet on the desk, staring at the newly painted ceiling and trying to put himself in the position of the dying man, cradled in Arbeit's arms, making a great effort to get out those three words. What had he tried to tell Max? That he had been killed by Piggott and Boyle? But that could not be true as there had been only one man in the car. Harland summoned up his sole image of the driver, again visualising the large face pressed close to the windscreen.

Harland's mind was floating away—Sylvester's violent death exerted a mysterious, intangible pull like the moon upon tides. He saw again Arbeit's woebegone expression, the stout man who had shouted out 'For God's sake get an ambulance', the pale schoolboy staring down from the bank. He was casting about once more for a possible explanation of 'General pig boil' when he sat up with a start, suddenly realising that he had a telephone number before him and that dialling it might produce some result. Impulsively, without thinking about what he

226

was going to say, he dialled the digits.

Within a few seconds a girl with a London accent repeated the number and said in a sing-song, oft-repeated way, 'Terry's Car Sales. Can I help you?'

'Is there a Mr T. Boyle I can speak to, please?'

The girl hesitated, saying, 'Er—well—reely—if it's about buying or selling I should put you through to our Sales Manager.'

'No, thanks, it's not a business matter. It's personal—I only want to talk to Mr Boyle.'

Harland heard the girl call out, 'Gent here, he wants Mr Terry. Says it's personal like.'

Another voice came on the phone, a woman speaking with lightly concealed impatience, 'Mr Boyle's secretary speaking. Mr Boyle is at a meeting. Can I take a message for him?'

'No, thank you. My name's Harland. I want to talk to Mr Boyle about a friend of mine, Rupert Sylvester. Perhaps I should phone later?'

'I see. Please hold a minute,' the woman said.

In less than a minute a male voice boomed in Harland's ear, so loudly that he had to hold the receiver an inch from his ear. 'Good morning to you, Mr Harland. Terence Boyle speaking. Now, just say again about this personal matter. What name did you mention, this friend of yours?' Boyle had a marked Northern Irish accent and his

227

booming voice resembled that of the Reverend Ian Paisley.

'Rupert Sylvester. An antique dealer at a village called Alderbury in Surry.'

'I see. No, sir, I think we may be at cross-purposes here. Now why exactly do you think I know this Rupert Sylvester?' The voice boomed even louder with a hectoring tone, but Harland thought he detected a hint of nervousness.

'Rupert had your name and phone number written down in a sale catalogue—for an auction held at Broomhill Park. Perhaps he thought something there might interest you?'

After a noticeable pause Boyle replied, 'Hold hard a moment now. Sylvester, yes I think perhaps I do recall that name. A shop in Surrey you said?'

'That's right, on the main road from Guildford.'

'Ah yes, I place it now. Well, Mr Harland, what can I do for you and Mr Sylvester?'

'Rupert's dead. He was run over on the road near Broomhill Park.'

'Was he indeed! Well, I'm sorry to hear that but . . .'

'There's something else written in the catalogue. I wonder if you can spare me a few minutes?'

'Are you speaking from London?'

'From Cecil Court, Charing Cross Road.'

'Come round here then, by all means, Mr

228

Harland. Terry's Car Sales, in Harrow Road. Corner of North Wharf Road, W.2.'

'I know Harrow Road. When shall I come?'

'Right now if that suits you. My meeting will be finished in a quarter of an hour and it will take you that to get here.'

'Fine.' Harland looked at his watch and saw that it was 11 a.m. Joan was using the car and he had arranged to have lunch with Max Arbeit at one o'clock. 'I'll probably get a taxi then. Your place will be somewhere near the back of Paddington Station?'

'Quite correct, Mr Harland. You'll spot our Union Jack and our red, white and blue motif. We're easy to find.'

Harland said goodbye and put down the receiver, grateful for relief from the booming voice. He studied a London street map and found the section showing Harrow Road. He folded the catalogue and put it in his jacket pocket.

At the top of the basement steps he saw that Mrs Cathcart was alone again and diligently typing. He waved to her, saying, 'Shan't be back till after lunch—say about two fifteen—so just close when you want to pop out. If Jack Quinn phones ask him when I can call him back. Did old Aspinall take the bait?'

Mrs Cathcart waved a cheque. 'He seemed delighted with it. And he asked me to keep

229

the Sir Thomas More aside for three days. Good eh?'

'Very good. See you later.'

CHAPTER TWENTY-ONE

Mickey Harland found a taxi in St Martin's Lane, gave the young, cheerful cabby the Harrow Road address and was soon speeding up Charing Cross Road. As he seldom used his car for short trips in London, Harland had considerable experience of driving in taxis and thought that cabbies fell into identifiable groups, including the eccentric veterans who had been driven half round the bend by their unenviable trade and were much given to talking to themselves. He had happened on a young speedster, subdivision: cheerful but silent, who liked to weave in and out of the traffic and jockey for advantage at the traffic lights.

When they reached the junction with Oxford Street, Harland watched with interest, knowing the obsession that many cabbies had for driving along Oxford Street even when it was jammed with traffic from end to end. Instead, the young speedster surged across into Tottenham Court Road, swerving in front of another taxi at the lights.

Taking out the Broomhill Park catalogue, Harland began to look through it more carefully, examining each page. He found a few more examples of Rupert's doodling, and on page thirty the name 'General Redvers Piggott' was decorated with stars and enclosed in an elaborate ornamental border as though to stress its importance. When he turned to the next page a small press cutting fell fluttering to the floor.

'REVOLUTIONARY' DIES

'Red' Trevor Allardyce, self-proclaimed 'revolutionary' and leader of a small group of political activists, was found hanged at his home in Old Forge Road, Layer de-la-Haye, Essex, yesterday. The police said they knew of no reason why Allardyce, a bachelor aged 33 and a former London bus conductor, might have wanted to take his life.

Frowning, Harland pocketed the catalogue and the cutting. It seemed quite hopeless trying to divine why Sylvester should have found the suicide of a former London bus conductor of special interest. He knew that most people have a secret life underlying the one that is public property, but he had always believed it to be an imaginative life that did not reach out into reality as Rupert's had seemed to do.

The silent cabby was driving along the Marylebone Road as though in a race with a big prize at the end of it, gunning the accelerator at each set of lights, weaving from lane to lane, never missing the chance to get ahead. Harland knew that fast cabbies were usually good at their job and it was the elderly eccentrics, talking in funny voices or gesturing as they drove, grinding along in a low gear, who were more prone to accidents. The taxi flashed up on to the flyover and dipped down to the left. Pulling up with a jerk, the curly-haired driver turned, grinning. 'Sorry I was slow, guv. I'll do better next time.'

Harland paid him, saying, 'Yes, thanks. Wings would help.'

When he faced Terry's Car Sales he saw that Boyle had not exaggerated in saying that his premises were easily identified. A large Union Jack fluttered above the white building and the effect of red and blue paint against the white background made the premises eye-catching if garish. Small Union Jacks adorned the corners of the showroom windows. Two glossy BMWs stood on the forecourt.

By the side of Boyle's building there was a crazy mirror underneath a sign reading 'No Matter How Odd You are We've Got Just the Car for You!' As he approached the mirror Harland saw a Daddy-long-legs version of himself with a pin-head, like one of Rupert's drawings. He straightened his tie in the mirror and instantly became a dwarf with a forehead several feet high.

The fairground impression was left behind when he opened a glass door to disclose ranks of gleaming cars and two men looking deep into the engine of an Opel. A blond young man in a three-piece grey suit negligently dropped a newspaper and walked towards him.

'Good morning. I've got an appointment with Mr Boyle.'

'Right, sir. And the name?'

'Harland, Michael Harland.'

'Just a minute.' The young man walked through a gap in a white partition at the back of the showroom and Harland looked round, noticing framed certificates on the walls and a large coloured portrait of the Queen.

An overweight woman with a jowled face appeared at the gap in the partition; she was heavily made up as though for a stage performance. She smiled, saying, 'Good morning, Mr Harland. Mr Boyle is expecting you.' From the mask of make-up her glittering eyes studied him with interest.

Harland followed her through the partition and up a white staircase covered in dark blue carpet. He could hear the clatter of typewriters and a booming voice. The woman knocked at the second door in the corridor, opened it and said, 'Mr Harland.'

A large man boomed 'So, thanks and

233

goodbye now' into a white telephone. He replaced the receiver and got up from behind a large desk. He was as tall as Jack Quinn, probably six foot two or three, but considerably bulkier. He wore a beige hand-stitched suit with tie, handkerchief and shoes in matching tone, all the colour of milky cocoa. His face was blotchy and an unhealthy red, but it was his eyes that struck Harland: they were greyish-green in colour and protuberant, like those of the driver of the VW Scirocco.

'Good morning,' Harland said.

'Good morning to you, Mr. Harland. Now sit yourself down.' Boyle looked at him with an expression that was not exactly friendly and pointed to a dark blue linen chair. Harland could not immediately classify Boyle's expression, but delved into his memory and came up with 'amused contempt', an attitude he had experienced in the Army from an RSM, a regular soldier, who had told him that his saluting and general attitude were just not good enough. The RSM had been about the same build as Boyle, but all muscle and a genuine tough guy, afraid of nothing. Harland had the intuitive feeling that there was more of the blusterer and bully in Boyle, that he was a man ever anxious to stress his masculinity.

A red telephone on the desk rang and Boyle said, 'Sorry about this,' before picking it up.

He listened for a few moments, said, 'Yes, Cindy,' in a normal tone and listened again.

Harland looked round the room. The principal decoration was a large photograph of the Queen on horseback in military uniform, reviewing her troops. Another photograph showed a parade of 'Billy Boys' in Belfast, serried rows of marching men, all in dark suits and bowler hats and sashes, carrying banners and Union Jacks. Seeing the Orangemen marching reminded Harland that Rupert had served in Northern Ireland in the mid-1970s and made him wonder if he had met Boyle there. If their relationship did indeed go back several years, then it was even stranger that Boyle should at first have denied knowing the name Sylvester.

Nervously drumming his left hand on the desk, which was bare apart from the two telephones, Boyle listened in silence with an attentive, somewhat obsequious expression. Saying solemnly, 'Yes, I see ... Yes, I understand,' he replaced the receiver and stayed quite still for a moment, plunged in deep thought.

Turning to Harland, Boyle said, 'Sorry, sorry about that interruption. Now that was bad news, what you told me about Mr Sylvester. A road acccident, I think you said?'

'Yes, he was run over just outside Broomhill Park—by a hit and run driver. The inquest has been adjourned.'

There was no flicker of guilt or emotion in Boyle's protuberant eyes which were the colour of stewed gooseberries. 'Quite so,' he said. 'You also mentioned something about a catalogue, I believe.'

Harland took out the folded catalogue and turned to the page where Boyle's name and telephone number were written. 'Does the name Redvers Piggott mean anything to you?' he said.

'No.' The denial boomed out as if the question touched on a sore point and was too quick and emphatic to be convincing. 'Now, why do you ask me that?'

'You'll see that your name was written down by Sylvester with that of Piggott. I just thought there might be a reason for putting them together. You understand Mrs Sylvester knows very little about the antiques business and some friends are trying to help clear up various matters.'

'Can I look at that catalogue?' Boyle's booming voice had a hectoring tone to it. Harland thought, Yes, it was probably you who drove the Scirocco though I couldn't be certain enough to swear to it in court. 'Of course,' he said, and pushed it across the desk.

Boyle turned the pages over quickly but he looked at each of them and his concentration was riveted on what he saw. 'I thought just by glancing through this I might happen on

236

some particular item which Sylvester thought would appeal to me,' he said. 'Some reason, you see, for my own name appearing here . . .' He broke off to point at something on the wall behind Harland's chair. 'I believe I bought that rather nice object at the shop in Alderbury.'

Boyle's last sentence had a ring of truth and Harland swung round to look at a barometer that appeared to be neither old nor new but somewhere in between, like many items in stock at Court Antiques.

When Harland turned back Boyle was still holding the catalogue open, giving one page grave consideration. He stopped reading at that point, put it on the desk and edged it slowly back. Halfway through the catalogue, Harland thought, that would be about page thirty where General Redvers Piggott's name is starred and enscrolled.

'So, Rupert Sylvester's dead, just like that.' Boyle snapped his fingers. 'A great pity. An attractive young man, as I recall, if I can say so without starting any hares and hounds.'

No, Harland thought, I'm not sure you can do that. There were no obvious homosexual mannerisms about Boyle but there was just something about him that made it seem highly probable that he had once found Rupert a very attractive young man. 'Well, thanks for seeing me, particularly at such short notice,' he said. 'I'm sorry to have bothered you, but with Rupert dying suddenly like that—it's left a lot of loose ends, so to speak. Puzzles that may never be solved...'

'Quite so. Probably the odd peccadillo too, I expect. Ah, well ... I would ask you to give his widow my condolences, but the fact is we never met.' Boyle signalled that the interview was at an end by pressing with both hands on the desk and raising his bulky figure.

'Thanks again,' Harland said. 'I can find my own way out.'

'Now turn left out of the showroom and then left again from Harrow Road into Eastbourne Terrace. That will take you down to Praed Street for buses or the tube. Goodbye for now, Mr Harland.'

Boyle's booming farewell echoed in Harland's ears as he walked along the corridor and down the blue-carpeted stairs. He thought, Will you be making an important phone call to General Redvers Piggott now, or did you in fact take it while I was in the room when you listened in obsequious silence?

Only the grey-suited salesman, lying back on a chair, was to be seen in the showroom and he did not raise his head from a newspaper. Once outside, Harland took deep breaths of fresh air. His mind was in a whirl; he was experiencing a heady mixture of excitement and fear, so that for a moment or

238

two he felt confused. Glancing down at his watch he saw that it was 12.15. He was due to meet Max Arbeit at one o'clock for lunch at Manzi's Fish Restaurant in Lisle Street, so he had plenty of time to walk down to Praed Street and catch a bus for Piccadilly Circus.

Excitement bubbled about inside him; he felt as if he had done something quite dangerous, rather like bearding a lion in his den. The fact that the lion had not stirred at all in his direction did not mean that the lion was without claws. He was now reasonably certain that it had been Terence Boyle who had run down Rupert Sylvester and that Max had been right all along in claiming that the death was murder, not manslaughter. Whether it could ever be proved was quite a different matter. As far as he knew he was the only witness able to identify the driver of the Scirocco and the police would need more than that to build up a case against Boyle. But what reason could there be for such a crime? Why should a prosperous London car-dealer wish to kill Rupert? What relationship could they have had? Was it a friendship dating from the time when Rupert had served in the Army in Belfast and Boyle was a hard-nosed Orangeman or possibly one of the notorious B Specials? Harland knew that friendships sometimes turned sour, could even change to antagonism—but murder? The idea seemed nonsensical to him, so why should the police believe in it?

The sky was still a clear blue, but a cold wind blew dust and scraps of rubbish along the dreary section of Harrow Road that bridged the railway lines into Paddington Station. Harland's mind was turning over what he had learned and sensed from the brief interview with Terence Boyle. Shortly he would be able to discuss it all with the Doctor but he did not think that would necessarily get them much further. Max was intelligent and perceptive, but it would again be a case of the blind leading the lame for they were both out of their depth in a murder investigation. Obviously, whatever Max thought, at some time he would have to go to the police.

Turning into Eastbourne Terrace, Harland found that it was comparatively busy with traffic to and from Westbourne Grove; but the image of cars and buses was replaced by a vivid mental picture of Boyle listening to the phone, his head inclined deferentially and saying only, 'Yes, I see ... Yes, I understand.'

Harland began to experience a different kind of excitement, more to do with discovery, such as a scientist must feel when certain facts tend to point to a conclusion. For more and more it appeared likely to him that Rupert had been involved with Terence Boyle in some kind of illegal activity and that

240

Boyle had carried out the murder not because he wanted to, but on the orders of a person to whom he never said no . . . Suddenly Harland heard the sound of heavy, pounding footsteps behind him, felt a powerful hand wrenching at his shoulder and spinning him round into the road. A moment later he was in the gutter, dancing on lifeless legs in front of a number 27 bus.

CHAPTER TWENTY-TWO

Jack Quinn stopped his Mercedes abruptly in Praed Street and set the handbrake with a nervous jerk. He was aware that he had driven badly from Westminster to Paddington with his mind not on what he was doing, making some of the nervy mistakes in heavy traffic which he found so irritating in other drivers.

It was a cool, cloudy evening and there had been just enough drizzle to make it necessary to use the windscreen wipers but not enough for them to function properly. Quinn looked out through the smeared glass at the tall, old building across the road. He had passed St Mary's Hospital scores of times driving down Praed Street and never given it a thought; now it seemed to loom over him like a minatory object. The plain fact was that he disliked hospitals, although he had little experience of them; illogically, he had come to look on them as places where people suffered and died just because that had happened to his father. Don't let Mickey give up like an old man, he thought. Quinn had only a handful of friends, which was perhaps the reason why he valued them so highly and felt that he could not afford to lose Mickey Harland whom he had known and liked since he was a teenager.

Quinn had planned a quiet evening at home, with a solitary fish and chip supper and a Richard Strauss concert on records. Now the fish and chips were congealing, still in their outer newspaper wrapping, in the kitchen of his house in Barton Street and he believed he had forgotten to turn off his record player. An excited phone call from Max Arbeit had dished his plans and led to him driving in a rush to Praed Street. The Doctor was never at his best on the phone: under the stress of calling from the hospital his message had been gabbled and confused, but Quinn gathered that Mickey Harland had been badly hurt in a street accident and taken to the casualty ward of St Mary's Hospital suffering from several fractures and concussion.

While locking his car Quinn could not help remembering the depressing series of visits he had paid to another London hospital, during which he had noticed barely perceptible changes in his father's condition as the old man lost his will to live. Crossing the road, he saw a coloured nurse scurrying along in the rain, holding a newspaper over her head.

'Can you tell me where I can make enquiries about someone in the hospital?'

Her hurried glance flickered over his scarred face. 'You mean a patient?'

'Yes, sorry. Yes, a patient—someone in a street accident.'

The nurse pointed to a gap between two buildings. 'The Norfolk Place entrance, the Porter's Lodge. They'll help you.'

Quinn called out 'Thanks' to the girl as she hurried away and walked along to the heavy iron gates which she had indicated. He was thinking of all the pleasant evenings he had spent in the Harlands' comfortable flat when Joan had played Chopin or Schubert on the piano before an informal supper. Joan often criticised Mickey but they were a loving couple whose marriage had lasted over thirty years.

The man behind the counter in the Porter's Lodge looked vague when the name Harland was mentioned, but responded quickly on hearing 'Arbeit'. 'Oh yes,' he said, 'Dr Arbeit left you a message. Your friend is in the Allcroft Ward, that's Orthopaedics. Jackson's going in that direction, he'll see you right.'

A man in brown overalls nodded and Quinn followed him into the main building and along a corridor, at the end of which he saw the diminutive figure of Max Arbeit holding a door open and conversing with someone in the ward on the other side of it. When Quinn was close to the Doctor he could see two patients in bed, one of whom was seemingly paralysed in an awkward posture, staring up at the ceiling; the other had stumpy wings made of snow-white plaster.

Max wore a vintage navy-blue suit with chalk stripes. He turned to smile fleetingly at Quinn but continued to converse with someone not visible, saying, 'Yes, understood, Sister. Very good. Better news than we expected, eh?' Still listening, he kept Quinn at bay with an uplifted hand holding a crumpled and stained copy of the Broomhill Park catalogue. He seemed very much at home in the hospital milieu, as if he were just about to don a white coat and make the rounds himself. Standing with his head on one side, he looked particularly wise and sensitive to what was going on around him.

Saying, 'Thank you, Sister. Yes, I'd like to pop back in ten minutes if I may, just to have another word with Mrs Harland,' Arbeit let the ward door close. He took Quinn's arm making him feel over-sized and clumsy.

'Good news, Jack! Mickey will be all right. Nothing to worry about. The concussion was slight. He has a couple of fractured ribs and a fractured collar-bone. They were worried about his arm. They thought it might be a comminuted fracture, where the bone is broken into pieces. But it's a simple, transverse fracture with a lot of bad bruising. Nothing that won't heal in a few weeks' time.'

'Your phone call had me worried, Max.'

'Yes, I'm sorry, but I telephoned when the position was less clear. I got here this afternoon. You see, Mickey was supposed to be lunching with me at Manzi's, so when he didn't turn up I went round to Cecil Court and got there just after the hospital had contacted Mrs Cathcart about this . . .' Arbeit hesitated for a moment as if unable to get his tongue round the word accident. 'This very disturbing affair. I can't call it an accident—Mickey is adamant on that point. He swears he was pushed in front of the bus . . .'

'Pushed!' Quinn experienced a sudden surge of anger within him. 'Can I see Mickey?'

'He's sleeping, Jack. Nodded off while Joan and I were talking at his bedside. A perfectly natural sleep. The best thing for him, nature's own antidote to shock. Will you have a cup of coffee with me? There's a good café across the street and we can talk more freely there.'

As they walked along the corridor and out into the fine rain Quinn strove to think

245

calmly; he had a short fuse at best, but temper clouded the mind. 'But why the hell should anyone push Mickey in front of a bus?' he said. 'And particularly round here. I've heard of someone being shoved off the pavement by a crowd in Oxford Street. But here? It doesn't make sense. What does Joan think?'

'Joan thinks it's all nonsense. She's convinced it's just a reaction to the shock or due to his concussion. I don't agree. The effect of serious concussion can be impaired vision and, at worst, a coma. Mickey had only slight concussion—no dizziness afterwards, no impaired vision, just a headache. But of course I didn't argue with Joan. She's feeling shaky herself as it is. I've no doubt at all that Mickey was pushed, but that can be gone into later. No point in upsetting Joan further at the moment.'

They hurried across the slippery road and into an Italian café. 'I'll get this as I'm going to have some sandwiches,' Quinn said. 'Won't you have something?'

'Perhaps a roll and butter, Jack. Thanks.'

Quinn ordered two black coffees, two salami sandwiches and a roll and butter. He noticed that Arbeit still held the crumpled catalogue like a valuable book, putting it on the table and staring at it reflectively.

When Quinn had sat down, Arbeit held up the catalogue. 'I think this is the cause of the trouble, the reason why our very good friend Mickey was nearly killed today. You see, when Rupert was run over I was the first on the scene. In fact he died in my arms. He said something to me, words which didn't seem to make sense at the time. But they were the names he had written down in this catalogue—Piggott and Boyle. Mickey found them and a phone number for Boyle, so he went to see him at his business address in Harrow Road. Minutes after leaving there he says someone grabbed him from behind and swung him round into the road. What do you think?'

Before replying Quinn made his point graphically by holding his nose with two fingers. 'It all stinks to me, Max. One road accident is possible, yes. Unlikely with someone as alert and agile as Sylvester, but still possible. Two road accidents in quick succession, no, I don't go for that at all. I'm sure Mickey was pushed and I'd very much like to have a chat with this bloke Boyle myself.'

Arbeit offered the catalogue to Quinn, who said, 'No, you keep that. Tuck it away somewhere safe. It may turn out to be quite a valuable document.' Quinn took out his pen and cheque-book. 'I'll just jot down those names. Like old Mickey, I don't carry a notebook. So, the names are Boyle and Piggott?'

'Yes, and Boyle runs a car business in Harrow Road, at the back of Paddington Station. The other name here is that of a General apparently, a General Redvers Piggott.'

'Right, I've got that. Now Mickey didn't mention another name by any chance, a Roscoe Starr?'

'No, why?'

'Oh, a friend of Polly's, her neighbour, seemed to think that Rupert might have been mixed up in something fishy with Roscoe Starr who appears to be a very dubious character. But I can raise that point with Mr Boyle.'

'So you will see Boyle? Is that wise, Jack?'

'I don't know if it's wise but I'm going to do it.'

CHAPTER TWENTY-THREE

'Assembly of God. Pentecostal Church'. The two signs in stark white lettering boldly proclaimed a place of worship but they were on a derelict building. It appeared to be in the course of falling down and was largely held together by grimy planks nailed across the front, together with two old doors. Obscene drawings and graffiti in red and black paint added further grotesque touches. Quinn had parked in front of the dilapidated church premises because it was close enough for him to study the freshly painted building occupied by Terry's Car Sales.

It was a very fine morning at the end of June, with a clear blue sky and a temperature in the high seventies kept free from humidity by a westerly breeze which tugged fitfully at the Union Jack flying over the car showrooms. But even on such a fine day the stretch of Harrow Road overshadowed by the flyover to the M40 was dusty, bleak and uninviting.

Quinn's eyesight was keen, so he was able to see small Union Jacks in the windows with twisted red, white and blue ribbons, and the printed sign: 'Always a fair deal with Terry Boyle'. He was interested in what made people tick and quite fascinated by Boyle's ultra-patriotic display. Was there some link between this and Rupert Sylvester's own right-wing brand of patriotism, always harping back to the Duke of Wellington and the days of imperial glory?

Quinn drove his Mercedes a short distance along the road and up on to the forecourt of the building, parking it cheek by jowl with a new Mercedes and two Opels. When he opened the glass door to Boyle's premises he was greeted by the vague background music usually heard in airport lounges. A youth with dyed blond hair, a sharp looking customer in a chocolate-brown suit, got up from a chair. His shifty eyes ran quickly up and down Quinn, trying to place him in a financial bracket. He said briskly, 'Morning, sir. Thinking of trading up?'

'What?'

'I spotted the old Merc, sir. Now, we could give you a very fair deal if you wanted an up-to-date model. Our guv'nor, he's quite keen on those old Mercs.'

'No, thanks. But I do want to see your Mr Boyle. My name's Quinn. Tell him I'm calling on behalf of Mr Harland who looked in here yesterday but is unable to call again today.'

The young man twitched his head to one side, a quizzical half-smile on his tiny rosebud mouth. 'Right, sir.' He nodded slowly as if memorising the message, with an air of insolent amusement. 'I see. Very good, sir. A Mr Quinn to see our Mr Boyle about a Mr Harland.'

'That's right.'

Walking back along the line of cars, the youth turned to give Quinn a final speculative look before disappearing through a gap in the white partition. After a minute or two a plump woman in a blue silk dress looked out from the partition, shading her heavily made-up eyes with one hand as she stared at Quinn. A moment later she was joined by a bulky man in a brown and cream checked suit.

Quinn turned his back on the partition and looked round the showroom. Despite the red, white and blue ribbons and the flapping Union Jack on top of the building, the stock of cars was largely of German manufacture.

'Mr Quinn.' Facing the partition again, he saw the plump woman was beckoning to him. Her make-up made her look like an ageing tart. 'You want Mr Boyle. Well, he's up there.'

When he reached the partition he saw the blue-carpeted stairs she was indicating with a crimson finger-nail so long that it looked like a tiny penknife blade. Quinn said, 'Thank you,' and walked up the stairs. As he did so he heard a male Cockney duologue below: 'Trouble? Who's that scarface?' 'One of those mad Micks, Paddy O'Quinn.' 'What's his game then?'

A male voice with a strong Northern Irish accent boomed out, 'In here, Quinn.' The bulky man stood by a desk, beating a regular tattoo on it with an ebony ruler. 'All right. I'm Boyle, so you've found me. Are you looking for trouble? This is my place of business, d'you understand? I'm not putting up with madmen barging in here and acting aggressive.'

'I wasn't at all aggressive. I just asked to see you.'

'That's what you say. Les said it came out

251

aggressive and I believe him. You've got aggression built into you.'

'Don't you want to hear why I came?'

'Not really. I bet it's got fuck-all to do with buying and selling cars and that's what I'm here for.'

'I thought you might be interested to hear that just five minutes after leaving you yesterday Mr Harland was pushed in front of a bus.'

Boyle said nothing but sat down heavily in his swivel armchair. With one hand on the desk he swung himself from side to side, studying Quinn from head to foot. 'So okay, now you've told me. Is that it?' he said. His expressionless face and dull eyes gave nothing away but Quinn knew from experience that liars were often let down by their failure to produce natural reactions. The bus incident was certainly not news to Boyle, but could it ever be proved?

'You're not upset by the news that Mr Harland is now in hospital?'

Boyle's heavy, red face remained impassive but a tiny yellow light came on in his eyes. 'Look, yesterday I didn't know Harland from Joe Soap,' he said. 'Once he'd gone out the door that was it. He's got troubles? We've all got troubles. Now, I'd like to get back to a little bit of business if that's okay with you.'

'Just two questions and I'll be off...'

Boyle laughed. 'Now I know how you got

your face in such a mess. You make a habit of this, pestering people with silly fucking questions.' He picked up a red telephone. 'Cindy, I want Ray and Dixy up here. Toot sweet.'

'Two questions then. I'll keep them simple. Can you give me General Piggott's address?'

Boyle looked as if he were going to say something but bit his lip instead, smiled and lounged back in his chair, beating the ruler against the palm of his left hand.

'Right, thanks a lot. Now here's the second question. Where can I find Mr Roscoe Starr?'

Yellow lights gleamed again in the dull pop-eyes. There was the sound of pounding footsteps and a muscular character wearing jeans and a black and white shirt chequered like the racing flag appeared in the doorway. He had black wavy hair and displayed a lot of curly chest hair at the neck of his shirt. He smiled broadly, saying , 'Yes, boss?'

Boyle permitted himself a lazy smile as he got up from his swivel chair. 'Ray,' he said, pausing to point at Quinn. 'What we got here is one of those big, awkward Micks. Now they've taken over all of Kilburn they want our little patch. So I'd like you to show him the Wharf Road exit. Is Dixy there?'

A man of medium height with a barrel chest, in greasy blue overalls, appeared at the door. His nose was no longer the shape that Nature had intended but considerably

253

flattened and he grinned with teeth that were perfect rather than realistic.

'Good,' Boyle said, 'now you'll give Ray a hand, Dixy? See that friend Quinn finds the way out all right?'

Quinn shrugged and walked towards the door, saying, 'I still have these two questions.'

With a theatrical sigh, Boyle said, 'See what I mean, boys?'

Ray took hold of Quinn's left arm. He said, 'Are you deef as well as stupid?' and propelled him into the corridor in the opposite direction to the stairs.

'This isn't the way out,' Quinn said.

'If I say it's the way out then it's the way out,' Ray said.

With a little chuckle Dixy added, 'Like—if he says it's Wednesday it's Wednesday.'

Quinn walked slowly along the blue-carpeted corridor, remembering his fight with the two policemen. It had been more of an ignominious scuffle than a fight and less than half-hearted on his side because after the very first blow he had known he was on a good hiding to nothing. With these two Cockney comedians he felt no such inhibitions but his face was criss-crossed with the recently healed cuts and any blow was liable to open them up.

'You can see by his face he couldn't read those instructions—you know, "Light the blue paper and retire immediately",' Ray said.

Dixy said, 'You heard the one about the Irish turkey? It was looking forward to Christmas.'

It was Quinn's turn to sigh. Was there any point in telling these jokers that he was a Londoner, born and raised in Hammersmith, who had never been to the Emerald Isle? He could foresee the cuts on his cheeks bleeding and the difficulties about shaving beginning again; and he looked villainous with a sandy beard. He could even visualise Madeleine's cold expression when she returned from America and found that he had sticking-plasters on his ugly mug once more. With another sigh he opened a door facing him at the end of the corridor. It led to a wooden platform, on an oil-soaked concrete base, that had steps going down into a messy yard, largely filled with boxes and crates. The concreted yard was surrounded by a high brick wall surmounted with barbed wire and any exit into North Wharf Road was obscured by the crates. In the corner an Alsation dog whimpered as it padded up and down a home-made cage of grimy planks and chicken wire. The Alsation made excited noises on seeing Quinn and began to jump up at the wire netting.

Quinn remained on the platform, looking at North Wharf Road which ran between the canal basin and a kind of dreary no-man's-land. There were no buildings along the road and no sign of activity. Ray stood close by him, following his inspection of the dismal area. 'Looking for a wolly? You'll be lucky. They don't trouble us round here.'

A hard, knuckled push in the back started Quinn on his descent of the stairs. 'Yes, Paddy, believe me, you're in shtook,' Ray said.

After going down three stairs Quinn looked round and called to Dixy who was in the doorway, 'Is he doing your thinking for you as well as the talking? I'm not even Irish, let alone a bomber.'

Ray gave him a jolting push. 'Maybe not,' he said. 'But you're fucking trouble. So we're going to give you a little lesson about that, down there where it's nice and quiet and private.'

Quinn leapt down the last four steps and spun round, searching desperately for the exit. He spotted a padlocked gate, half hidden by a particularly large crate and realised that if he could clamber up on to the crate he could then climb over the wire on the wall.

'Trouble,' said Ray, punching Quinn in the chest. 'Trouble—we can—do—without.' He punctuated the warning with punches. Ten years in the forward line of a rugby team had given Quinn a chest which could absorb a few

256

punches; he was back-pedalling like a boxer in trouble, holding his open hands high to fend off any blows aimed at his face. He noticed that Dixy still held back, high up on the steps, as if satisfied to be an interested spectator. A minute, he thought, that's all I need to clamber up on to the crate, only a minute but one in which no one is tugging at my legs. He saw that Ray moved his right arm awkwardly in delivering punches and that left a gap in his defence.

The Alsatian's excited whimpering changed to snarls and Quinn realised that he was close to the cage. His attention distracted, he slipped on a patch of oil and Ray caught him with two hard punches to the face. The second one, connecting with his mouth and nose, was particularly painful. Quinn tasted blood and, out of the corner of his eye, saw some spurt from a cut on his cheek. A rising red haze of temper completed the crimson colour scheme. A moment later he caught Ray with a clubbing left to the head and a mighty right upper cut to the throat. He saw Ray wobble and punched him in the throat again. Ray rocked and Quinn kicked him on the knee. Ray sat down and the Alsatian went wild with excitement, throwing himself repeatedly at the netting, anxious to join in the fray.

Dixy rushed down the wooden steps but Quinn took off at the same time, catching

Dixy in a low tackle, propelling his big, fourteen-stone, frame forward regardless of where it took him. The two men collided with a crate in a bone-jerking crash. Dixy took the brunt of the impact on his spine and it knocked the wind out of him. Quinn drove his fist into Dixy's white face, scrambled to his feet and raced back across the yard, leaping up desperately for the top of the crate. Inspired by the threat of what lay behind him he managed to scramble up on to the crate, but a redoubled burst of snarling made him think that the Alsatian had got free and in a nervous grab he cut his right hand on the barbed wire.

He stood by the wall for a few moments, catching his breath before negotiating the wire. Sliding down the other side he fell awkwardly, but he was more concerned that he had a mouthful of blood. He had to spit twice to clear it before he ran to the corner of North Wharf Road and round to the forecourt of the car premises.

Seated in his Mercedes Quinn remained still for a minute or two, a tremor of nerves shaking his right arm. In the driving mirror he saw that two cuts on his cheeks were bleeding freely. More blood spattered his shirt and jacket. He pulled some tissues from a box he kept on the dashboard and dabbed the cuts. Spitting into the tissue and probing with his tongue, he said 'Sod it' in a thick voice. The punch full in the mouth had loosened one of his front teeth. 'And sod that dog,' he added fervently as he started the car. No one emerged from Terry's Car Sales as he drove away.

CHAPTER TWENTY-FOUR

'Christ! You are an impetuous sod!' Charlie Saunders sounded genuinely annoyed. He and Jack Quinn were seated in the former's BMW, parked outside the derelict Pentecostal Church, positioned so that Quinn could keep an eye on the to-ings and fro-ings at Terry's Car Sales as it closed down for the night.

Quinn had asked Saunders to drive him there because he realised that his old Mercedes would probably be spotted by someone at Boyle's premises. 'All right,' he said, 'if you don't want to be involved,' putting his hand on the car door.

'Sit still! Look, I'm *not* involved and I'm not going to be. You asked me to drive you here—okay, it's a small favour and I'm glad to do it for you. You want me to drive you somewhere else afterwards? Fine! If you want me to drive you to Edinburgh I'll do it as long as I get a chance to phone Lilian first. No problem. What I do object to is the way you behave, barging about looking for trouble. Your Dad said you inherited that unfortunate trait from his old man. Now, you could say I was looking for trouble on that beach in Normandy, June the sixth, 1944. And I found it all right. Bit of my foot blown off and I've been hobbling about ever since. But I had to go there. You don't *have* to be involved in this messy business.'

'Someone murdered Sylvester. I'm positive of that now. Someone also tried to push old Mickey under a bus. I want to find out why.'

'Simple answer. Go to the police.'

'Ah, my friends the police!'

'Now, that's something else I've been meaning to talk to you about. The first time I met you, Jack, you were still in short trousers. Six, seven? Anyway, there was a time when you used to call me "Uncle Charlie". So that allows me to talk to you like a Dutch uncle. Right?'

'Right. Go ahead.'

'Okay. Well, I think you behaved like a right prick with those two coppers. You don't like being pushed about—that's understood. And you're a big chap so it doesn't happen often. But Christ Almighty, you must realise that coppers in the East End at night are expecting a bit of trouble. You want to give it to them? Fine. They lap it up.'

'I do know that, Charlie. I realised I was an idiot the moment I pushed that copper. I behaved very stupidly—no argument about that. But this is different. I think if I can just get to meet this General Piggott I may be able to make some sense of what happened. Terry Boyle is a thug. Maybe I'm naive but I don't think a former British General will be a thug too.'

Saunders shook his head pityingly. 'Listen, from what you've told me there seems to be some organisation which gets rid of people who make trouble for them and they do it with "accidents". Now, that's a clever wheeze. I mean, I'm in the sea with Lilian and I hold her under—someone on the shore may think they saw me commit a murder, but ten to one someone else will say how I was trying to save her. Where no weapon is involved in a killing it must be hard to *prove* anything. That makes this group very dangerous indeed. You get in their way and the next thing I'll be reading about how you fell under a bus...'

Quinn held up a finger. A tall, bulky figure in a dove-grey suit had emerged from the showrooms and he needed to concentrate to be sure it was Terence Boyle. The tall man paused to look in the plate-glass window and then adjusted his tie in a long mirror on the wall. Quinn saw the bald patch at the back of the man's head and the hunched way in which he held his heavy shoulders and knew it was indeed Boyle. The man got into a

261

brown Audi and accelerated off the forecourt at a rate that was fast enough to be flashy and attract attention.

'That's him.'

'I know, I know,' Saunders said, raising his eyebrows repeatedly in a comic way. 'Follow that car.'

'You don't *have* to.'

Saunders said nothing but drove along Harrow Road, pulling funny faces as if conducting an interior monologue. He drove with skill, as was to be expected from someone who covered a huge mileage every year. The Audi went down Eastbourne Terrace and turned left at the traffic lights into Praed Street.

Saunders said, gesturing at the sun perched in a clear blue sky, 'Fine evening like this you should be out getting some healthy exercise. Swimming, tennis. Didn't you say Madeleine could still beat you at tennis?'

'Do you always take good advice, Charlie? When I heard someone had actually tried to push old Mickey under a bus I thought "To hell with that!" Same as I would if it had happened to you.'

Charlie shrugged. 'That's disarming certainly. I'll shut up. No, I won't. One more word of advice. That Roscoe Starr sounds a right chancer. I'm sixty-four but I've only known two real chancers in my life. Weird! You look in their eyes and there's nothing and you know they really don't give a damn—about anything. Take my tip—if you meet a real chancer you back off. Understand?'

'T. Boyle's no chancer. He's just got so used to pushing people around it comes natural to him. I'm simply going to ask him two questions. As long as I get straight answers there won't even be a scuffle.'

'I should think not. Look at your face. What will Madeleine and the little girls think?'

The brown car turned right into Sussex Place and overtook a taxi with a burst of acceleration. 'Your friend seems to be in a hurry,' Saunders said. 'Unless he always drives like that. Supposing he's bound for a booze-up with some of his cronies?'

'I shall just have to give up—for now.'

As the Audi turned into Strathearn Place it was caught in a stream of traffic, so that Saunders had to slow down. 'One thing, Charlie,' Quinn said. 'I'm fairly certain he's not going to Edinburgh.'

Saunders shook his head with a serious expression. 'There definitely is a streak of something in you, Jacko—I don't know exactly what—as if you were looking for trouble, like your old grandpa. You've got a lovely wife, two smashing kids, a nice home, a good business, enough cash ... I can't understand it.' He had to slow down again as the Audi was stationary once more, held up at a mini-roundabout leading into Hyde Park Street. 'But then character is fate—well, that's what the ancient Greeks believed. I read it somewhere.'

Boyle drove into Connaught Street and swung over on to the right-hand side of the road, parking his car outside a house facing the Duke of Kendal pub. Saunders drove past it and stopped about fifty feet further down on the left-hand side. Quinn saw that Boyle was going into a house painted blue and white. 'Well, that's it. Thanks, Charlie—and for the good advice. I do mean that,' he said.

After Quinn had got out of the BMW, Saunders moved across to stick his bald head out of the offside window, calling, 'Good luck! I shan't be going out this evening and you know the number.'

'Yes. And I promise—to look before I leap.' Quinn stood still for some minutes after Saunders had driven off, bound for his house in Golders Green and the Jewish supper he preferred. Quinn had been a guest to meals there on countless occasions and he did look on Saunders as a kind of uncle, partly because he was over twenty years older and also because Charlie had been a good friend for as long as he could remember.

Quinn looked at Boyle's house and then above it at the sky which was subtly changing colour all the time as the sun slowly descended towards a solitary small bar of cloud, gilding the top edge and making it appear like a mysterious island in an even more mysterious sea. Charlie was right: on such a fine summer evening he should have been out seeking healthy exercise, though he knew, all things considered, he would have preferred to drive to Alderbury to spend a few hours in Polly Sylvester's company. Momentarily he forgot about Terence Boyle in thinking of Polly and Rex Bealby; they made a very unlikely couple and yet he had undoubtedly intercepted loving glances between them.

Walking back along Connaught Street, mingling with a jolly group converging on a French restaurant, Quinn gave some thought to his imminent encounter with Boyle. He certainly did not fancy any rough stuff with an overweight, middle-aged man who moved ponderously and was short of breath. However, Boyle might have delusions about his own fitness and see things differently. Quinn knew he could not single-handedly solve the mystery of Rupert Sylvester's murder, but he felt that if he could meet the elusive General Piggott, for whom there was no entry in *Who's Who*, at least he might be able to understand what lay behind the killing.

When he knocked on Boyle's front door, Quinn had no idea what scene might lie ahead. Terence Boyle appeared to be a man capable of producing a gun or of other dramatic action; there was something of a fanatic, as in many Orangemen, hidden behind that phlegmatic face.

No sound came from the house so Quinn knocked again, much more loudly. There were faint footsteps and the door opened. Boyle looked out, without showing any emotion. He still wore the dove-grey trousers but had changed into a navy-blue cardigan and black leather slippers. He pulled a rueful face. 'Ah yes, I thought I might see you again. Come in.' The Northern Irish accent was still noticeable but his voice did not boom at all; it was as if he adopted a different persona away from his place of business.

Boyle turned back into a faintly gloomy hall in which there were several old engravings on the wall, including a portrait of King William of Orange. There was something of an unaired and uncared-for atmosphere in the house like that Quinn found in his own home when Madeleine was away.

The only furniture in the room they entered consisted of three armchairs grouped round a television set which was switched on and showed a mens' singles match being played at Wimbledon; the walls were bare apart from one engraving. Boyle hovered over the television for a moment before switching

266

it off. While his back was still turned to Quinn he said, 'That was a bad mistake—what happened this morning.'

'I find that very hard to believe.'

'I tell you it was a mistake. I meant that Ray should just give you a warning and the bum's rush. I said nothing about any beating. I apologise. Please sit down.'

'All right.' Quinn sat, feeling relieved that he was not going to tangle physically with an ageing man who looked tired if not ill, with a very unhealthy complexion.

'You see, when your friend Harland came to talk to me I was angry that he seemed to think I had something to do with Rupert Sylvester's death. I've checked up on that date and I was definitely in London on the first day of the sale at Broomhill Park. I have half a dozen witnesses to prove that. Then you came along with more questions, more accusations . . .'

Quinn said nothing but thought, Yes, I bet you have witnesses and just as many to swear that you never left your office the morning that Harland took a tumble in front of a bus.

Boyle sat without speaking, gently massaging his chest, staring hard so that his dull eyes protruded even more than usual; he seemed to be trying to read Quinn's mind. Still holding his chest, he stood up abruptly. 'I need a drink. Some brandy. I don't feel too good. Will you join me?'

Quinn snorted a laugh. 'That's rich. This morning you tell your men to beat me up—or throw me out. This evening it's drinks. No thanks.'

'I admitted I did something foolish this morning—I panicked a bit when you called in. You appeared so aggressive, as if you were just looking for a chance to throw your weight about. And I was angry, hearing more accusations. Nothing that would ever get into court, mind you. Look, I'm going to answer your questions. Have a drink. Gin, whisky?'

'No thanks.'

'Just hold on a minute.'

When Boyle left the room Quinn wandered over to examine the framed picture. It was a Victorian steel engraving, giving a stereotyped impression of the Battle of the Boyne, fought in July 1690 between the armies of William III and James II. Boyle was obviously a fanatical Orangeman. Had he once been a member of the paramilitary group in Northern Ireland which was trained by the mysterious Roscoe Starr? And what was the real reason for this volte-face about answering the questions?

Boyle returned holding a balloon glass and a slip of paper. 'I have no idea why Sylvester should have jotted my name down with that of General Piggott. But then who knows what goes on in other people's minds?' He raised the glass. 'This is fine old Armagnac. You should join me.'

Quinn shook his head and Boyle sat down heavily, with a weary sigh. 'But I do recall, now, that it was at the General's place I first saw Sylvester. On a course.'

'A course? What do you mean?'

'Oh, lectures, debates, that kind of thing. The General conducts seminars, weekend courses during which he lectures on politics and military history.'

'Is that his address you're holding?'

'It is. You've got a long drive if you really mean to see him.'

Boyle handed over a small piece of paper with a typed address: 'The Castle, Vomit Point, Dale, near Haverford West, Pembrokeshire.'

'Vomit Point? Is that a joke?'

'Not at all. You can check it on a map. It's a house built in the remains of a castle, right on the coast—been in the General's family for centuries.'

'Okay. So that's the first question answered. And what about Mr Roscoe Starr?'

Momentarily Boyle's face darkened. Quinn felt the other bullying, loud-mouthed persona might emerge; that the gentle invalid mask was to be dropped. But Boyle made a dismissive gesture with his thick arm, staring at Quinn in the fading light as if trying to get him into focus. 'I've never heard of the man. You draw a blank there. And the answer would be the same if you were to knock me down like you did young Ray.'

Quinn looked back scornfully. He did not believe he was being told the truth about Starr, but to meet the General would be to take a step forward. He got up, saying, 'Don't worry. There's no fear of that.' He walked out of the room and along the dismal hallway.

CHAPTER TWENTY-FIVE

On the last day in June, a splendidly fine one, Jack Quinn drove towards Dale with an ailing car which he knew would shortly require attention. He was not mechanically minded but having driven the Mercedes for over a hundred thousand miles in five years he knew the noises it should make and was always alert to any changes in sound. It was in descending a steep road in the ancient city of Carmarthen that he had first heard a grating noise from the front brakes and the sound had grown steadily worse. The front brake pads were protesting that they were nearly worn out and metal was beginning to jar on metal. But by driving slowly and using his gears on corners Quinn was confident that he could get to Dale and have the brake pads changed there.

The drive from London along the M4 and

across the Severn Bridge to the Welsh border had been so swift and the subsequent journey skirting the Black Mountains so enjoyable, that Quinn had decided he would shortly revisit the area, purely on pleasure, with his two daughters. His wife disliked what she termed 'bucket and spade holidays', having had them annually when she was young, but Quinn had never been to the seaside as a child and he fancied the idea. Both of his girls were keen on nature and he was sure they would enjoy a week of swimming, looking in rock-pools, walking and picnics. Madeleine had taken them to Vermont for three weeks—it was reasonable that he should have the pleasure of their company for a week in Wales.

As he drove along the minor road that led from Haverfordwest and ended in the village of Dale, Quinn felt quite happy and relaxed. The previous night, instead of having a nightmare about murder and violence, he had experienced a delightful dream of living in an idyllic country cottage with his daughters and a wife who was a strange amalgam of Madeleine and Polly. The drive over rolling hills and through river valleys had reinforced the relaxed feeling; he could not remember a car journey of comparable length which was free of traffic frustrations and which held so much pleasure for the eye. And all the time the sun shone down from a clear blue sky and only a slight westerly breeze ruffled the trees. He might not get to meet the General who chose to live within leaping distance of the Atlantic or the meeting with him might prove to be a dead end; nevertheless the day would not have been wasted.

There was a first, tantalisingly brief, glimpse of the sea and then the road began to rise and dip, with a succession of longer sea-views and Quinn had to drive with extreme care; fortunately he had the road to himself, but the grating noise got on his nerves. Rounding a wooded bend, the road descended steeply to a narrow strip of beach with the sun sparkling on the sea and a number of yachts moored in the bay. At the far end of the beach he saw a tiny harbour tucked away in a corner, with rising wooded land immediately behind it.

Quinn passed by cottages and beached yachts and spied petrol pumps, feeling like someone happening on an oasis. When he drew up to the pumps a grey-haired, friendly looking man emerged from a hut and listened, nodding, to a description of what was ailing the Mercedes.

'I don't do repairs myself, haven't the time,' he explained. 'But I've got a friend who'll tackle it, do a good job. You'll have to leave it overnight. Changing pads only takes an hour or so, but happen he'll need to go to Haverford or Pembroke to get 'em.'

'Fine. I didn't really fancy driving back to London tonight. I did want to drive out to General Piggott's house, but it seems I'll have to walk.'

'Oh, you wouldn't want to drive there anyway. Very rough, old track it is to Vomit Point. Bad enough for them Range Rovers the General has. It would ruin a car like this. You can get there on foot quite easy. Lovely walk along the coastal path.'

'Good. I'll do that then. Shall I be able to find somewhere in the village to stay tonight?'

'Yes, the pub has vacancies at the moment. Be different next month, what with all the schools breaking up.' The grey-haired man turned to point to the yachts bobbing about in the glinting water. 'Now that isn't the open sea, that's the Haven, safe for boating.' He swung round and pointed in the opposite direction, across the promontory. 'The Atlantic is over the other side, if you see what I mean. Now take that little road, cross two fields and you'll come to the cliffs. Turn left on the coastal path. There's a series of headlands—Long Point, Short Point, Little Castle Point. Vomit Point is just after Frenchman's Bay. But you'll spot the Castle easily enough. Take about half an hour ...' He looked down at Quinn's long legs. 'Say twenty minutes for you.'

Quinn tried to push a pound note into the man's hand but he said, 'Oh, no need for that. Perhaps I'll see you in the pub this evening. Wouldn't say no to a pint then if you pressed me.'

'You can rely on it. I shall enjoy a pint or two myself.'

The lane the man had pointed to was obviously little used by cars and led past an old church which Quinn decided to look at the next day. It was good to walk after being cooped up in the car for five hours. Seagulls were flying over the fields he crossed, doing lazy aerobatics and mobbing a crow. When he came to the cliff top he looked down on a delightful small bay with a sprinkling of bathers. There were rocky headlands on either side. It was apparent that the tide was coming in and some children were building a sand wall which they evidently hoped would keep the sea from invading the upper beach.

The cliff path was narrow and further confined by straying, spiky sprays of gorse and bramble above which butterflies and bees hovered. Quinn stopped at the top of the first steep part of the path to take off his jacket and survey the magnificent vista of sea and sky. Starting to walk again, he was disturbed by an oppressive memory of Boyle's house, its depressing, stage-like aspects and the ageing man living there alone. Don't let me end up like that, he pleaded to Fate. 'Character is fate'; the Greek notion quoted by Saunders echoed in his head. He knew that he had an

274

unsatisfactory character, containing one man inside another as it were: from his mother he had inherited his passion for books and music and a strain of sensitivity; but the other man was like his grandfather with a tendency to seek out trouble and drink too much.

A denser growth of bushes, thistles and tall grasses in places obscured the view on both sides, so that he had only a distant prospect of the sea. Plodding on, he found that his shirt was sticking to his back; the temperature would be high in the seventies, if not more, and the sun appeared like a great ball of fire. With a mocking, melancholy cry a gull glided past close at hand before describing a lazy descending circle, taking it out of sight towards the sea.

When he first caught sight of the house-cum-castle built behind the headland called Vomit Point, Quinn stopped to cool down and give himself time to think of what he would say to General Piggott. He thought it was quite possible that Terence Boyle had gone to the Castle on a course, as he had said, of lectures on politics and military history. It was also likely that such a seminar would have appealed to Sylvester. But even if that were the case, why should Rupert have mentioned the General's name with his dying breath? It seemed an inscrutable mystery. Better brains than his would have to find the final solution and systematic police work would be necessary to bring whoever was guilty to court.

After climbing a stile into a field which had a 'Private' notice, Quinn had a much better view of the General's house. It had been converted from the ruins of an ancient castle with great skill and feeling for the site, retaining old towers and walls some of which formed an integral part of the house. Stone steps connected terraces at various levels, so that the occupants would always be able to find a seat in the sun that was out of the wind. Staring hard at the house, Quinn was startled to hear someone calling out, 'Lost your way?'

A young man with closely clipped blond hair, dressed in tennis shirt, shorts and shoes, walked towards him across a field of springy turf in which there was as much thyme and clover as grass. He called out, 'Sorry, but this is private property! You have to stick to the coastal path for St Ann's Head.' He looked very tanned and fit.

'Yes, I know. I was hoping to see General Piggott.'

The young man came nearer and looked closely at Quinn's scarred face as if he were going to comment on it. Instead he said, 'I see. You're not a local, are you?'

'No, I've come from London.'

'To see the General? He will be flattered. What do you want to see him about?'

'It's a rather complicated, private matter.'

'And you are?'

'Jack Quinn.' He dug a card out of his jacket pocket and handed it over.

'Right. I should think the General will see you.' Glancing down at his watch, the man with the military haircut said, 'Half three. But he won't be able to spare you much time. I know he's expecting someone about four. Anyway, come on. I'll have a word on your behalf.'

As they walked across the spongy turf, Quinn began to struggle into his jacket.

'I say, don't bother with that. It's all very informal here and you look rather hot.'

Quinn was, in fact, sweating freely. The heat, exertion and a touch of nerves were conspiring to make him feel hotter minute by minute. 'Yes, too much beer and not enough exercise recently.'

'Oh, I don't know about that. It's a good pull up and a scorcher of a day. Eighty-four in the shade. God knows what it is out here!'

A flinty, chalky track ran through the field and a gap in the stone wall, then divided into two. One path led up to the house and the other to stone outbuildings in front of which there were two red Range Rovers. A dark young man with similarly cropped hair was washing one of them.

'A variety of entrances here. We'll go in by the side. A nice cool room, or at least it will be for an hour or so. It faces due west.'

277

They climbed steps to a grassed-over terrace and then up another flight to a stone balcony. There was a superb commanding view of the Atlantic and Skokholm Island. French windows, with the curtains partly drawn, led into a large shady room containing a full-sized billiard table.

'Do take a pew, Mr Quinn. Would you like a drink? We can offer most kinds.'

Quinn sat down in a green leather armchair. 'No thanks.'

'Right then. I shouldn't think he'll be long.'

If the atmosphere of Boyle's house had been the depressing one of a bachelor pigging it alone, with worrying overtones for Quinn of things as they might be if he left his wife, that of the General's residence was of subdued luxury. Everything was immaculate. On a white wall facing the french windows there were two framed photographs of soldiers grouped round army tanks. The central decoration was a large drawing of a coat of arms with the motto: *'Sauve qui peut'*. Quinn translated this as 'Every man for himself', thinking, To hell with that.

He sat completely still, aware that sweat was still trickling down his neck, very thankful that he had thrown clean pants and a shirt into his hastily packed overnight bag. The door burst open and a man propelled himself quickly into the room in a wheelchair.

278

He was a heavily built, elderly man with a big head and thick, steel-grey hair. He had sharp, grey eyes under bushy eyebrows, a jutting chin and a thin mouth that was partly obscured by a pepper-and-salt moustache. He was dressed in a cream silk shirt and cavalry twill trousers; trouble had been taken to give his reddish-brown shoes a mirror-like shine.

'By God, Mr Quinn!' the man said explosively. 'You've had a very long journey to see me. I only hope I shan't disappoint you.'

Quinn stood up, but the man said, 'Oh, do sit down. Relax!'

Quinn did so, saying, 'Thank you for seeing me, General. It was kind, at such short notice.'

'Quarter of an hour,' Piggott said, pulling off his wristwatch, which was on an expanding steel bracelet, and hooking it on the arm of his wheelchair. 'Sorry about rationing the time. Don't want you to think I put a premium on it like some ghastly business wallah. It just happens that I have a friend arriving for tea. But I can answer a hell of a lot of questions in fifteen minutes, you'll find.' He looked down at his legs which appeared to be immobile and were positioned so that the gleaming shoes were placed exactly together. With a faintly bitter smile he said, 'That's what I do largely, nowadays.'

'Someone told me you held seminars here.'

'Ah yes, but you didn't expect to meet such an old crock! Be honest! Rather a joke really. Or one of life's little ironies, of the kind that fascinated Thomas Hardy. I had six years of active service, you see. Emerged unscathed. Then, a few years ago, I foolishly made a trip to that great metropolis of ours, dined at a fashionable Chelsea restaurant and some left-wing lunatic spoilt my dinner with his bomb! The spine, you see, is very vulnerable. Yes, that young Trotskyite bomber dished me . . . But you haven't driven all that way for my reminiscences.' The severe grey eyes had been summing up Quinn while the oft-told tale was re-told. At the same time Quinn had seen a likely link between an embittered old General who lectured on politics, a reckless mercenary, a fanatical Orangeman and a reactionary Tory such as Sylvester had proclaimed himself to be.

'A friend of mine died recently, knocked down by a car,' Quinn said. 'Rupert Sylvester, an antique dealer in Surrey.' He paused but the General did not comment, though he nodded gravely.

'We found that Rupert had written your name, together with another man's, in a sale catalogue. In fact he was holding the catalogue when he was killed.'

'Very odd, that! Sylvester, Sylvester.' Piggott looked solemn as he repeated the name, but Quinn wondered if there was not a

280

hint of amusement in the dark grey eyes. 'The name does seem to ring a bell, but a very faint one. Excuse me just a moment, Mr Quinn, I don't want to appear rude but I have to keep my other guest in mind.' He swivelled his head stiffly as if he wore a plaster collar and called out, 'Hugh. Hugh!'

The blond young man's smiling face appeared at the open door.

'Don't forget our other guest, lad! Just do a quick recce and see if you can spot him.'

With a vague half salute the blond man disappeared.

Piggott swivelled his head back to face Quinn and momentarily the awkwardness of the movement made him appear like an over-sized ventriloquist's dummy. But Quinn did not underestimate the immobile ex-General and thought that anyone who did so would be extremely stupid. Redvers Piggot might be confined to a wheelchair but he exuded courage, intelligence and willpower. He said thoughtfully. 'Yes, now, Rupert Sylvester. It is just possible that he came here once. What did you say the other name was?'

'I didn't mention it but it was Boyle, Terence Boyle.'

'Ah, now I remember Mr Boyle very well indeed. He was certainly here, on a course. Very good value, as I remember, in the debates. A loudish voice and tended to go on a bit, but said some trenchant things

281

nevertheless.'

'Mr Sylvester's widow had never heard your name and so she wondered why he would have made a note of it. Do you think he may have been going to contact you?'

Piggott said slowly, 'I think, Mr Quinn, that Boyle's name might be the clue here. Did your friend know Mr Boyle?'

'Yes, he did.'

'Well, there we have it. Quite possible that Mr Sylvester fancied a seminar and was going to contact Boyle regarding same.' He gave Quinn a level, judging look. 'Sorry indeed not to be more helpful, but that's the best I can do, I'm afraid.'

'Well, it is an explanation . . .'

'Of sorts,' the General completed Quinn's sentence with a smile that for the first time disclosed his narrow, ivory-coloured teeth; momentarily it gave him a wolfish look. Quinn had the strong impression of being face to face with a man who was both courageous and ruthless, the kind of general who would have enjoyed the war and said, 'Right, gentlemen, now let's give Jerry hell!'

Quinn glanced at the nearest photograph on the wall and the General followed the movement of his eyes. 'Simpler days those, my dear fellow,' he said regretfully. 'Yes, indeed they were. A time when one knew what was what and where one stood.' He fumbled in his shirt pocket, appearing to have trouble in extricating something. 'Well, Mr Quinn, I have your card here which I noticed gives both your home and office addresses. You live in a street I know well. So if any other thoughts occur later I can let you know. I quite understand that Mrs Sylvester would like to have any little mysteries cleared up.'

The blond man appeared in the doorway. 'All serene, General. Your guest has arrived.'

'Good,' Piggot snapped. 'Well, the guests arrive and the guests depart, I'm afraid, Mr Quinn.'

Quinn stood up, noticing as he did so an unguarded look in the General's eyes, a flash of envy, and realised the endless frustration endured by the once vigorous leader of men. 'Thanks again, General,' he said. 'You have a beautiful house, and I've found it all very interesting.'

'Have you? That's good. Hugh, be a kind fellow and put Mr Quinn on the right path.'

As they left the billiard room Hugh paused on the balcony, gesturing vaguely at the view. 'Lovely day for a swim, but the sea's still icy.'

'You've sampled it then?'

'Every morning. Part of the régime here. Are you going to stay in the village?'

'I hope so. At the pub by the harbour.'

'Oh yes, very nice little place.'

They made their way in silence down the steps. Hugh glanced twice in Quinn's direction and as they passed through the gateway in the stone wall he asked, 'Did you go through a windscreen?'

'Yes. No safety belt.'

'Ah, I see.'

Walking along the track he said, 'You'll find you make much better time going back to Dale. It's downhill a lot of the way.' He pointed to the stile. 'Cheerio then.'

When he had left the rough track Quinn heard the sound of a car being driven at speed behind him and turned to see a Range Rover belting along. He waited in case he was going to be offered a lift back to the village, but the red vehicle did not slow up and swerved off in the other direction. As it did so Quinn could see that the man sitting next to the young driver had black and white streaked hair, like a badger's coat; the man smiled sardonically and waved farewell while the car accelerated away to the other side of the field. Quinn watched till it disappeared from view, convinced that he had glimpsed the notorious Roscoe Starr, ex-war hero and mercenary who had turned house burglar, according to Rex Bealby.

Walking over to the stile, Quinn decided that he had not wasted his time in visiting Dale even though the General's replies had been as few and unsatisfactory as he had expected. He had decided to see the police immediately he was back in London. He would go with Max Arbeit and together they should be able to convince someone in the C.I.D. that Sylvester's death and Harland's injuries had not been accidental. Further enquiries by the police should then uncover the conspiracy that he was sure existed between Boyle, Starr, Piggott and others as yet unknown.

The coastal path was indeed more down than up on the way back to Dale and that was welcome, but steep chalky paths were not easily negotiated in shoes with leather soles. Half sliding, half stumbling down a particularly tricky slope, he saw that a young man in dark blue shirt and trousers was waiting a little further on, at a sharp bend in the path. The man was poised up on his toes as though to leap forward. He had dark brown hair and eyes and a handsome face that was vaguely familiar, like that of a film or television actor. A flick-knife appeared in the man's right hand and the blade flicked out. 'No way through, John,' he said.

'What do you mean?'

'I mean—no way through. So what you going to do about it?' The man had a lop-sided grin as he waited for Quinn's reply. 'You're a big bloke ... but you got to think ... are you fast enough for me? Or could you ... get back up that slope ... before I got to you? It's important, John.'

The warning was given in a flat, South London voice, in a way that made it seem like

285

an ordinary conversation, but Quinn's neck had become tense and stiff, his palms were wet, his breathing fast and shallow. This is what real fear is like, he thought. He realised he might be killed on that remote cliff and never see Dolly and Liz again.

The grinning man waved the switch-blade about as if he were joking but his left hand was bunched into a fist that looked like another good weapon. There was something about his carelessly arrogant manner, even the way he stood on his toes in scruffy white tennis shoes, that was familiar. His handsome face was unmarked but there were signs of scar tissue around his eyes. Suddenly Quinn recognised him as a boxer he had once seen fighting in a London ring—Frank something. He looked into the man's eyes and saw that he did not really think that what was going to happen was important and that he did not really care about anything. He had met a chancer of the rare kind Charlie Saunders had described, but Saunders' advice to 'back off' was useless.

'Time up, John. Time to make a move.' The man took a step forward and made a casual pass with the flashing blade.

Quinn lowered his head and charged forward like a bull, catching the man in a low tackle. At the moment of impact he felt a searing pain in the back of his left bicep and a hard punch high on his right cheek.

Nevertheless Quinn's weight and power forced the man back through the bushes and off balance, so that he ran backwards on staggering feet. Pain made Quinn hardly aware of where he was until he realised that there was nothing beneath his own feet, and he experienced the horrible sensation of falling endlessly. He cried out but continued to hold on to the other man and together they performed an acrobatic feat of turning over and over in the air.

Hitting the surface of the sea at speed took Quinn's breath away and he lost grip of his aerial partner. Total immersion in the chilly water constricted his chest still further. He sank with such force that his legs and feet struck rocks at the bottom and when he dazedly looked up it was through perhaps twenty feet of water. The other man lolled close by on a giant bank of kelp, with a deep bleeding gash in his forehead and a silly grin on his mouth as if he were pleased with his dire position. Quinn reached out to touch him but as he did so the blue-garbed man slid down further into a mass of slippery kelp. Quinn's lungs felt as if they were bursting so he propelled himself upwards by kicking his feet, finding that he could only use his right arm as he struggled up to the glinting surface. Once there, he floated on his back, breathing in deeply while he kicked off his shoes and struggled out of his trousers.

Taking a great gulp of air Quinn duck-dived, threshing his legs as hard as he could, aware that he was not very good at underwater swimming. He spied the knife safely lodged in a rock pool shaped like a hand-basin, but the man had slipped even further into the kelp so that only his shoulders and head remained in view. Quinn tugged at the man's shoulder with his right hand and managed to raise him a few inches, but the inert body slipped again. The man was unconscious or already dead. Quinn's own consciousness was leaving him as he continued to struggle feebly. Finally all he could see of the man were strands of dark brown hair waving together with the lighter brown weed. With a convulsive effort Quinn propelled himself up to the sun-dappled surface of the sea.

Supine, exhausted, yet disturbed that his efforts had only helped to entomb the man in a grave of seaweed, Quinn did nothing but float for some minutes. He felt sick but when he vomited it was only salt water. Above him a cliff of rock, perpendicular and perhaps seventy feet high, loomed threateningly. Moving his head awkwardly from side to side he could see that to the left of the towering headland, about a hundred yards away, there was a small bay with a narrow strip of sand and a comparatively low cliff that looked scaleable. Very slowly he made his way towards it, floating and propelling himself just by kicking his legs.

When he stood up in the shallow water at the edge of the sand Quinn felt so dizzy that he fell forward to his knees. He crawled out of the water and fell forward again. Lying on the wet sand, he was aware only of the pain in his left arm; he felt remote and the world seemed to spin beneath him. When he sat up he saw that only his left arm had been bleeding badly, though he had half-a-dozen other cuts and scrapes on his body. He sat gripping his left bicep, pinching it so hard that eventually the flow of blood stopped. Above his head a group of seagulls swooped and glided as if exulting in their graceful, careless flight. In a strange way their presence gave him hope: life was going on all around him and with luck he would take part in it again.

He was satisfied that he had found a vital part in the Sylvester mystery jigsaw; but it was more like one of the paper puzzles that had been popular when he was a child, the kind in which dots appeared to be distributed purposelessly on a page until they were connected by lines and an image appeared. And when the police finally drew a line linking the conspirators to the nameless boxer/assassin on the cliff, some image would certainly appear.

Half lost in a nightmare memory of seeing

the man's head slip down into the kelp, Quinn heard a distant noise which changed to the sound of voices. Feeling ridiculously weak he got to his knees and saw that a young boy and two girls, all carrying towels, were gradually descending a rocky path down the cliff. He managed to get to his feet and call for help in a feeble voice that sounded nothing like his own. There was an answering cry and the boy dropped his towel and descended the cliff at speed. Quinn sat down again heavily, trying to remember something that seemed important but eluded him. I've lost a lot of blood and that's why I can't do anything or even think straight, he thought. But he remembered as he heard the boy racing towards him across the sand and rehearsed it aloud, saying, 'Ah yes, my friends the police!'

CHAPTER TWENTY-SIX

The first Saturday in October occurred in a period of halcyon weather that was much appreciated by the villagers of Alderbury. They all agreed that the summer weather had been very disappointing—too hot and humid in early June, too cold in July and much too wet in August. After several cricket matches had been cancelled due to rain or the pitch being so wet that it squelched when walked on, Stanley Prince, the butcher, called the summer 'a bloody washout' and it became a popular catch-phrase with which the villagers greeted each other during August as they sheltered under the damp awning of the butcher's shop or scampered home from the tiny post office as 'the skies just opened' or 'it poured down in buckets'. Even the Reverend Arthur Owen appeared nettled when the church fête was rained off the Vicarage lawn and a much modified version had to be staged in a leaking marquee.

The halcyon weather set in during the third week of September. Equinoctial storms did not materialise and in the early part of the month the days gradually became more dry and warm. By the third week an area of high pressure was stationary over Southern Ireland, leading to the weather being 'set fair' as Stanley Prince declared it to be on the perfect day when he scored a century with four boundaries hit clear out of the ground. Then there was a long-seeming succession of fine days which mirrored each other in that they all began with cool, misty dawns and ended with spectacular sunsets. Stanley Prince was up betimes to see some of the misty dawns because he had heard a rumour that boys had been fishing very early in the morning in the Alder Pool and had caught a monster carp, possibly one of the specimen fish which his father, Reuben, had placed in the pond some forty years previously. While patrolling the rushy boundary of the Pool, when even the purple loosestrife looked grey in the mist, he would watch the sun rising and the sky gradually become a light, translucent blue. And, as he declared, the best part of these glorious days was that even the midday sun had only a benign warmth without humidity, just right for the fruit and crops and not too hot for people who had to work.

If the summer weather had been largely unsatisfactory, the villagers of Alderbury could not consider the season had been a disappointment in other ways. There had been a series of surprising events and all of them pleasant. First Brigadier Bealby informed the Parish Council that he was offering them the freehold of a meadow he owned by the river on the understanding that it would be used, in perpetuity, as a playing field for children. Hardly had this information been digested than Bealby told Dr Frederick Benson, the new chairman of the Council, that he was going to give them a strip of land where council houses could be built.

While these gifts were being widely discussed, it was noticed that changes were also afoot at the Hall which had been little altered during the previous century. A firm of landscape gardeners were hard at work for a fortnight, removing decaying trees and great masses of undergrowth which had given the old house its faintly gloomy aspect. No sooner was the landscaping finished than the builders, Harding Townshend, moved in to carry out a programme of alterations and decorations which they informed the landlord of the White Rose would take three or four months to complete. Village estimates of the cost of these renovations reached staggering heights when it was realised that four men would be working there full time. One substantial alteration was the transformation of a small kitchen, scullery and breakfast room into a large modern kitchen with an all-cream colour scheme, including a cream double Aga. Cuthbert Barfoot wagered the cost 'would break the bank of Monte Carlo', but little Mrs Watterson, who ran the post office and knew practically everything about everybody, declared that the Brigadier was an extremely wealthy man who had always preferred to hide the fact rather than boast about it.

Alice Prince, the butcher's wife, had other things to gossip about but she was aware that 'something was in the air' concerning Polly Sylvester. She noticed that Polly and Louise Simpson had become very close and then she heard that Louise had been given Rupert's mare. The two young women were sometimes to be seen walking arm in arm along by the river, talking animatedly, and Mrs Prince said she would like to be a dragonfly for a few minutes in order to hear what they were discussing. Then Mrs Watterson, who not only ran the post office but also arranged the delivery of newspapers and thus had three young spies at work, began to behave oddly as if she knew something quite sensational but was loath to disclose it. After that the Vicar's wife let slip at a W.I. meeting that the church was reserved for the morning of the first Saturday in October. Barbara Owen did not give a reason but ingenuously went on to say how well the Brigadier, or 'dear Rex' as she called him, was looking, having quite lost the image of someone frail and under-nourished.

Alice Prince left the W.I. meeting brooding on this information and also the fact that Polly Sylvester was ordering more meat than one would have expected a young woman on her own to eat. She came up with the surprising prediction that the Brigadier and Polly would be married in Alderbury on the first Saturday in October, at the church where generations of the Bealby family had been christened, married and buried for over two centuries.

Only a few days after Alice Prince had spread this unlikely rumour Barbara Owen confirmed that it was a matter of fact and put her seal on the marriage by saying as an old friend of the Brigadier's how glad she was about the rapidly approaching event. The villagers pondered the marriage. Mrs Watterson said that Polly was thirty-five but she was a Scorpio and so would be thirty-six in October; Rex Bealby was only just seventy-one since he was a Cancer with a July birthday. The arithmetic still did not come out too well because, as Mrs Prince never tired of pointing out, 'When she's only forty-five he will be eighty-one,' and so on, but everyone wished the couple well. Polly was widely popular and most people admired the gentle, unassuming Brigadier. Even Judy Browning, usually the odd one out in village matters, declared she would be going to the church ceremony as she wanted to show her appreciation of Bealby's generosity in giving the land to build the council houses which Rupert Sylvester had so strongly opposed.

On the first Saturday in October the marriage was in everyone's mind and the post office, butcher's shop and baker's had all arranged to close early in order to attend the ceremony which was to take place at eleven-thirty. It was made known that the Brigadier and his bride would depart for London Airport immediately they left the church, bound for Rome. But the Brigadier had arranged for a champagne buffet to be served after their departure, in the newly decorated dining-room at Alderbury Hall and all those who attended the wedding service would be welcome. During that Saturday morning the church bells rang out with a joyful refrain.

At eleven-fifteen that morning Mickey Harland was still driving to the village, negotiating the tricky, long bend which curved back on itself by a copse of oaks. He knew that he had the reputation of being a slow driver and was sometimes laughed at for his reluctance to drive in London and for preferring to park at the very edge of a town. Jack Quinn had once said to him, 'Christ, Mickey! You're the only bloke I know who makes a big deal out of driving into Oxford.'

Harland had underestimated the time required to get through Guildford on a fine Saturday morning when the streets were thronged with shoppers. Another factor hindering him was the stiffness of his broken arm. A physiotherapist had assured him that the fracture had mended perfectly but he was still not used to it feeling strange and awkward. 'As if,' he had explained to Joan, 'it had a life of its own.' He sometimes made a joke of this by moving his arm round, crooked at chest level, as if it had moved of its own accord. Occasionally he felt like Lionel Atwill in an absurd horror movie where Atwill was a mad German professor with an artificial arm in which he stuck darts.

296

Although it was not unduly hot Harland was sweating as he drove along, nervously humming and whistling. He had made the mistake of wearing a new suit and shirt which compounded his feeling of stiffness; anxiety at the idea of being late for the wedding was another factor. When he caught sight of the village pubs he murmured fervently, 'And get me to the church on time.' If only Joan had decided to go to the wedding, he thought, she would have made sure that they left in plenty of time. Joan's name had been on the invitation but she had turned the idea down, making a big thing of Polly being *his* friend, as though he had been having an affair with the girl instead of occasionally looking in at Court Antiques to help her price books. And Joan had gone to town about Polly after Max Arbeit had been extolling her virtues and had exclaimed, 'Who is this Polly who turns all men's hearts to flame?' And as he was setting off to drive to the wedding she had said, 'Oh, it's Polly this and Polly that.' To which he had succinctly replied. 'Oh, balls.'

Harland slowed up by Court Antiques and noticed that the window looked slightly different under the new régime. It still appeared spick and span, but the non-antique copper and brass items had been dropped so that it looked less like a Middle Eastern bazaar.

After parking his car behind Arbeit's green

Mini close to the butcher's shop, Harland had trouble in undoing his safety belt and pushed his dodgy arm out of the way as he had done in the days just after the plaster cast was removed. Catching sight of his sweaty, anxious face in the driving mirror he pulled a silly, sinister smile in the Lionel Atwill style. He left his car unlocked and ran down the road as fast as he could, determined not to arrive at the church just as Polly drove up.

The churchyard was empty and looked quite different in brilliant sunshine; it was apparent that it had recently received a good deal of attention with a general tidying up and the grass being closely cut. Harland could hear the organ playing and for a moment he thought it might be the *Wedding March* and his heart thumped. He forced himself to stand still and catch his breath. If the bride was already walking down the aisle there was nothing he could do about it. He looked about, noticing that Rupert's grave was marked with a white headstone and half covered with fresh flowers, wondering if they had been placed there by Polly or by the mysterious Mrs Simpson.

When Harland stepped into the church it seemed dark after the bright sunlight and he could make out very little. Someone close by murmured something but he could not take it in. Momentarily he felt strange owing to the panicky drive and half wished he had not come. Then he caught sight of Quinn's tall figure at the end of a pew tucked away at the back of the church. He walked round to join him but paused to look at the slightly built bridegroom in a dark blue suit, standing next to a veritable giant of a man who was similarly dressed. The exceptionally tall man was very distinguished-looking despite being bald.

When Harland got to the obscurely placed pew, half hidden by a pillar, he saw that Quinn, Peter Rawlins, Max Arbeit and Charlie Saunders were all sitting there together. 'What's this then, the Rogues' Gallery?' he whispered.

Saunders hissed back, 'Do you mind! Do me a favour. No connection with any other firm.'

'Oh yes, it's very nice being here with blokes who know how to behave in church,' Rawlins said.

Quinn shook his head disapprovingly. 'By God, Mickey! You cut it fine! You're not a bridesmaid you know.'

'Yes, I do realise that, old lad. I got caught in a traffic jam in Guildford.' Harland stood at the end of the pew in a particularly dark corner, with the unpleasant sensation of feeling cold sweat trickling down his spine. 'Does anyone know who the best man is?' he asked. 'Must be even taller than you, Jack.'

Arbeit whispered, 'Polly said he was a very old friend of Rex's. Known each other since their school days. Piers Mortain, a shipping magnate, I think.'

Saunders pretended to fish around in his pockets, saying, 'Sounds like real money to me. Perhaps I should hand out a few cards.'

Harland craned his head round to look at the two men standing silently together at the front of the church, looking relaxed and unself-conscious. He noticed that they both wore Old Etonian ties. Piers Mortain had a striking profile like the head on a Roman coin.

There was an excited stir in the congregation as people rose to their feet and the organ played Mendelssohn's *Wedding March*. Harland had to crane his head in the other direction to catch sight of Polly, in a light-grey suit with a cyclamen coloured blouse and matching Juliet cap on her blonde hair; she looked very lovely as she walked down the aisle, arm in arm with the bluff-looking man who had sat near her at the funeral.

Harland watched as the Vicar stood with Bealby and Polly, saying, 'Dearly Beloved, we are gathered together here in the sight of God . . .' but his mind was elsewhere. He was thinking of all the events that had stemmed from Rupert Sylvester's death. The police had found a mechanic in the Harrow Road firm who was willing to talk about a silver VW Scirocco, and Terence Boyle was at present remanded in custody waiting to be tried for murder; Boyle himself had talked, and another man, Colonel Bertrand Moilliet, had been arrested on the same charge. Boyle had also revealed the existence of a right-wing organisation, dedicated to the execution of 'left-wing fanatics', and its link with the ex-boxer, Frank Shields, who had tried to murder Quinn on the cliff at Dale. The right-wing conspiracy had been broken and its leaders, a General Piggott and a Major Starr, had fled the country, surfacing in South Africa.

Holding his head awkwardly to one side in order to look round the pillar Harland stared at the bride and groom, trying to concentrate on the ceremony and not 'moon about'. Although she had turned down the invitation Joan would nevertheless want a full report even on such details as what the bride's mother had worn. But his attention was sidetracked by noticing the carving on a marble panel let into the church wall. It was a memorial plaque to a Joshua Seymour Bealby who had died in Alderbury in 1781; it showed a man with frilled cuffs and a curled wig holding an open book and standing at his back the figure of Time holding an hour-glass and a scythe. The finely carved border included symbols of time, eternity and mortality: a serpent biting its own tail, a winged hour-glass, a bird and a bat.

Underneath there was a simple, haunting text: Be ye ready. Harland was struck again by the oddity of human existence. In May Rupert Sylvester would have attended services in this church; in June he had joined Joshua Bealby and the great majority; in October his widow was marrying old Joshua's descendent. Be ye ready.

The congregation sang 'O Thou Who Gavest Power to Love' and Harland pretended to sing too, opening his mouth but emitting no sound. A sidelong glance showed him that Jack Quinn made no pretence of singing and was staring ahead with a faintly depressed expression. Quinn had been rather low in recent weeks, as if something was constantly on his mind that prevented enjoyment. Perhaps he feels some guilt because Frank Shields drowned, Harland thought. It would be absurd to feel guilty over such a death but guilt did not work on a logical basis.

As the newly married couple disappeared through a door with the Vicar and a handful of other people, the congregation relaxed; there was some clearing of throats and Max Arbeit coughed. Charlie Saunders turned round and winked. Harland thought, I wish I were like Saunders, always optimistic, always positive, always interested and busy; I bet he never feels guilty about anything.

The couple reappeared and began to walk

back up the aisle. Polly was flushed which suited her, giving her cheeks a bloom like roses. Harland made a mental note not to mention that little detail to Joan. As Polly and Bealby left the church, Quinn said quietly, 'I could do with a drink.'

'There's going to be a champagne buffet.'

'You're going to that then?'

'Of course I'm going to it,' Harland said. 'Should be fun. Don't slope off to the pub, Jack! Adele and Pam said they were looking forward to seeing you again—said you hadn't looked in at the shop since they've been running it.'

'No, I—oh, I've been feeling rather down recently. No point in spreading it about.'

'Have some champagne then. Pam said that the Brigadier had ordered crates of the stuff. And from what I hear he can afford it. So, let's get drunk.'

'I think not. But I'll go to the buffet and have a chat with Adele, she's a nice woman.'

Making slow progress out of the church, Harland was trying to imagine what it would be like to be Rex Bealby, embarking on marriage again at seventy-one, beginning that long process of getting to know nearly everything about another human being. Unsought, an image of Polly, flushed and with unpinned, long blond hair, in a nightdress, appeared in his mind. He got rid of it by saying out loud, 'Be ye ready.'

303

'What?' Rawlings asked.

'Nothing. Just be ye ready, old son.'

Outside there was an excited crowd round Polly, but she took a step in Quinn's direction. He bent down but only brushed her hairline with his lips. Harland kissed the girl's warm cheeks and said, 'Good luck.' He thought she smelt and looked quite delicious but that was something else that Joan would not hear from him. Bealby was busy shaking hands, looking round with calm blue eyes. It was the candid, tranquil gaze of a happy man.

Quinn had moved away and was talking earnestly to Adele Rogers. Charlie Saunders said to Harland, 'What's up with Jack? Lately he's been moving about like a car with its brakes full on.' He spoke out of the corner of his mouth, which he sometimes did in relating confidential matters but without talking any quieter than usual. Harland shrugged and Saunders went on, 'I can't understand him lately. When you could get bugger-all of interest at Court Antiques he was often in there, sorting out those flashy bindings for Rupert. Now that there's a steady trickle of really choice items from the Hall, Jack steers clear of the place.'

Quinn returned as if he had heard his name mentioned. As the newly married couple made their way through the cluster of people by the lich-gate he turned to Rawlins and asked, 'Jealous?'

Rawlins hesitated and looked surprisingly serious when he replied, 'Yes and no.'

Polly and the Brigadier got into a dark blue Rolls Royce, followed by Piers Mortain. Saunders said, 'I hear the Silver Spur belongs to Mortain. Cost about fifty grand, they do. I might put him on my mailing list. Can't be more than one Piers Mortain in the book.'

The car drove off to resounding cheers. Max Arbeit lifted one finger, as he did when quoting something noteworthy. 'Marriage is the beginning and end of all culture ... The scale of joy and sorrow is so high that the sum which two married people owe one another is incalculable ...'

'Who wrote that, Max?' Quinn asked the Doctor.

Arbeit replied, 'Goethe, his *Wolverwandtschaften.*'

The Rolls stopped by the butcher's shop as a very old man hobbled up in order to shake hands with the bride and groom. When the car had finally disappeared from view Harland remained staring in its direction, feeling that he had a sad and envious expression glued to his face, one that he could not get rid of.

Peter Rawlins asked him, 'Jealous?'

Harland moved his stiff arm round slowly, crooked at chest height, like a model man in a shop window. He said in his Lionel Atwill voice, '*Ach! Nein!* Such pleasures are not for the likes of me.'

Rawlins and Quinn laughed. The Doctor said, 'Thank God for the gift of laughter.'

Quinn asked him, 'More Goethe?'

The small man pondered for a moment and then said slowly, 'No, my dear, I think that's Arbeit.'

Photo   by
REDW   hire.